He must have sensed her presence.

Because he suddenly turned and looked straight at her. She found herself catching her breath, because he was the most handsome man she had ever seen in her life.

He smiled at her, put his finger to the brim of his hat and tilted it towards her. Her answering smile lit her face, as if she had suddenly met someone she had known long ago and hadn't seen for a while.

'Esme, how could you?' Rosemary took Esme's arm and almost dragged her away.

Esme looked back over her shoulder and discovered the young man was staring after them…

Born in Singapore, **Mary Nichols** came to England when she was three, and has spent most of her life in different parts of East Anglia. She has been a radiographer, school secretary, information officer and industrial editor, as well as a writer. She has three grown-up children, and four grandchildren.

Recent novels by the same author:

THE HONOURABLE EARL
THE INCOMPARABLE COUNTESS
LADY LAVINIA'S MATCH
A LADY OF CONSEQUENCE
THE HEMINGFORD SCANDAL
MARRYING MISS HEMINGFORD
BACHELOR DUKE
AN UNUSUAL BEQUEST
TALK OF THE TON
WORKING MAN, SOCIETY BRIDE

A DESIRABLE
HUSBAND

Mary Nichols

MILLS & BOON

Pure reading pleasure

First published in Great Britain 2007
Harlequin Mills & Boon Limited,
Eton House, 18-24 Paradise Road, Richmond, Surrey TW9 1SR

© Mary Nichols 2007

ISBN: 978 0 263 85192 2

Set in Times Roman 10½ on 12½ pt.
04-0907-84378

Printed and bound in Spain
by Litografia Rosés S.A., Barcelona

A DESIRABLE
HUSBAND

Chapter One

March 1850

'Are we nearly there?' Esme turned from watching the countryside flying past the carriage window at a speed that would have frightened her had she been a young lady given to attacks of the vapours, which she certainly was not.

It was not her first ride in a train because she had travelled by this means the short distance from her home in Luffenham to Leicester to visit her married sister, Lucy, but that went at the pace of a snail. This was the first time she had undertaken such a long journey, and without her parents, too. Lucy had intended to accompany her, but five-year-old Harry had gone down with a cold and she would not leave him. So here she was, being escorted by her brother-in-law, who had business in town, and Miss Bannister, her old governess, who was going to act as companion and maid.

'Not long now,' Myles told her. 'Are you tired?'

'Not especially, I'm simply impatient to arrive.' Papa had said he could not give her a Season—at least, not one befitting the daughter of the Earl of Luffenham—and she would have to take her chances on finding a husband among the local gentry, which would be very nearly impossible. She knew them all and there wasn't one she liked well enough to want to spend the rest of her life with. The whole family talked about it, arguing to and fro as if they were talking about what to do with a problem servant. Both Lucinda and Rosemary had had come-out seasons and it didn't seem fair that Esme should be deprived of one, for how else could she find a suitable husband? In the end, Rosemary, who was married to Rowan, Viscount Trent, and lived in a smart mansion in Kensington, had persuaded her husband to provide the wherewithal. Esme could not wait to see what social occasions had been arranged for her.

At nineteen, the youngest of the Earl of Luffenham's three daughters, Esme was as excited as a child. With her flawless skin, rosy cheeks and big blue eyes, she looked younger than her years—a state of affairs she was anxious to correct. She was a young lady, a marriageable young lady, and she wished everyone would not treat her like a schoolgirl. Mama and Papa and Lucy had spent the whole of the day before giving her advice on how to behave. 'Do this. Don't do that. Remember you are a lady. Be courteous and friendly, but do not allow any of the gentlemen to whom you are introduced to take liberties.' She wasn't quite sure what they meant by liberties; she supposed kissing her would be one. She wondered what it would be like to be kissed by a man, but she hadn't dared ask.

The journey had begun very early when they boarded the local train at Luffenham Halt to take them to Peterborough, where they changed on to the London train. It was all made easy for them because Myles was someone important in the railway world; porters and guards and everyone working on the railway, fell over themselves to ease his passage. But even so, sitting in a closed carriage for five hours was about as much as she could bear.

'Another few minutes,' he said. 'We are slowing down already.'

She turned her attention back to the window and realised they had left the countryside behind and there were smoke-begrimed buildings on either side of the line. A minute or two later they drew into the Maiden Lane terminus and the platform came into view with people standing about, perhaps to meet others coming off the train, perhaps to board it for its return journey. Porters scurried here and there, carrying luggage, mysterious parcels, boxes of cabbages and crates of squawking chickens. A dozen empty milk churns stood ready to be sent back whence they came, no doubt to be returned full the next morning.

They stopped in a hiss of steam and the door of their carriage was opened by a porter. Myles stepped down, then turned to help her. She remembered just in time that she was supposed to be a decorous young lady and resisted the temptation to jump down on to the platform and allowed him to hand her down. Miss Bannister followed while he was giving instructions to the porter about the delivery of their luggage.

Esme felt firm ground beneath her feet; she was here at last, in the great metropolis. The excitement bubbling up in her was hard to contain, but overexuberance was one of the things Mama had warned her against, so she walked sedately beside Myles as they left the station and he hailed a cab to take them to Kensington. Familiar only with Leicester and Peterborough, the two towns nearest her home, the city seemed never ending: warehouses, shops, poky little houses and grand mansions in juxtaposition lined their route, and then a long wide avenue running alongside a park.

'That's Green Park,' Myles told her. 'Buckingham Palace is on the far side of it. We'll come to Hyde Park soon. That's where the Exhibition is going to be held next year.' He leaned forward and pointed. 'That's the Duke of Wellington's house.'

'Shall I meet him?'

'I don't know. You might.'

'But he is your friend?'

'He is certainly an acquaintance, I would not be so presumptuous as to claim him for a friend.'

'Shall I meet Prince Albert? Will he be present when I make my curtsy?'

'Goodness, child, I don't know.'

'I am not a child, Myles. You sound just like Banny.'

He grinned ruefully at Miss Bannister while addressing Esme. 'Then I beg your pardon. I shall remember in future to address you as my lady.'

'Now you are being silly.'

Nothing could repress her for long and she was soon smiling again. A few minutes more and the cab driver turned into a wide street lined with imposing town villas and pulled up outside one of them. 'Trent House,' he announced.

Myles got out, handed Esme down and then her companion. He was always courteous and polite to Miss Bannister and treated her like a lady, for which he received her undying support.

Esme was standing uncertainly, looking about her, when the front door of the nearest house was opened and her sister, in a dove-grey dress and white cap, stood waiting to greet her. Esme started to run to meet her, but remembered in time that running was not ladylike and walked to the door.

'Here at last.' Rosemary offered her cheek to be kissed. 'Did you have a good journey?'

'Yes, very good, but I'm so glad to be here.'

'You are very welcome, sister dear.' And to Myles, offering her hand, 'Myles, welcome. Come along in. I'll take you to your rooms, then when you have settled in, we shall have some refreshments and you shall tell me all the news from home.'

Ignoring Miss Bannister, she led the way into an imposing entrance hall and up a flight of stairs. 'The drawing room,' she said, waving at a closed door. 'And that's the dining room. The door farther along is the small parlour where we sit when we are alone. That's where I shall be, so come there when you are ready.' On she went up a second flight of stairs. 'Bedrooms on this floor,' she said, flinging open a door. 'This one is yours, Esme. I have put Miss Bannister next door, for your convenience. Myles, a room has been prepared for you at the far end of the corridor.' She pointed at a farther flight of stairs. 'Nursery suite and servants' quarters up there, though they have their own staircase. That's it, except for the ground floor, which contains ante-rooms, a large room we use for dancing, soirées and suchlike, the library and Rowan's study. I'll show you those later.'

Miss Bannister and Myles left them and Rosemary followed Esme into her room and sat on the end of the bed to watch as her sister removed her gloves, cloak and bonnet to reveal a tiered skirt in a soft blue wool. It was not new. Nothing she had was brand-new. 'Esme, did you have to wear that dress?'

Esme smoothed her hands over her waist. 'What's wrong with it? Mama said it was perfectly adequate for travelling.'

'It's years old. I remember you having that when I was still at home.' She stopped speaking to answer a knock at the door. Two footmen had arrived with Esme's trunk. They were waved inside and told to put it on the floor at the foot of the bed. They had no sooner gone than Rosemary had it open and was pulling out the contents. 'Esme, I could swear this was Lucy's jacket. And this skirt.' She delved deeper into it. 'And this gown…'

'So they are—Mama said no one would ever know.'

'Haven't you brought any clothes of your own?'

'Not many,' Esme confessed. 'They are all so old and some of them are too short for a young lady and Lucy said I could have these. She has grown a little plumper since she had Vicky and they are the very best materials. We hardly had to alter anything, except to shorten them. Lucy is inches taller than I am.'

'Whatever was Mama thinking of, to send you with nothing but hand-me-downs? You'll never find a husband that way.'

'No one knows they are hand-me-downs.'

'Myles knows.'

'Of course he does, but he's family, and Lucy asked him if he thought it was all right for me to have them and he said they were her clothes and she could give them to whomever she pleased.'

'He would.' There was a deal of meaning in those two words and conveyed perfectly what Rosemary thought of her brother-in-law. He was an upstart, a nobody, for all he was Lord Moorcroft's heir; it was a new peerage and meant nothing at all, except that the working classes were aspiring to become nobility, which they never could do. They did not have the breeding. She tolerated him, even managed to be polite and treat him like an equal, but that was for Lucy's sake, not his. 'I can't take you out and about unless you are dressed appropriately. Whatever will people think of me?'

'I shouldn't think they will think anything of it.' Esme had forgotten how repressing Rosie could be. Nothing and nobody was good enough; even her poor husband was bullied into conforming to her ways.

'Nevertheless, you shall have a new wardrobe. Thank goodness the Season hasn't started yet and there will be plenty of choice in the shops and dressmakers with little enough to do.'

'I am sure Papa cannot afford it. He has been lecturing us for years about not being extravagant and it's got worse since he lost money investing in the Eastern Counties railway.'

'More fool him for doing it. No doubt he listened to Myles.'

'It wasn't Myles's fault, he advised against it. I believe it was Viscount Gorridge, though his lordship cannot have taken his own advice because he is richer than ever.'

'Well, whatever it was, you are going to have new clothes. Rowan will pay. He always gives me whatever I ask for.'

'Aren't you lucky,' Esme said, which made her sister look sharply at her, but there was no malice in Esme's expression.

'Yes, I am.' She went to the door to the adjoining room. 'Miss Bannister, Esme requires your help changing her dress.' To Esme she said, 'Hurry up. I've lots to tell you. And I want to hear how Mama is.' And with that she took her leave.

Esme turned to look at the room. It had a large canopied bed, a huge walnut wardrobe, a table and two upright chairs, a little desk with another chair, a chest of drawers and, beside

the bed, a bookcase containing several matching books. She
went over to the window, which had view of a park, neat
gardens and a stretch of water.

'Did you hear all that?' she asked Banny, who had joined her.

'Yes.'

'She made me feel like a poor relation. I was so pleased
when Lucy gave me those clothes; they fit me very well and
I do not feel such a schoolgirl in them. I am not a schoolgirl
and I do hope that Rosie isn't going to buy me a lot of silly
frilly stuff. I am grateful to her for having me, but I want to
be me, not her baby sister.'

Miss Bannister smiled. 'I think you can stand up to her,
my pet, but take my advice, be diplomatic about it. What
shall you wear now?'

'I don't mind. It's not important if I am going to be
lectured about it.'

Twenty minutes later, washed and dressed in a green-and-
yellow striped jaconet with her hair freshly brushed and held
back with combs, she went down to the small sitting room
to find her sister presiding over the teapot. Myles was
standing looking out of the window. He turned to smile at
her as she entered and she felt at least here she had an ally.

They drank tea and nibbled little cakes; Myles told
Rosemary all the news of Lucy and young Henry and baby
Victoria and was regaled in turn with the cleverness of Master
John Trent, who had just had his first birthday. Esme sat and
appeared to be listening, but her mind was wandering. In
spite of her defence of Lucy and her gratitude for the clothes,
she was looking forward to having a wardrobe of her own,
something bought and made especially for her. Shopping
would be a rare treat, but after that...

Mama had told her what her own come-out Season had been like and said all Seasons followed an established pattern. The first and most important event was her presentation to the Queen. Along with a long line of others, she would have to walk sedately into the room without falling over her ten-foot train and on reaching her Majesty make the deepest curtsy, until her knee was almost on the floor, and hold that position while kissing the Queen's hand and bowing her head. And then she had to get up again without falling over. The trickiest bit was scooping up her train and making her way backwards out of the room.

After that she would be well and truly out and could accept invitations to soirées and routs and balls at which she would meet many new people, including some young men out looking for a wife, who would flatter and cajole. She was not, under any circumstances, to have her head turned by them. Rosie would say who was and who was not suitable and whom she could safely encourage.

She came out of her reverie to hear Rosemary saying, 'Esme is a hopeless romantic and is unlikely to make a push to find a suitable husband herself, so I will have to take her in hand and point her in the right direction.'

'Is it like a paper trail, then?' Esme asked and was gratified to see a smile crease Myles's face, which he quickly stifled.

'Don't be flippant, Esme,' her sister said. 'It is a serious business. You have to choose a husband carefully because you have to spend the rest of your life with him.'

'But the same must be said of him, surely? He has to spend his life with me.'

'It's different for a man.'

'How?'

Rosemary looked discomforted. 'It just is. A man is looking for a lady to be an asset to his position in life, someone to be a credit to him, someone to manage his household, entertain his friends, be a good mother to his children, look elegant on his arm.'

'What about being in love?'

Rosemary suddenly found it necessary to fiddle with the tea caddy and it was left to Myles to answer her. 'He must be in love with his wife and she with him, that goes without saying, otherwise the marriage is doomed to failure.'

'Well, of course,' Rosemary said, and rang the bell for the parlour maid to come and remove the tea things. As soon as they had been taken away, she stood up. 'I always have a half hour with John about this time before he is put to bed. Would you like to come and say hallo to him, Esme? Myles, I am sure you can amuse yourself. There is a newspaper on the side table. There's little enough news in it, except the plans for the Exhibition. "The Great Exhibition of the Industry of All Nations." What a title!'

The proposed exhibition was the brain child of Henry Cole, a man of many talents, who had been involved in smaller exhibitions all over the country. He had approached Prince Albert with the idea of combining the art and manufacture of the whole world in one enormous exhibition and his Highness had embraced it enthusiastically and become its principal patron. It was why Myles had come to town, invited to a banquet by his Royal Highness and the Lord Mayor of London aimed at furthering the project among influential people in the provinces.

Esme followed her sister from the room. She wanted to be married, like her sisters, but she was not going to let herself be pushed by Rosemary into marriage with someone she did not love. Myles had said it was important and so had Lucy. Lucy had managed to win Papa round to let her marry Myles who was not at first considered a suitable husband for the daughter of an earl, being a man who liked to work and was not afraid to dirty his hands, though he was rich enough not to have to. Since then he had been a rock for all the family, the man they all turned to for help and advice—all except Rosemary, of course. She had never changed her original opinion of him; he was a labourer, one of the operative classes and far beneath her. Esme would be happy if she could find another Myles, but she did not suppose there could be two such as he.

Having admired her nephew, watched him being petted by his mother until he dribbled all down her gown and was hastily handed back to his nurse, Esme returned to her room to rest before dressing for dinner. At the sound of the first gong, signalling that dinner would be in a half hour, Miss Bannister helped her into one of the gowns Lucy had given her. It was a cerise silk that had suited Lucy, who was darker than she was, but Esme was not sure that it was the best colour for her pale complexion, but she would never have dreamed of hurting her sister's feelings by saying so.

She heard the second gong as she was going down to the drawing room where she found the family gathered. She barely had time to greet Rowan before dinner was announced and they went into the dining room and took their places at the long table.

Esme had met Rowan twice before, once when Rosie had first become engaged to him and then again at the wedding at which she was a bridesmaid. He was tall and thin and had a long nose, which was unfortunate because it seemed as if he was perpetually looking down on everyone. Except Myles, of course; no one could look down on Myles who was well over six feet tall.

While the meal was being served they exchanged pleasantries, but the conversation flagged after that. It was then Rowan filled the void by asking Myles what had brought him to London, apart from escorting Esme.

'Myles has an invitation to Prince Albert's banquet at the Mansion House,' Esme put in before he could answer for himself. 'It's huge. It has gold letters and a gold border and his Highness's coat of arms on it. You should see it.'

'Is that so?' Rowan turned to Myles. 'Am I to conclude you are going to add your name to that ridiculous idea for an exhibition?'

'I do not consider it ridiculous,' Myles said evenly. 'It will be a showcase for everyone, no matter what country, creed or branch of endeavour they are engaged in. It will show the world that Britain leads the way in innovation and engineering and bring exhibits and visitors from all over the world.'

'That is just what I have against it,' Rowan said pithily. 'We shall be inundated with hoards of people roaming the streets, filling the cabs and omnibuses, frightening the horses and servants who will not dare venture forth on their lawful business for fear of being set upon by thieves and cut-throats. And there is the risk of troublemakers from the Continent spreading discontent among our own workers who will undoubtedly find the means to flock into London. And with all that building going on, goodness knows what it will do to property values in the area, and that includes this house.'

'I am given to understand the building will only be a temporary one and will be taken down as soon as the Exhibition is over.'

'And how long do you think that will take?'

'I cannot say. I am sorry you do not feel inclined to support it, Rowan.'

'Inclined to support it!' Rowan snapped. 'I am totally against it and intend to do all I can to prevent it from happening.'

'Then we shall have to agree to differ.'

Esme, who had been listening to the exchange with growing dismay, wished she had never mentioned the invitation. Lucy had been so proud of it when she showed it to her and it seemed a good way to counter all Rosemary's boasting about how well-thought-of in society her husband was, how everyone envied her taste in her furnishings and the cleverness of her precious child, and now she had set the two men against each other.

'Esme, let us retire to the drawing room and leave the men to continue their argument over the port,' Rosemary said, rising from her chair.

'I didn't mean to cause dissent,' Esme said as she followed her sister to the drawing room. 'I had no idea—'

'No, that's the trouble with you, Esme, you tend to speak before you think. I beg you to curb it or you will upset the very people you should be pleasing.'

'I am sorry, Rosie. I know you have put yourself at great inconvenience to bring me out and I am truly grateful. I will try very hard to be a credit to you.'

'Then we will say no more. Men like to argue, especially strong-minded men like Rowan and Myles, but I don't think it will lead to a serious falling out.' She busied herself with the tea things while she spoke. 'Now, let us talk of other things. We will go shopping tomorrow and see if we can get you kitted out ready for the season, though it will not get properly under way for a good two weeks. We shall have to amuse ourselves in the meantime.'

'Oh, I am sure we can do that. We can go for walks and visit the sights and I should like to ride. Will that be possible?'

'Perfectly possible. Hacks are easily hired.' She handed Esme a cup of tea. 'Do you know how long Myles is planning to stay in town?'

Myles, when he offered to escort Esme, had been invited to stay at Trent House while he was conducting his business, but at that time she had expected Lucy to be with him. She had no idea of the nature of his business, whether it was simply to attend the banquet or if it were something to do with his railway or engineering concerns.

'I know he is anxious to return to Lucy and see how Harry is, so I think he cannot be planning to stay above a couple of days. Are you wishing you had not asked him?'

'Good gracious, no! He is family and it would have looked most odd not to have invited him. I cannot think why he does not buy a town house; he could easily afford it.'

'Lucy prefers to live in the country and says it would be a dreadful waste to keep a house and servants in town when she would hardly ever be in residence.'

The men joined them at that point and appeared to have overcome their hostility. They sat and drank tea and made light conversation, most of it of a social nature, carefully avoiding renewing the subject of the Exhibition and the Prince Consort's banquet.

Rowan agreed that it was impossible for Esme to go out and about in Lucy's cast-off clothes, which very nearly started Myles off on another argument, but he wisely held his peace. The carriage was put at Rosemary's disposal for the next morning so that she could take her sister shopping and Rowan readily agreed to foot the bill for the new wardrobe.

When they dispersed to go to their beds, Esme contrived to walk a little way with Myles. 'I am so sorry,' she whispered. 'It was not my idea to buy new clothes and I would not for the world have Lucy think ill of me.'

'I am sure she would understand.' He grinned. 'And it will be grand to have a new wardrobe, won't it?'

'Yes, as long as I am not put into frills and flounces. I hate them.'

The shopping expedition was not a leisurely affair; Rosemary knew exactly what was wanted and was determined Esme should be a credit to her good taste. In every shop they entered the assistants hurried forward to serve her, though Esme would have liked a little more time to browse and view what was on offer, she was obliged to admit that Rosemary's choice was excellent and flounces, frills and bows were kept to a minimum. 'You have a very good figure,' Rosemary told her. 'Simple clothes will show it off to advantage.' The material and pattern of the gown she would wear for her curtsy to the Queen took the longest to be decided upon and was to be made up by Madame Devereux, Rosemary's own dressmaker. The bodice of the dress had to be low cut and the skirt very full with a long train. Accessories like slippers, fan, jewellery and feathers had to be chosen with care to conform to the rigid rules laid down by protocol.

By the middle of the afternoon, they were on their way back to Trent House with the carriage loaded down with purchases and more to be delivered in the coming days.

Shopping with her mother in Leicester and Peterborough was never like this. There, it would be an all-day affair with her mother complaining of the lack of choice and the high prices and wondering aloud what her father would say when presented with the bill, though it never stopped her buying something she wanted. Rosemary had never once mentioned the price of anything.

They turned from Oxford Street, where Rosemary had purchased some lengths of ribbon, into the northern end of Park Lane. Esme glimpsed green grass through the trees and longed to go for a walk. At home in Luffenham she walked or rode everywhere and already she was missing her daily exercise. 'Is that Hyde Park, Rosie?' she asked.

'Yes.'

'Is it possible to walk home through it?'

'Yes, perfectly possible.'

'Then do let's walk. Banny can take the coach home and put the shopping away.'

'We have to go to Lady Aviemore's to tea.' Her ladyship was, according to Rosemary, a notable hostess and knew everyone of any importance and she could—if she took to Esme—be influential in introducing her to other young people, among whom might be a suitable husband. She would know the history behind every one of them. Who could safely be cultivated and who best to avoid. 'Once you are out, she can help us get you seen and noticed,' Rosemary had told her sister. 'So it is important you make the right impression.'

'That is hours away. Come on, Rosie, I want to explore.'

'Very well.' Rosemary asked the driver to stop and they left the coach and entered the park by Brook Gate and were soon strolling along one of the many walks towards the Serpentine.

In spite of the fact that London was, according to Rosemary, quite empty, they met several people she knew and they stopped to chat. Esme was presented to them and exchanged the usual pleasantries, but she was not particularly interested in what they had to say and her attention wandered to her surroundings. The park, once on the outskirts but now in the heart of London, was an oasis of green. There was a wide tree-lined carriageway and several paths for pedestrians and the famous Rotten Row where horsemen and women showed off their mounts. Her curiosity was aroused by a slim young man in a single-breasted green riding coat and biscuit-coloured riding breeches, who was very deliberately pacing the ground and making notes on a pad he was carrying. Every now and then he looked up at a group of elms that graced that corner of the park and appeared to be sizing them up and drawing them. She took a step closer to see what he was about.

He must have sensed her presence because he suddenly turned and looked straight at her. She found herself catching her breath because he was the most handsome man she had ever seen in her life. His eyes, she noted, were greenish brown and they were laughing, not at her, she was sure of that, but in a kind of amused empathy, as if he understood her curiosity and was not in the least put off by it. His hair, beneath a brown beaver hat, was a little darker than gold and curled into his neck. His hands, holding his notepad and pencil, were lean like the rest of him, the fingers tapered. An artist, she decided. He smiled at her, put his finger to the brim of his hat and tilted it towards her. Her answering smile lit her face as if she had suddenly met someone she had known long ago and hadn't seen for a while.

'Esme, who is that?' Rosemary had said goodbye to her

friends and turned to see her sister apparently on nodding terms with a young man.

'I've no idea. I've never seen him before, but he's handsome, isn't he?'

'Esme, how could you?'

'Could I what?'

'Smile in that familiar way at a man to whom you have not been introduced.'

'But he smiled first and—'

'Then he cannot be a real gentleman. It is the lady's prerogative to acknowledge a gentleman when she is out and until she does so, it behoves a gentleman to show no sign of recognition. You should have ignored him.'

'Would that not have been impolite?'

'Not at all. Now come away before he decides to approach us, for I should feel mortified to have to speak to him.' She took Esme's arm and almost dragged her away.

Esme looked back over her shoulder and discovered the young man was staring after them, which made her giggle.

'Esme!' Rosemary reprimanded her. 'I see I shall have to take you to task about what is and what is not acceptable behaviour. You do not smile at strange men. Goodness, it is asking for them to take liberties.'

'What liberties?' Esme asked. 'Do you mean kissing me?'

'Good heavens, I hope not. I mean speaking to you without an introduction.'

'Oh, that.' Esme was dismissive.

Rosemary's reply to that was a decided sniff.

Felix watched them go, wanting to laugh aloud. The young lady, who was very lovely with her rosebud complexion and neat figure, was evidently being given a scolding, but it did not seem to be subduing her. He wondered who she was. Was she one of those young ladies who came to London for a Season with the express purpose of snaring a husband? It was early in the year for that and she seemed a little young to be tying herself down to marriage.

His mother might not agree; she had been urging him ever since he returned from France without Juliette to find himself a bride. 'Someone young and malleable,' she had said. 'Then you can mould her to your way of doing things. Besides, a young bride is more likely to produce healthy offspring.' He smiled to himself; this particular young lady did not look as if she were especially malleable, not that he would want a wife who dare not say boo to a goose. He pulled himself up short. How could the sight of a pretty girl make his thoughts suddenly turn to marriage. He wasn't ready for that yet; time, the healer, had yet to do its work.

He was not a hermit by any means. To please his mother, he had attended tea parties and dances in the assembly rooms in his home town of Birmingham, taken tea with the matrons and danced with their daughters, making superficial conversation, even flirting a little, but, as his mother was quick to point out, that could hardly be called a serious pursuit of a bride. He supposed he would have to marry one day, but he never felt less like falling in love again and it would be unfair on any young lady to use her simply to beget an heir and have an elegant companion, if she were expecting a husband to love her. It would be better to choose someone more mature than the young miss with the friendly smile, someone worldly wise who wouldn't expect declarations of eternal love, but would be content with wealth and position.

He smiled ruefully to himself; whatever had set his thoughts on marriage had better be stifled. If this idea of a great exhibition came about, he would be too busy to think of anything else. He looked down at the pad in his hand. There was a series of measurements and a rough sketch of the elm trees, which were going to be a stumbling block to any good design. The Exhibition building committee were working on a design but he thought it was ugly, and it took no account of the trees, assuming they would have to be felled. Even the committee was dissatisfied with it and an idea was being mooted for a competition to design the building and he thought he might enter it.

His pencil moved over the pad, roughing out the plan of a building with an open central courtyard to accommodate the elms and then for no reason that he could fathom, added people to his drawing: the urchin bowling a hoop, a man on a horse, a carriage on the drive, the cake-and-fruit stall beside the water and the two ladies he had just seen. He laughed at himself for his fancifulness. Pulling his watch from waistcoat pocket, he was startled to discover it was already four-thirty; his valet would be dancing up and down in impatience. He hurried to where he had tethered his horse and cantered off in the direction of Hyde Park Corner and his house in Bruton Street.

'Rosie, could we not go and see the guests arriving for the banquet?' Esme asked when they were on their way home in the carriage after Lady Aviemore's tea party. Esme had expected the company to be mixed, but they had all been ladies, some young, some older, who spent the time between sipping tea and nibbling wafer-thin sandwiches, in exchanging gossip, some of it shockingly malicious, but the outcome was several invitations to soirées and musical evenings and little dances.

'It is too early in the year for balls,' her ladyship had said. 'But I intend to hold one as soon as the town begins to fill up. Lord Aviemore is on the committee dedicated to raising funds for the Exhibition and we thought a subscription ball would be just the thing. Very exclusive, of course. You will come, dear Lady Trent, won't you, and bring your delightful sister?'

Rosemary declared she would be delighted, which surprised Esme, considering Rowan's implacable opposition to the project, but a look from her sister stopped her making any comment.

'Lord Aviemore is to attend tonight's banquet,' her ladyship continued. 'It is being held to encourage the towns in the provinces to raise funds. After all, it is a countrywide endeavour, not just for the capital.'

'I thought it was an international project involving the whole world,' Esme put in.

Lady Aviemore looked sharply at her as if surprised to hear her daring to take part in the conversation. 'Indeed it is,' she said. 'But it is the idea of our own dear Prince and it is this country which will organise and build it.'

'I believe the banquet is to be a very grand affair,' one of the other ladies put in. 'I intend to go past the Mansion House on my way home to see the guests arrive.'

It was that which had prompted Esme's question. Ever since she had returned from her walk in the park, she had felt unsettled, as if she were waiting for something extraordinary to happen, though she had no idea what it might be. The tea party had done nothing to dispel it. They had no engagement for the evening and, as both Rowan and Myles were to be out and they only had themselves to please, she could not see that a little diversion would do any harm. Myles was off to the banquet at the Mansion House and Rowan was going to have dinner with Lord Brougham, a former Lord Chancellor, who was one of the prominent figures working to scotch the idea of an exhibition. She smiled to herself in the darkening interior of the carriage, wondering if Myles and Rowan had encountered each other on their way out and, if they had, what they had said.

'Whatever for?' Rosemary demanded.

'It will be such fun to see all the coaches and carriages arriving and the guests dressed in their finery. I should like to be able to tell Mama and Papa I had seen Prince Albert. Oh, do tell the coachman to take us that way.'

Esme could see she was tempted to see the spectacle herself, though she still hesitated. 'What Rowan would say I cannot think.'

'Why should he say anything? You do not have to tell him.'

'Goodness, Esme, I would never deceive him or keep anything from him, and I sincerely hope that when you are married, you will be completely honest and open with your husband.'

'I am sure he would not begrudge me a sight of the Queen's consort arriving for a banquet.' She did not add that if he did, she would have made a terrible mistake in her choice of husband. She was beginning to think this idea of deliberately setting out to find a husband was full of pitfalls and she must be on her guard. 'Go on, Rosie, it won't take long, will it? There is no one waiting for us at home.'

'Oh, very well. I suppose it cannot do any harm.' She used her fan to lean forward and tap the coachman on his back. 'Croxon, take us round by the Mansion House.'

Without giving a flicker of reaction to this strange way of getting from Russell Square to Kensington, he obediently turned the carriage and headed down Kingsway to Aldwych, Fleet Street and Ludgate Hill, an area new to Esme. This was the financial heart of the City and was a mixture of imposing buildings and little alleyways and courts. They began to notice the crowds as they approached St Paul's and from then it was difficult for the coach to proceed. 'There's nothing for it—but we shall have to get out and walk,' Esme said when the carriage finally came to a stop, closed in by the hordes, and, before her astonished sister could stop her, had opened the door and jumped to the ground. Rosemary felt obliged to follow.

They pressed forward until they managed to find themselves a good position where they could see the guests arriving, with Rosemary grumbling all the way. 'We'll be trampled to death,' she said, holding tight on to Esme's arm.

'Of course we won't. You saw how everyone made way for us, they probably think we are guests.'

'I don't think there are any lady guests. They will all be men.'

'Really? Then we shan't see any sumptuous dresses.'

'No, did you think we would?'

Esme did not answer because the police were forcing everyone back to make way for the cabs and carriages bringing the guests. There may not have been any ladies, but the men were got up like peacocks. There were foreign ambassadors in court dress, high-ranking military men in dress uniform, glittering with medals, mayors from provincial towns in red robes and regalia, bishops in their vestments, others in colourful livery, who Rosie told her were the Masters of the City Guilds, and there were men in plain evening dress, wearing honours on their breasts.

'Oh, look, there's Myles,' Esme said, pointing. 'Doesn't he look grand?'

Myles was wearing a double-breasted black evening coat, narrow black trousers, a blue brocade waistcoat and a shiny top hat. He did not appear to see them as he walked into the building beside the Mayor of Leicester.

But someone else did notice them. The young man they had seen in the park was right behind Myles. His evening coat sported several decorations. His waistcoat was black with silver embroidery, which glittered as he moved. And he moved gracefully, Esme noticed, a sight which set her heart pumping. Oh, but he was handsome! He turned to follow Myles and caught sight of her animated face under a fetching blue bonnet and, smiling, stopped to doff his hat and give her a slight bow of recognition before disappearing inside.

'The effrontery of the man!' Rosemary exclaimed. 'You should not have encouraged him to be familiar, Esme.'

'I didn't encourage him. I cannot help it if he chooses to tip his hat to me. I do not know why you are making such a fuss.'

'It is the second time today. I begin to wonder if you do know him after all and that is why you wanted to come here.'

'No, Rosie, I promise you I have never met him. It is pure coincidence.'

'If you ever meet him again, I want you to cut him dead. I cannot have him think you wish to know him.'

Esme did not answer, though she could have told her sister she would not mind knowing him. He must be someone of importance if he had been invited to the banquet. Instead she turned back to the road in front of them as a crescendo of cheering signified that Prince Albert was arriving. Dressed, according to Rosemary, as an Elder Brother of Trinity House, he was met at the door by the Lord Mayor of London in full regalia, as soon as they had gone inside, the doors were closed.

'There's nothing more to see,' Rosemary said. 'We might as well find the carriage and go home.'

It was easier said than done; the crowd seemed reluctant to disperse and were still milling about talking of what they had seen and those guests they had recognised. Rosemary and Esme linked arms and pushed their way through. By the time they reached the carriage, Rosemary's bonnet was awry and she was decidedly nervous, unlike Esme who did not realise the dangers inherent for two women walking about the city streets alone after dark, for night had fallen while they had been standing and it was now nearly seven o'clock.

'Thank heaven for that,' Rosemary said, when they had gained the safety of the carriage and she was able to set her hat straight. 'Don't ever inveigle me into doing anything like it again, Esme, for I declare I'm done in.'

'Oh, but I shall have such a tale to tell Mama and Papa when I write.'

'No, Esme, I beg you not to. They will think I do not know how to look after you and Papa will come and fetch you back and you will have no come-out. It will make me look an idiot to my friends and all those people who have invited you to their homes. You wouldn't want that to happen, would you?'

Esme agreed that she wouldn't. After all, there was a handsome young man in town whom she seemed destined to run into and who was she to argue with destiny? She could not help wondering about him. He was very self-assured, perhaps a little conceited, but he had every right to be, considering how handsome he was. She wondered how many young ladies were falling over themselves to be noticed by him. If he was still around when the new débutantes were released on to the town, he would be seized upon by every hostess and hopeful mama and bombarded with invitations.

Unless, of course, there was something unacceptable about him—a shady past, some scandal, or perhaps he was not as financially independent as he appeared. Oh, she did hope that was not the case.

Chapter Two

Felix followed the procession of guests down the corridor, lined with greenery, to the Egyptian Hall where the banquet was being held. In honour of the occasion, the columns round its walls were decorated with symbols to represent the different British counties and their products. At the head of the table were two figures representing peace and plenty and at the other Britannia holding a plan of the Exhibition, which could only have been the committee's own plan, surrounded by four angels delivering invitations to all the countries in the world to send exhibits. 'What do you think of that?' he murmured to the man beside him, nodding at Britannia.

'The statue?'

'No, the plan of the building in her hand.'

'I think we could do better.'

'I am sure we can.' He held out his hand. 'Felix Pendlebury.'

'How do you do?' Myles took the hand and shook it. 'Myles Moorcroft.'

'Oh, I've heard of you. A railway entrepreneur, aren't you?'

'Among other things. I have heard your name somewhere, too. Lord Pendlebury, if I'm not mistaken. Something to do with the manufacture of glass.'

'Among other things,' he said, echoing Myles's own words.

'You intend to submit an exhibit?'

'More than that—I'm going to have a go at designing the Exhibition hall. It needs to be light and airy, something to make people want to come to visit, not a mausoleum.'

Myles laughed. 'Glass?'

'Well, why not?'

'No reason at all, if it can be made safe.'

'I think it can. Glass is much tougher nowadays than it used to be.'

They stopped speaking as Prince Albert arrived and took his seat. 'Have you met His Highness?' Myles ventured.

'Yes, we both belong to the Society of Arts, which is how I came to be involved with the idea of the Exhibition. What about you?'

'I met him through the Society to Improve the Condition of the Working Classes. We are both passionate about that.'

'Ah, now I place you. You're the gentleman who calls himself a navvy. I heard tell of a wager about filling a truck with forty tons of earth in a day. Is it true? Did you do it?'

'Yes, though that was some time ago. Nowadays I only go on site to inspect the works and make sure the men are content. A contented workforce works better than one that is constantly bickering.'

'Then we are in agreement. What is your interest in the Exhibition?'

'Apart from raising funds, I might be interested in supply-ing the builders with girders and other metal products from my engineering works in Peterborough. And I would like to exhibit a locomotive.'

'A locomotive! How would you bring it to the site?'

'Ah, that's the challenge.'

Felix laughed and they continued to talk animatedly through all the courses—turbot soup, fish, lobster, game pies, pigeon and mutton, fruit cakes and ices—and only stopped when the traditional loving cup was passed round the whole company. After that the loyal toast was drunk and the National Anthem sung before the speeches. First to speak was Prince Albert, who outlined the reasons for having an exhibition and was vigorously applauded when he said it should be paid for by public donation and not government funds. 'Which is the reason we are all here,' Felix murmured.

The Prince was followed by several more, all echoing the same theme. Sir Robert Peel, an elder statesman and former Prime Minster, said he was confident they would succeed in spite of the objections of some, a pointed reference to people like Rowan. The Earl of Carlisle was the last speaker and he said the Exhibition should encompass all nations, classes and creeds, saying it was predominantly intended as a festival of the working man and woman.

'Which hardly includes anyone here,' Felix said, as everyone applauded.

The evening was judged a great success and everyone went away determined to drum up support from their own towns, villages and industries. Felix and Myles strolled out side by side, still talking. 'Can I offer you a lift?' Myles asked as he hailed one of the many cabs that had arrived touting for business. 'I'm going to Kensington.'

Felix accepted and asked the cabbie to drop him off at the end of Old Bond Street. 'I can walk from there,' he said.

Before they parted they arranged to meet the following afternoon at Brooks's club to continue their discussion.

Felix was in a mellow mood as he made his way to Bruton Street, where the family's London house was situated. It had been a successful evening, he mused, everyone was enthusiastic and it looked as though they might soon sink the opposition. He had met a new friend, a man whose outlook on life and championing of the working classes matched his own and, besides all that, he had glimpsed one of the loveliest young ladies he had seen in a long time.

He wasn't quite sure what it was that made her lovely. Was it her perfectly oval face, or her nose, which was neither too big nor too small, or her blue eyes, which were large and intelligent, or perhaps her trim figure with its small waist and rounded bosom? Was it all those things or something else entirely, the essence of the woman that shone through and set his pulses quickening? Judging by the way she reacted to her companion's scolding she was a spirited chit, not one to be easily cowed. And then to see her again outside the Mansion House, dressed simply but elegantly, hemmed in by the hoi polloi, had made his day, especially when she responded to his salute with a brilliant smile. But who was she?

He ran up the steps and let himself into the house, chuckling at the memory. He didn't know why, after so long, he suddenly found he could laugh again when thinking of a woman, but it felt good.

Esme woke next morning to find the sun shining and the birds singing. After a very wet winter, spring was at last on its way. She scrambled out of bed, washed in water from the ewer on the washstand, dressed in a light wool gown in a soft lime-green and hurried downstairs to greet the new day. She found Rowan sitting in the breakfast room munching toast and marmalade.

'Good morning, my lord,' she said, helping herself from the dishes on the sideboard: scrambled eggs, a rasher of bacon and a slice of toast.

'Good morning, Esme, you are up betimes.'

'Yes, it is too nice to lie abed. I was hoping I might ride today. Rosie said you could find me a mount.'

'Croxon will hire something for you, but you are not under any circumstances to ride alone. It is not done in polite society and, besides, your parents would never forgive me if you took a tumble while in my care.'

'I won't take a tumble. I haven't fallen off a horse since I was five years old and that wasn't my fault.'

He smiled. Everyone smiled at Esme, even when scolding her. 'Nevertheless I want your promise.'

'You have it. Shall I go and ask Croxon now?'

'No, I will do it. He is no doubt preparing the carriage. I shall want it today.' He rose as Myles came into the room. 'Morning, Moorcroft.' The greeting was polite, certainly not jovial.

'Good morning.' In contrast, Myles was very cheerful. 'Did I hear you talking about riding?'

'Yes,' Esme put in. 'Rowan is going to ask Croxon to hire a mount for me.'

'No need to trouble Croxon,' Myles said, addressing Rowan. 'I can save him the bother. I was going to Tattersalls to hire one for myself. I'll do the same for Esme. We can take a ride together.'

'My thanks,' Rowan said. 'I am somewhat busy today.' And with that he left the room.

Esme laughed. 'I don't think he likes you, Myles.'

'He doesn't like what I stand for. I don't think it's personal.' He helped himself to food and sat at the table opposite her.

'Did you have a good evening?' she asked.

'Yes, it was a great success.'

'Oh, that is why Rowan is so grumpy.'

'Is he? I hadn't noticed.'

'We saw you going into the banquet, Rosie and I. We were standing on the pavement, watching everyone go in, and there you were. I thought you looked very elegant.'

He ignored the compliment. 'How did you get there?'

'In the carriage. At least as far as St Paul's. We walked from there.'

'I am surprised at Rosemary agreeing to it.'

'Oh, I think she secretly wanted to go.' She paused. 'Myles, can I ask you something?'

'Ask away.'

'Is it very wrong to smile at a gentleman when he doffs his hat and bows to you?'

'No, why should it be?'

'Rosie said I should have ignored him. You see, we had not been introduced. He was a complete stranger.'

'Oh, I see. Then your sister was probably right.'

'But I'm sure he was a gentleman. We saw him going into the banquet and he was so handsome and elegant and his smile was catching. I could not help responding.'

'I think,' he said solemnly while trying to hide the twitching of his lips, 'that you had better be guided by Rosemary.'

She sighed. 'I don't suppose I shall ever see him again, so it does not matter.'

'Bear it in mind if you meet other men who smile at you.'

'Oh, I am sure I shall not be tempted by other men.'

He looked sideways at her and decided not to comment. 'What else did you do yesterday?'

'Shopped for clothes. I think Rowan must be very rich because Rosemary did not once query the price of anything. It is all very extravagant and I feel dreadful.'

'Because of the extravagance?'

'Not only that, but because Lucy gave me all those lovely clothes and I shall not wear them.' She brightened suddenly. 'I will wear the riding habit though, if you will take me riding. You did mean it, didn't you?' There was a new forest-green habit, among the clothes being made for her, but that had not yet arrived.

'Yes, but it will have to be this morning. I have an appointment this afternoon and tomorrow I must go home and leave you.'

Rosemary entered the room and bade them both good morning before helping herself to some breakfast and sitting at the table opposite Esme.

'Myles is going to hire hacks and take me riding this morning,' Esme told her. 'Shall you come? We are going as soon as I have changed and Myles has arranged for the horses.'

Rosemary, who had been denied the use of the carriage that day, agreed that a ride would be just the thing to blow away the cobwebs and asked Myles to instruct a groom at the mews to saddle her horse, then both ladies finished their breakfast and went to change.

Esme came downstairs half an hour later in Lucy's riding habit, a dark blue taffeta with military style frogging across the jacket. The matching skirt was plain and the hat was a blue tricorne, with the brim held up one side by a curling peacock feather. Rosemary joined her five minutes later and by that time Myles had returned, riding a huge mount and leading two others, one Rosemary's own horse and another for Esme.

They mounted and set off, entering Hyde Park by a gate close to Knightsbridge barracks, and were soon riding down Rotten Row.

'I suppose we shall be denied this pleasure when they start building the Exhibition hall,' Rosemary said.

'Possibly,' Myles agreed. 'The details have yet to be worked out.'

'Well, I think it is too bad. It is so handy for me if I want to ride or come out in the carriage and it will all be spoiled. I am disappointed in you, Myles, really, I am.'

'It is not my project, ma'am.'

'You support it. I should have thought you would have had more family feeling.'

'My feelings for the family have not changed. I support the idea of an exhibition because I think it will be good for the country and good for the working man.'

'You will give him ideas above his station. There will be unrest and violence, fuelled by all the foreigners roaming about with nothing to do but cause trouble. Indeed, Rowan thinks...'

'Oh, please, do not argue over it,' Esme put in. 'It is too nice a day to be at odds with each other.' She looked about for a way of diverting them. 'Oh, look, there's that gentleman we saw yesterday.'

'What gentleman?' her sister asked.

'That one.' She lifted her crop to point him out. The young man, dressed in a single-breasted brown wool jacket and matching trousers, was busy as he had been the day before, sketching and making notes.

'Oh, no. I do believe he does it on purpose.'

Felix looked up and, catching sight of them with Myles, stood watching them approach.

'Do you know him?' Myles asked.

'No, we do not,' Rosemary said sharply. 'But he is insufferably impudent. He seems to think he can smile and doff his hat and that is as good as an introduction.'

'Oh, in that case, let me do the honours.' Myles drew rein beside Felix and the two ladies had perforce to stop beside him. 'My lady, may I present Lord Felix Pendlebury? Pendlebury, Viscountess Trent. And this…' He turned to Esme with a twinkle in his eye, which told her he had connected her question earlier that morning with Rosemary's comment about smiling and doffing hats. 'This is Lady Trent's sister, Lady Esme Vernley.'

'Ladies, your obedient.' Felix bowed to each in turn.

Rosemary's slight inclination of the head was the smallest she could manage without snubbing him, which she could not do, since he had now been properly introduced.

'Oh, it is so nice to have a name for you, my lord,' Esme said. 'What are you drawing?' She indicated his sketching pad.

'It is an imaginary scene, my lady.' He proffered her the pad, which she took.

'And you have put us in it. Look, Rosemary, there's you and there's me.' She held it out for her sister to see, but Rosemary hardly glanced at it.

'If it is meant to be us, then I think it is an impertinence.'

'None was meant, my lady,' he said. 'I was simply drawing what I thought the scene might look like when the Exhibition building is completed.'

'I like it,' Esme said, handing it back to him. Their hands

touched as he took it from her and she found herself tingling all over from the shock of the contact. But it was far from an unpleasant feeling and she wondered if he felt it, too. He was looking up at her in such a strange way, his eyes moving over her face, as if he were studying her features, trying to memorise them. She found that that was what she was doing to him, storing up a picture of his lean face, high cheek bones, the well-defined brows, green eyes with their little flecks of brown, his smiling mouth, his proud chin held above a purple silk cravat. Was he teasing her? Did she mind? She did not.

'I did not know you knew Myles,' she said.

'We met last night at the banquet and found we had much in common.'

'He tells me it was a great success. Did you find it so?' She ignored Rosie's fidgeting beside her.

'Indeed, I believe it was.'

'Did you come to town especially for it?'

'No, I have other business and visits I must make on behalf of my mother.'

'Then perhaps we shall come across each other again. I am here to visit my sister for the summer—'

'Esme!' Rosemary's tone was furious. 'I am sure Lord Pendlebury does not wish to know that.'

'On the contrary, my lady, I am delighted to hear it,' he said. 'Since my father's death brought me back from the Continent two years ago, I have been kept busy at home in Birmingham and have sadly lost touch with the *beau monde;* I shall be glad to see someone I know.'

'The horses are becoming restive,' Rosemary said. 'Come, Esme, it is time we resumed our ride.'

'Then I bid you au revoir, ladies.' As they moved off, he

turned to Myles, who had watched the exchange with some amusement. 'Until this afternoon, Moorcroft. Two o'clock we said, didn't we?'

'Yes, two o'clock,' Myles answered and hurried to catch up with his sisters-in-law.

'Esme, your behaviour has put me to the blush,' Rosemary was saying. 'You were openly flirting with the man and we have no idea who he is or anything about him. I am ashamed of you.'

'Why, what did I do wrong?'

'Telling him you were here for the summer and hoped to meet him again. I never heard anything so brazen. You would have been asking him to call on us if I had not stopped you.'

'Oh, no, I wouldn't do that,' Esme said blithely. 'It is your home, not mine; besides, if he came to the house he would only quarrel with Rowan, considering they are on opposing sides over the Exhibition.'

Myles was chuckling. Rosemary turned to him in exasperation. 'It is all very well for you to laugh, Myles, you do not have the responsibility for this wretched sister of mine. I shan't be able to let her out of my sight for an instant all summer long. She will talk to anyone. I cannot remember Lucy or I being allowed such licence.'

'Times are changing,' he said evenly. 'Young ladies are allowed a little more freedom to say what they think nowadays.'

'That is what worries me. Just who and what is Lord Pendlebury? I have never heard of him. He says he has returned from abroad. Where abroad?'

'France, I believe. Or it might have been Venice. He was working abroad when his father died and he returned to take over the family estate near Birmingham.'

'Working! Oh, now I see what you have in common, you both like to get your hands dirty.'

'He doesn't have dirty hands,' Esme protested. 'They are very clean and long-fingered, an artist's hands. Is he an artist, Myles?'

'I have no idea,' he said. 'But judging by that sketch he was doing he has a talent in that direction. I believe his business is in the manufacture of glass.'

'Well, I think he is an artist,' Esme said.

'What you think of him is of no account,' Rosemary said. 'He is a manufacturer, a tradesman, and you will not think of him at all, do you hear?'

'I hear.' Esme told her, but she didn't see how she could obey. Her thoughts could not be commanded like that. They wandered about in her head, jumping from one subject to another, and she could not say when a thought of the handsome Lord Pendlebury might pop into her mind, let alone tell it not to. She was thinking of him now, especially of his eyes. She had thought at first they were laughing; indeed, they had been full of amusement when Rosemary had been so haughty towards him, as if he understood and did not care, but when he spoke of being abroad, a shadow had passed across them, like a cloud on a summer's day suddenly excluding the sun. There had been unhappiness in his life. She wondered what it was that made him suddenly sad and wished she could banish it and bring back the sunshine. Which was nonsense, of course.

Felix watched them go and then break into a canter. The ladies were both accomplished horsewomen and he could admire that, even in the stiff-backed Lady Trent. As for her sister… Esme, a pretty name for a pretty young lady. He flipped over the page of his sketching pad and began drawing her face, every line of which seemed to be etched into his memory.

He was being a fool, he knew that. He knew nothing about her. Was she, for instance, capable of breaking hearts? He rather fancied she was. He was beginning to envy the young men who might aspire to court her, but he did not envy them their broken hearts when she tired of them. He looked at what he had drawn and knew he had failed utterly to reproduce the *joie de vivre* that showed in her eyes, in her smiling mouth, in her trim figure, which seemed to buzz with barely controlled energy. Her whole demeanour seemed to say, 'Here I am, ready for anything, put me to the test.' He did not suppose that she, watched over and cosseted, had had a moment's unhappiness in her whole life. She did not know what it felt like to be betrayed, to discover that what you had fondly believed was honest and wholesome was nothing of the sort. He hoped she never would.

He saw the trio returning back at a neat trot and hastily flipped back to his plan, pretending to concentrate on the lines of his proposed building. He looked up as the horses approached him and tipped his hat to the ladies. Rosemary dipped her head in brief acknowledgement, but Lady Esme, riding slightly behind her sister, lifted her crop and gave him a broad smile. It was almost conspiratorial. It was the memory of that smile he carried back to Bruton Street with him.

He was still thinking of it when he met Myles at Brooks's later that day. The club was quiet at that time and the two men found a corner to enjoy a bottle of wine and talk, and though he would have liked to talk about Lady Esme Vernley, that was not the reason for the meeting and they settled down to discuss the Exhibition and how they could promote it. Knowing that it was meant to celebrate the work men and women did and the things they achieved, most of those who were referred to as the 'operative classes' were as enthusiastic as he was and were already giving their pennies and sixpences to the fund.

'It won't be enough,' Felix said. 'It's the business owners we must aim at, people such as we are with money to spare. If we set a good example...'

'I have done so already,' Myles told him. 'I do not doubt we shall manage it if we keep the momentum going. We have to. Already there are inquiries from abroad to display their wares.' He chuckled. 'My brother-in-law, Viscount Trent, is convinced that the capital will be overrun with foreigners, none of whom are honest or clean, and if they have nowhere to stay will be living in parks and doorways. Not only that, he is positive they will stir up unrest among our own workers.'

'Accommodation will have to be provided for them and the troublemakers weeded out. The Duke of Wellington won't hear of enlisting the help of foreign police. He is relying on our own police and the army to keep order. I know because he has asked for my help, on account of the fact that I came into contact with some of the revolutionaries when I was in Paris and was able to pass on intelligence to our government. I think he is worrying unduly, but I have said I will do what I can. We are to meet next week to discuss it.' He paused. 'I tell you this in confidence, of course.'

'Of course. You will be staying in town, then?'

'For the moment.' He smiled suddenly. 'I also have courtesy visits to make to my mother's friends, which I had been looking on as an irksome duty, but if your delightful sister-in-law should happen to be present at any of their at-homes, it will change from a duty to a pleasure.'

'She is a delight,' Myles agreed. 'And I hope nothing happens to spoil that.'

'Why should it?'

'Because she is an innocent and ripe for adventure and could easily be led into accepting flattery and flirtation as reality and falling head over heels in love when the attraction might well be that she is the daughter of an earl.'

'Are you warning me to stay clear?'

'I would not be so presumptuous. I hope you are old enough and wise enough to understand and perhaps look out for her.'

'Does she not have a dragon of a sister to do that?'

Myles laughed. 'Oh, she will contrive to slip her rein if the watchfulness becomes too unbearable.'

'A scatterbrain, then.'

'Far from it. She is the youngest daughter and her parents and sisters, Rosemary in particular, tend to treat her like a schoolgirl and a delicate one at that, but she is twenty in two months' time and not nearly as fragile as she looks. She embraces everything with enthusiasm and is afraid of nothing, but underneath it all, I think she is capable of deep feeling.'

'You know the family well, then?'

'I am married to Esme's other sister, Lucinda—have been for six years now. Esme is more like Lucy than Rosemary, a free spirit. I wish I could stay and keep an eye on her, but I am anxious to return to my wife and children. Henry, our three-year-old, had a nasty cold and Lucy would not leave him to accompany me and I am not comfortable in the Trent household without her. I am the upstart, a man who likes to earn his living, and though the Earl, their father, has come to accept me, Rosemary has never thought me quite good enough for her sister. Matters are made worse by my support for the Exhibition. Trent is implacably opposed.'

'I see I shall have to avoid crossing swords with him. When do you leave town?'

'Tomorrow morning.'

'Then I shall bid you adieu now. No doubt we will meet frequently as the year advances.'

'I certainly hope so.' He paused, smiling. 'Does your mother count Lady Mountjoy among her friends, my lord?'

Felix's grin was one of understanding. 'Do you know, I believe she does.'

They left the building together and parted on the street, Myles to return to Trent House, Felix to take a stroll about the town. It was necessary to become familiar with every street, every alleyway, every court, every hotbed of dissent if he were to discharge the duty the Duke of Wellington had set him.

It was at the end of that perambulation, when he was on his way home again, that he decided to call on Lady Mountjoy in Duke Street.

Her ladyship received him in her drawing room. She was thin as a rake, dressed in unrelieved black, even down to black mittens and a black lace handkerchief. He bowed and explained the purpose of his visit was to pay his respects to his mother's old friend.

'Fanny Pendlebury,' she mused. 'Haven't seen or heard of her in years. What made her suddenly think of me?'

'Unfortunately she seldom comes to town nowadays,' he

said. 'But one day she was indulging in a little sentimental remembrance and spoke of the times when you both arrived in London for a come-out Season and what happy times they were. She wondered what had happened to you and how you did, and I undertook to make inquiries. I have lately returned from a protracted stay on the Continent and am rediscovering London.'

'You will not find it much changed, except for all the new houses and railways stretching into the countryside. And I am, as you see me, widowed and living alone.'

'My condolences, my lady.'

'It happened many years ago and I have become used to pleasing myself. I have a great many friends. I go out and about and entertain. I am about to go out now, so I am afraid I cannot stay and entertain you, but come back another time. I am at home on Tuesday afternoon. Married, are you? Or affianced?'

He thought briefly of Juliette and nearly changed his mind about the whole idea. It was all very well for Myles Moorcroft to ask him to look out for Lady Esme, but Moorcroft did not know the story. Nor, for his pride's sake, would he tell him, or anyone else, for that matter. 'No, not married,' he said. 'Nor yet affianced.'

'Good. How old are you?'

'Twenty-seven, my lady.'

'Old enough to settle down.'

'That is what my mother tells me.'

'Ah, now I see. She sent you to me, knowing I knew everyone in town and could help you find a wife.' She did not give him the opportunity to confirm or deny this before going on. 'Have no fear, I will introduce you to some nice young fillies. A handsome man like you should have no trouble. No trouble at all.'

He bowed and took his leave, wondering what he had let himself in for. If Lady Mountjoy wrote and told his mother of their conversation, she would die laughing. Or perhaps she would not; perhaps she would thank her ladyship for taking her recalcitrant son in hand.

Esme felt she had lost an ally when Myles went home. Rosemary was becoming impossible, lecturing her morning, noon and night and ordering Miss Bannister to keep a close watch on her. 'See she does not speak to any strange men,' she told the old governess when they went out without her. 'Before we know where we are, she will be carried off and goodness knows what ills will befall her. Just because a man has a title does not mean he is a gentleman.'

'You cannot mean Lord Pendlebury,' Esme put in.

It was Sunday and they had just returned from morning service at St George's Hanover Square, where, to Esme's astonishment, Lord Pendlebury had been in the congregation. Rosemary had been outraged, convinced he was hounding them, but when Esme pointed out that he had a perfect right to attend whatever church he chose, just as they had done, considering St George's was not their nearest place of worship, she was forced to agree. He had not approached them, which in one way had disappointed Esme, but in another she had been relieved. Even so, the sight of him tipping his shiny black top hat to them in the churchyard after the service had set her sister off again.

'I speak as I find,' Rosemary said, drawing off her gloves and removing her hat and handing them to her maid. 'We do not know him, we do not know his background and yet you smile and flirt with him like some…some… Words fail me.' Her fine blue wool coat followed the hat and gloves.

'He cannot be so objectionable if he is known to Myles and Myles saw fit to present him,' Esme protested, taking off her own outdoor things and giving them to Miss Bannister who had accompanied them to church.

'Myles only met the man the evening before, so that does not signify.'

'I think it is unkind of you to judge him badly on so little evidence. A man may smile, may he not?'

'Not at a young unmarried lady to whom he has not been properly introduced.'

'Myles did—'

'We will hear no more of Lord Pendlebury, if you please. Peers who go into trade and manufacturing are betraying their birthright and not to be considered. I can and will introduce you to other young gentleman who will make far more suitable husbands.'

'Rosie, I was not thinking of him as a husband.'

'I am glad to hear that. You are in London to see and be seen in the hope of finding a husband, as you very well know. It is why I offered to sponsor your come-out and keep you by me for longer than a Season, which is too short when all is said and done. You are here ahead of the others and that will give you a flying start. You are, after all, the daughter of an earl.'

'I sincerely hope no one considers that the prime reason for marrying me. If I thought that, I should most certainly turn him down.'

'Of course it must not be the main reason, but it certainly makes a difference. Is that not so, Banny?' she appealed to Miss Bannister, who nodded sagely. 'There, you see! I am right. Now let us go into the drawing room and have a glass of something before luncheon is served. I want to tell you about the outings I have arranged for next week.' She led the way into the drawing room, leaving Miss Bannister and the maid to toil up the second flight of stairs with the discarded outdoor clothes.

'Now, let us see what is on offer,' Rosemary said, picking up her engagement diary. 'Nothing much happens on a Monday, so perhaps a little sight-seeing. There is St Paul's or the Tower, though I find that a dismal place. We could go to the British Museum or the National Gallery. If you like, I am sure Rowan could arrange for us to see round the new Houses of Parliament.'

'I should like to see it all.'

'Not all at once, I hope.'

'No, a little at a time whenever you have the time to spare.'

'We shall see, but once you are out and the town fills up, we shall be inundated with invitations. You know how many we received when we went to Lady Aviemore's. On Tuesday, for instance, we are expected at Lady Mountjoy's at-home.'

'Are we? I don't remember her.'

'She was the tall, thin lady in widow's weeds. She is another like Lady Aviemore, a prominent figure in the *beau monde,* knows everyone. She can do you a great deal of good.'

'How?'

'By introducing you to other important people who will introduce you to more. Before you know it, you will be the asked out everywhere.'

'Will you be doing any entertaining?'

'Of course, invitations must be reciprocated. And I have it in mind to hold a ball for you later, when the Season gets under way.'

'Really? Oh, Rosie, you are so kind. I shall like that,' Esme said, thinking of Lord Pendlebury. She had managed to banish him from her thoughts for all of half an hour, but now he was back, filling her mind with an image of him in evening dress, taking her on to the floor to waltz. She would be in a beautiful ball gown with her hair done up in coils and jewels at her throat, and they would dance and dance in perfect harmony and smile at each other. But it was a futile image because he would never be invited.

What had made him so unacceptable? The fact that he smiled and tipped his hat to her? The fact that she had smiled back? Or was it that he was an acquaintance of Myles, and Rosemary had always looked down on Myles, for all he was Lord Moorcroft's heir and one of the richest men in the kingdom, certainly richer than Papa. Or was it that he supported the Exhibition, which Rowan was determined to sink without trace? Or that he manufactured glass? What was wrong with making glass? Some of it was very beautiful.

'If we cannot find you a suitable husband by the end of the Season, I shall have failed utterly,' Rosemary said.

'Suitable does not necessarily mean desirable,' Esme said. 'I should like to desire the man I marry.'

'Esme!'

'What is wrong with that? Did you not desire Rowan?'

'That is none of your business.' Her sister's face had turned bright pink. 'And not a subject for an unmarried lady.'

'Surely it is too late after one is married to discover that one's husband is not at all desirable? Suitable would not mean much then, would it?'

'You don't know what you are talking about.'

'No, I don't and I wish I did. What is it like to feel desire, Rosie? Is it the same as love? Shall I recognise it?'

'Oh, you are giving me a headache. Go and ask Miss Bannister your foolish questions.'

'Oh, do you think she might know the answers?'

'I do not know, do I? I never asked her.'

Esme did not ask Miss Bannister because Rowan came in at that moment and a few minutes later luncheon was served.

Lady Mountjoy did not believe in seating her guests unless they were very frail, on the grounds that they should move about and mix with each other. It also meant they did not become too comfortable and overstay their welcome, but for some reason her at-homes were very popular. Esme found herself in a crowded drawing room, trying to keep firm hold of a cup of tea in case it was knocked out of her hand by the constant stream of people who came and went.

Nevertheless her ladyship made sure that every young lady who arrived with her mama or guardian was introduced to every other young lady and every young gentleman, whom they outnumbered by at least four to one. Esme found herself trying to memorise their names, while listening to Rosemary explaining who they were. 'Toby, the son of old Lord Salford, very wealthy but something of a rake; James, Lady Bryson's son and the apple of her eye, and Captain Merton. As an army officer he would never be at home, though his wife might travel with him; and there is Lord Bertram Wincombe, the Earl of Wincombe's heir.' She stopped speaking suddenly and gave a little gasp of annoyance. Esme, who had her back to the door, turned to see what had caused it. Lord Pendlebury, smart in a blue tailcoat and narrow matching trousers, was striding into the room and making for Lady Mountjoy.

His entrance had caused a sudden lull in the conversation and everyone turned as the handsome stranger bowed to his hostess. 'Lady Mountjoy, your obedient,' he said, taking the hand she offered.

'You are welcome, young man. Let me make you known to everyone. Take my arm and we will perambulate.'

Esme giggled at her antiquated turn of phrase. She wouldn't be a bit surprised if the lady did not think of herself as one of those old-fashioned matchmakers who did nothing but suit young men to young ladies and she wondered how successful she was. Everyone had stopped talking to watch the two proceed round the room and more than one mama nudged her daughter into showing some animation at being introduced to this handsome creature. He was charming, re-membered their names, made some flattering comment to each and passed on. By the time he reached Esme, she had put her cup and saucer down to stop it rattling and was trying—and failing—to hide her laughter.

'Lady Trent, may I present Lord Pendlebury,' their hostess addressed Rosemary while looking severely at Esme.

'We are already known to the gentleman,' Rosemary said stiffly. 'Good afternoon, your lordship.'

'Lady Trent.' He bowed. 'Lady Esme.'

She looked up into his face and realised he was also trying to control his laughter. It made it all the more difficult to keep a straight face. 'My lord, I did not expect to see you here.'

'Lady Mountjoy is an old friend of my mother. I came to pay my respects. It is a small world, is it not? You said we might come across each other and you were right.'

'Yes.' She wished he had not reminded her of that comment. She still smarted from the dressing-down she had had from Rosemary over it. When she said it, she had had no idea the significance her sister would put on it, nor that he would remember it.

'Are you enjoying your stay in town?' He did not take his eyes from her face, though some part of him registered that she was wearing a pale blue gown that was plain apart from a few narrow tucks and satin ribbon trimming, but its very plainness spoke of quality cloth and superb workmanship. It made her stand out from all the other young ladies in their fussy lace and flounces.

'Oh, very much. We went to the National Gallery to look at the pictures yesterday.'

'What did you think of it?'

She was acutely aware of Rosemary standing beside her, unable to stop her speaking to him and thoroughly put out that he was undoubtedly acceptable in society when she had made up her mind that he was not. 'Wonderful. It made me realise how poor my talent is.'

'You like to paint?'

'I draw a little and paint in water colours, but I am not very good at it. I envy people who can draw a few lines and produce a likeness without apparently trying very hard. It did not take you many strokes of your pencil to draw Rosemary and me the other day and we were instantly recognisable.'

'You are kind, Lady Esme, but I cannot reproduce your animation on paper. I only wish I could.'

She smiled at the compliment, but did not comment, being more interested in finding out all she could about him. 'You are not an artist, then?'

'No, a designer. I like to design things to manufacture.'

'What sort of things?' The noise that came from Rosemary's throat sounded very much like a snort. Both ignored it.

'Anything that takes my fancy—household articles, inventions, but particularly objects made of glass.'

'Drinking glasses, bottles, that kind of thing?'

'Yes, dishes, vases, ornaments. I have a small manufactory in Birmingham.'

'Is that where you live?'

'Just outside it. The estate is called Larkhills. I live there with my mother.'

'Is your mother in London with you?'

'No, she rarely travels these days. I came down for the Mansion House banquet.'

'But that is over and you are still here.'

He smiled, amused rather than annoyed, by her questions. 'There are other attractions to keep me here.'

'A lady?'

'That would be telling.'

She heard Rosemary's sharp intake of breath and knew she had breached another of her sister's strict codes. 'Oh, I should not have asked.' She saw his lips twitch and nearly laughed aloud. Instead she posed another—to her, less contentious—question. 'What were you doing in the park when we saw you sketching? You spoke of the Great Exhibition. Are you an architect, too?'

'No, but I thought I might try my hand at designing something to house the exhibits.'

'Has that not already been done?'

'There are architects working on it, but nothing has been finally decided.'

'Then I wish you luck with it. Has it been decided where the building is to be sited?'

'I think it is fairly certain to be in the corner of Hyde Park where we encountered each other.'

'And that was why you were on that particular spot?'

'Yes. No doubt I shall need to go there again to check my measurements.'

It was a mundane conversation, apparently meaningless, but Esme knew there was more to it than that. They were communicating with their eyes, with the way they looked at each other, even in the way they stood and occasionally lifted a hand to emphasise a point. There was empathy in the very air around them. It was a wonderful feeling that left her slightly breathless.

She did not realise it also made her cheeks rosier than usual and her eyes bright as stars. Felix saw it and felt it. Here was a child of nature, someone so open, so unafraid, he was afraid for her. He was afraid of life treating her badly, of his own emotions, which at that moment were playing havoc with his peace of mind. He had no right to feel like this, no right to engage her feelings when he had sworn never again to let a woman into his heart. She was too young to understand what was happening, too young to be hurt. He did not want to hurt her.

He bowed. 'I must not keep you from your friends. Good day, Lady Trent, good day, Lady Esme.'

He moved on and Esme found herself watching his back disappearing through the throng and wanting to cry. His departure had been so abrupt, as if she had said something to upset him. But she hadn't, had she? She had complimented him on his drawing skill—that wouldn't make him want to disappear, would it? Perhaps he found her conversation boring? Or had he realised Rosemary had not spoken a single civil word to him since her first formal greeting? Was he sensitive enough to feel her sister's animosity? If she met him when Rosemary was not present…

She pulled herself together to listen to Rosemary making arrangements with Lady Bryson to attend a charity concert the following week, after which they took their leave and returned to the carriage which took them back to Trent House. The whole journey was one long scold, mainly directed at Lord Pendlebury and the way Esme had encouraged him.

'I cannot understand what you can have against him,' Esme said. 'I think you made up your mind not to like him right from the first when he tipped his hat to me and smiled. It was just his way of being polite.'

'Impudent, you mean, and then to draw pictures of us without even a by-your-leave.'

'You surely did not mind that. It was only a sketch and very tasteful.'

'I mind when my sister, for whom I am acting *in loco parentis,* makes a fool of herself,' she said, as Esme followed her. 'And of me.'

'No one is making a fool of you, except yourself, Rosie. Lord Pendlebury is accepted in society. Why, you could see all the unmarried ladies falling over themselves to attract his attention.'

'That does not mean you have to. Always remember you are the daughter of an earl and should behave with more dignity.'

This business of protocol and etiquette and what was and was not proper behaviour was full of pitfalls and she seemed to be falling into every one of them. The trouble was, she did not know they were there until she had tumbled into them. The result was that, as soon as they arrived home, she was given a book on etiquette and told to study it.

Chapter Three

Esme's study of the book of manners soon palled and, since Rosemary was otherwise engaged with household affairs the following morning, Esme prevailed upon Miss Bannister to accompany her on a walk in the park. 'I might sit and sketch the riders,' she said, picking up a pad and several newly sharpened pencils.

'Don't you think that is a little advanced for you?' the governess queried mildly.

'Perhaps, but I mean to try, then I can send it back to Mama in my next letter.'

If Miss Bannister thought her erstwhile pupil was up to mischief, she did not say so, but fetched her coat and bonnet and prepared to humour her.

It was the first really mild day of the year and the good weather had brought out the populace who had nothing better to do than stroll in the park, ride in their carriages or show off their riding skills. There were some workers among the idlers: road sweepers, park attendants, street vendors, grooms holding horses, coachmen who drove the carriages in which the rich paraded, cabmen hoping to pick up a fare, a soldier or two on his way to or from the barracks. Esme in a patterned gown in several shades of green from palest aquamarine through apple green to dark forest green and a long matching jacket, was alive to it all, drinking in the sights and sounds, chatting animatedly to Miss Bannister, all the while searching around her for a particular figure. He had meant he would be in the park, hadn't he? But perhaps not today.

Miss Bannister was old and becoming frail and it was not long before she declared herself exhausted. 'I must sit on this bench awhile,' she told Esme, indicating a seat beside the carriage ride and suiting action to words.

Esme sat beside her and began sketching. Before long she was aware of gentle snoring and smiled to herself as she tried her best to draw the scene before her.

'Very good,' said a quiet voice behind her. 'But you have made the horse's neck a little too long and his head too small.'

Her heart began pounding, but she did not turn round. 'I told you I was not very good, didn't I?'

'I didn't mean it was bad.' He walked round the seat and sat beside her. 'Here, let me show you.'

She looked apprehensively at Miss Bannister as he took the pencil from her trembling fingers. The old lady gave no indication she had seen or heard the newcomer. 'We must not wake your duenna.' It was said in a whisper.

'No, she is quite old and tires very easily.' More whispering. She felt like a mischievous child, glorying in doing something forbidden. It would not have been the least bit necessary if Rosemary had not taken against his lordship, she excused herself, they could have met openly. But, oh, the need for secrecy was fun.

He moved closer, so that he was very near indeed, his grey

trousers brushing against the folds of her skirt and his warm breath on her cheek. 'Now, you do this. And this.' The pencil skimmed over the page. 'Think of the muscles in the horse's neck, how strong they are, how they support the head and how they are attached to the shoulders.'

'Oh, I see what you mean. It is perfect now. Is it the same for drawing people?'

'Of course. It is the bones and muscles that govern the shape of everyone.'

'Fat, too, or lack of it?'

'Yes, but that you can add that afterwards, along with the clothes, when you have the underlying structure right.'

She smiled mischievously. 'You mean I should imagine everyone naked?'

He laughed aloud and then stifled it when he heard Miss Bannister stir. 'If you like.'

'I do not think I could do that. It would be most improper and Rosemary has been lecturing me on being proper. I am, according to my sister, a very improper young lady. Myles says I must be guided by her, but it is so difficult, when I want to ask so many questions. It is not polite to quiz people, so I am told.'

He gathered from that statement that she had been scolded over her questioning of him the day before. 'I do not mind it,' he said. 'But I can see that a lively curiosity might lead you into trouble.'

'You were not offended? My sister said that was why you hurried away from us yesterday.'

'Did I hurry away?'

'Oh, yes. We were in the middle of a conversation and you suddenly took your leave. Were you angry?'

'No, of course not.' But he had been angry, not with her,

but with himself. He had found himself succumbing to her charm, a charm she seemed completely unaware she wielded. Or was she? Ladies could be accomplished deceivers. It was that which had driven him from the room. How could he so soon forget the vows he had made to himself? He was sorry afterwards and afraid he had hurt her feelings, which was why he was here with her now. And it was happening all over again. Would he never learn? 'I had an appointment.'

'Then I forgive you.'

He smiled. 'I am obliged, though I do not remember asking forgiveness.'

She let that go. 'How is your design for the Exhibition hall coming along?'

'I do not seem able to concentrate on it.'

'Oh, the lady.'

'What lady?' He was genuinely mystified.

'The lady who is so attractive she is keeping you in town when you ought to be going home.'

'Oh, that one.'

'Yes. I am a little jealous of her if she commands so much of your time.'

'No need to be. I—' He stopped suddenly as Miss Bannister gave a loud snort and opened her eyes to find her charge apparently in intimate conversation with a strange young man. She had heard Lady Trent scolding Esme—Rosemary never had learned to lower her voice—and it was plain that a young gentleman was involved. No doubt this was he.

'Miss Bannister, may I present Lord Pendlebury?' Esme said, knowing perfectly well that she was flattering the old lady by the formal introduction. One simply did not introduce one's servants to one's acquaintances. But Banny was more than a servant—she was a friend, a confidante, an ally.

Miss Bannister hastily adjusted her bonnet. 'How do you do, my lord?'

'Banny is my dear friend and companion,' Esme told him.

'You are indeed fortunate,' he told Esme while smiling at Banny and quite winning her over, though she knew she had been very remiss in her duty towards her charge.

'His lordship is an accomplished artist,' Esme said. 'He has been showing me how to draw a horse.'

'So I see.' She stood up a little shakily and Felix rose to take her elbow to steady her, but let her go the moment she had found her balance. 'Now I am rested and it is time we returned home. Come, my lady.' The formal address was for his lordship's benefit. 'Good day to you, my lord.'

Esme gathered up her sketching pad and pencils and murmured, 'Goodbye, my lord', before following her.

He sat down again, picking up his own sketching book from the seat beside him. He flipped over the top page on which he had outlined his building and worked on the drawing of Esme. If only he could get her to sit for him, he could really make a shot at making the picture come to life, but that would need the permission of the dragon who resided at Trent House and he knew he would never get that.

'I suppose I am to say nothing to your sister of that young gentleman?' Miss Bannister said, as they walked.

'We met by accident, Banny. He saw what I was doing and stopped to help. There was no harm in it. He behaved perfectly properly.'

'I do not think your sister would agree.'

'But you won't say anything, will you? She will only give me a scolding.'

'Esme, you are nearly twenty years old, a grown woman,

and it is time you learned to behave like one. If you want that young gentleman to court you, then you must persuade Lady Trent to accept him, not meet him in secret.'

'There was nothing secret about the park, Banny. There were hundreds of people there.'

'That's what I am afraid of,' her mentor said repressively.

'Banny, how shall I know when I am in love? And what is the difference between love and desire? Is there one?'

'My dear child, you are asking quite the wrong person,' Miss Bannister said. 'Your mama should be the one to speak to you of such things and no doubt she will do so when the time is right.'

'And when will the time be right?'

'Why, when you have become betrothed, a day or two before your wedding day.'

'It will be too late then. Banny, I do not want to make a dreadful mistake.'

'You won't make a mistake, Miss Esme, you are too level-headed for that.'

'I am not, I am feeling all topsy-turvy, very far from level-headed. How will I know if I have met my match? And what if he is not at all acceptable to Rosemary? She is determined to find me someone she calls suitable. I have a dreadful feeling that her idea of suitable and mine are not the same thing at all, and Mama and Papa are bound to be guided by her.'

'Your sister can be a little dogmatic, I own,' the old lady said. 'But she is only thinking of your good.' She paused and laid her gloved hand over Esme's. 'I fancy these questions have been sparked by that particular young man, is that not so?'

'Is it so obvious?'

'I am not blind, child, I can see he is having a very powerful effect upon you, but do not be misled into thinking it is love.'

'You don't think it is? When he looks at me, my knees wobble and my heart beats so fast I can hardly speak.'

'Goodness, that sounds alarming.'

'Have you ever had that feeling, Banny?'

'Once, but it doesn't signify.'

'Why not?'

'He was most unsuitable and in the face of my papa's opposition he disappeared. I believe he married a servant girl in the end.'

'Oh, how sad for you.'

'No, for I think he went to the bad and I had a lucky escape. So you see, it pays to listen to one's parents and those who know more of the world. All the glisters are not gold.'

'Oh, I wish I had not asked you. You are no help at all.'

'Because I did not tell you what you wanted to hear.'

Esme did not answer and they walked the rest of the way in silence.

Almost the whole of the following week was taken up with preparations for her presentation at Court. For some reason Esme could not fathom, a feather headdress was a must and as her Majesty disliked small feathers, they had to be large enough to be seen by her when the débutantes entered the room in a long line, one behind the other together with their sponsors. In Esme's case that would be Rosemary who rehearsed her over and over again until she was reduced to a trembling jelly. 'Esme, for goodness' sake, Mama taught us all to curtsy, do you have to look so clumsy? If you fall over, I shall die of embarrassment.'

The evening arrived at last and she set off with Rosemary to make her début into society, resplendent in a dress of pure white silk and a white gauze veil topped with the mandatory feather headdress, which made her keep her head bowed in the carriage. The journey took only a matter of minutes but there was a long line of vehicles outside St James's Palace and they had to sit there for over an hour until it was their turn to enter. Others, whose fathers were not so high-ranking as the Earl of Luffenham, had even longer to wait. By the time they were called, Esme was shivering with cold and nerves, especially as no cloaks, capes or shawls were allowed. Once in the palace they waited in line in the gallery until it was their turn to move forward. Esme looked at Rosemary and received a smile of encouragement as she finally entered the throne room.

A couple of attendants helped to arrange her train and she walked slowly and sedately forward, following the girl in front of her, until she found herself standing before her Majesty, who was seated surrounded by standing courtiers. After Rosemary had presented her, she sank down into her curtsy and took the hand that was offered, kissed it, bowed and carefully straightened her knees, quickly righting herself when she began to wobble. The Queen was smiling at her. She dipped her head again and felt behind her for her train. A waiting footman picked it up and laid it over her arm and then indicated the direction she should take. Slowly, step by step, she retreated backwards until she was at the door.

'Good,' Rosemary said, taking charge of the train. 'That's over. Now, you are out.'

'Out' meant she could take her place in society and attend balls and functions and meet that desirable husband. All that expense, all that practising, all those jangling nerves, for the sake of two or three minutes in a crowded room and even less time in the presence of her Majesty.

They were soon outside, a shawl put about her shoulders because it was very late, and on their way back to Trent House. Tomorrow her Season could begin.

Between visits to Rosemary's friends, tea parties, the odd soirée and a concert or two, Esme amused herself by riding, when she was accompanied by Rosemary, or walking when her companion was more often than not Miss Bannister. On one never-to-be-forgotten day, she and Rosemary were walking home through Hyde Park after a shopping expedition, having dismissed the carriage in Park Lane, when they found themselves being jostled in a crowd of people craning their necks to see something going on in the middle of the park. Esme, ever curious, pushed her way through, with Rosemary reluctantly behind her.

'Why, it's a balloon,' she said as she came to a roped-off enclosure in the middle of which a long colourful mass of silk material was being gradually inflated.

A man with a megaphone was explaining to the crowd how it was being filled with hydrogen gas. 'The gas is made by the action of sulphuric acid and water on the iron-and-zinc shavings in those casks over there,' he said, pointing. 'In passing through the water, the gas is rid of its impurities and is passed through a tube into the neck of the balloon. The gas displaces an equal volume of atmospheric air and, because it is lighter than air, the balloon rises until it reaches a layer of air equal in density to its own and there it remains, floating above the earth with the basket beneath it.'

'How d'you get down again?' someone shouted.

'We let the gas out a little at a time and admit an equal

quantity of atmospheric air. The balloon descends and reaches the ground when all the gas has been expelled.' As he spoke the balloon rose above them and the basket, which had been lying on its side, righted itself, held beneath the balloon by a network of ropes. Only the tethering ropes held the whole contraption to the ground. The crowd, including Esme, looked upwards as the huge globe, painted in red, blue and yellow, filled up. 'Now we are ready to ascend,' he said, standing beside the basket. 'I can take three passengers. Who will come with me on a voyage of a lifetime?'

There was no immediate response, possibly because the watchers were mostly ladies and a few gentlemen who were out for an afternoon's stroll, and would not demean themselves by volunteering. One lad walked across the grass and shook hands with the balloonist and clambered into the basket. 'Any more?' the man shouted. 'Come along, the panorama of London at such a height is a wonder to behold. You won't be carried away. The balloon will be tethered at all times. You will return to this very spot.'

The prospect of such a ride was too much of a temptation for Esme. 'Oh, Rosie, wouldn't it be fun? Shall we try it?' She looked round for her sister, but Rosemary had been swallowed up by the crowd and was some distance away. Undeterred she ducked under the ropes and walked across the grass towards the balloon, unsure if she really would have the courage to step into the basket.

'Why, here's a little lady putting you all to shame,' the balloonist called out, as he bowed to Esme and took her hand. 'Well, miss, are you game?' he asked.

She nodded. He opened a little door in the side of the basket and, picking her up, deposited her inside it beside the boy. She looked round her and was met with a sea of faces, all smiling and cheering. Except one. Rosemary had made her way to the front and was looking wildly round her as if appealing to someone, anyone, to fetch her sister back. Esme could not hear what her sister was saying, but she was already beginning to regret her foolhardiness. Pride would not allow her to change her mind, especially when the balloonist began shouting again, 'Come on, you brave men, you aren't going to let the little lady show you up, are you?'

A man pushed his way through the onlookers and began sprinting across the grass, followed by several others. They were making a race of it, each wanting to be the last passenger. Esme, who had recognised the front runner, willed him to win, which he did, jumping into the basket and closing the gate as the men helping the balloonist let out the slack in the tethering rope.

'You are quite mad, you know that, don't you?' he told her.

She smiled a little weakly as the balloon rose and began to sway as the breeze caught it. 'I wanted an adventure.'

'Now you have it.'

'Yes.' Her voice conveyed her nervousness and made him smile. 'What about you?'

'The same, I especially could not forgo the pleasure of having it with you. Are you afraid?'

'Certainly not!'

'Good.' He grinned. 'Then let us enjoy it. Look down there.'

Tying her bonnet firmly under her chin, she peered downwards. Already the people watching them were colourful dots and the houses little squares with tiny gardens and the parks large green patches. Apart from the wind in the rigging, there was little sound. 'See, there is the Thames and that's

St Paul's and there's the Tower. And just down there is Buckingham Palace and, if you look over this way, you might be able to pick out Trent House.'

It was wonderful and as the wind lifted her hair she looked back at him with shining eyes. 'I'm flying!'

'Yes, you are.'

The balloonist smiled at her. 'She has courage, that one,' he said to Felix.

'Yes, she has.'

Higher and higher they went. Noticing she was shivering in the cold air, he took off his coat and put it round her shoulders. He did not take his hand away, but kept it across her shoulders, steadying her, as he listened to the aeronaut explaining the technicalities of ballooning, the size of the balloon, the weight in the basket, the height they had attained, the rate of ascent and descent, all of which he found fascinating. 'When we take passengers, we remain tethered, not only to give them peace of mind but in order to return to the spot from which we started,' he said. 'When we fly free, we are looking for wind and currents of air to carry us along.'

'I should like to try that some time,' Felix said.

'How far can you go that way?' Esme asked. With Felix beside her and the confident tones of the balloonist explaining everything she did not feel afraid. She felt exhilarated. But the ground was an awfully long way down and she hoped the mooring ropes would hold.

'Flights have already been made between England, France and Germany,' he said. 'Perhaps, who knows, one day a balloon will circle the earth.'

They were no longer rising, but suspended in space. For a few minutes they enjoyed the view of London and even some of the surrounding countryside spread out beneath them. 'It makes me feel humble,' she whispered. 'Human beings are such small things when you think of the vastness of the universe.'

'Yes, but small does not mean insignificant. The human race and its endeavours are what makes the world go round. It is the men of vision that keep us moving forward.'

'Yes, I can understand why you and others like you are so keen on the Exhibition.' She was aware of his hand on her shoulder and knew she ought to object to his impertinence, but it was reassuring to have it there and she let it lie.

It was only when the balloonist busied himself with the descent that she began to worry about what Rosemary would say. The nearer they came to the ground, the more apprehensive she became. But it wasn't only Rosemary she had to face—it was a battery of reporters who circled the descending balloon. 'Oh, dear, I did not expect that,' she said. The balloon touched down with a jolt that sent her into the arms of Felix as the basket tipped over.

'Are you hurt?' Felix asked as the balloonist apologised for the hard landing and his helpers sprang forward to stop the deflated silk dragging the basket along the ground.

'No, not at all.' She sat up and put her bonnet straight. 'I landed on you. Are you hurt?'

'No.' He scrambled out of the basket and held his hand out to help her. Then he replaced his jacket round her shoulders and turned up the collar before hurrying her away from the inquisitive reporters who clamoured to know her name, where she lived, why she volunteered, had she been afraid. She answered no to the last question, before Felix placed himself between them. 'Don't answer,' he told her. 'It will only encourage them.'

Somehow he made a way through them, shielding her face

with his jacket. 'Keep going,' he said, making her run. 'I left my cab on the carriageway. I only hope the driver obeyed my instructions to wait.'

To his intense relief it was still there and he lifted her into and jumped up beside her. 'Go down Piccadilly,' he instructed the driver.

'But that's the wrong way,' she protested.

'We need to put them off the scent. We can't have them following us to Trent House, can we?'

'What about Rosemary? I left her in the park.'

'I am sure she will have seen what happened and had the good sense to return home incognito.'

A half hour later after a ride in a cab that took her all over the west side of London, he instructed the driver to make for Kensington and she arrived home to find he had been right. Rosemary had waited until she saw her sister safely on the ground again and had crept away. To say she was displeased would be an understatement; she was furious. She managed a grudging word of thanks to Felix at the same time as she berated him for not making her sister come out of the basket before it took off.

'I might, if I had been given the time,' he said evenly. 'But no sooner had I stepped in than we left the ground. There was nothing I could do after that until we returned to earth.'

'Which we did with a bump,' Esme said, refusing to be cowed, though she realised she had frightened her sister to death.

Rosemary gave her a withering look and turned again to Felix. 'My lord, I thank you again, but I will take care my sister's feet remain firmly on the ground from now on. You do understand?'

'Yes, my lady, I understand. Good afternoon.' He bowed formally. 'Good afternoon, Lady Esme.'

As soon as the front door had closed on him, Rosemary turned on Esme. 'I never felt so humiliated in my life,' she said. 'I know you are up to all sorts of tricks, but I never thought you would be so mad as to deliberately get us separated so that you could embark on that imbecile adventure. Anything could have happened, you could have been carried away, hurt, even killed....'

'But I wasn't. It wasn't dangerous at all. You should have come, too, you could see for miles and miles.'

'Certainly not. Just look at the state of you. Your hair is all over the place and there is a tear in your skirt. If it wasn't dangerous, how did that happen?'

'Oh, I expect when we landed. The basket turned over, that's all.'

'That's all! It will be all over the papers tomorrow.'

'No, it won't, they have no idea who I am. Lord Pendlebury shielded me from the reporters when we landed and the cab brought us home by a roundabout way.'

'Let us hope you are right. Heaven knows what Rowan will say.'

'I suppose it is no good asking you not to tell him?'

'No good at all.'

But for some reason she did not say a word. It might have been that Rowan was too busy with his campaign to have the Exhibition stopped, which was gaining momentum day by day, and was not in a mood to listen to domestic problems. He made no comment at all when the exploits of an unknown young lady who had dared to ascend in a balloon pushed the Exhibition and the arguments for and against off the front pages. Headed, 'The Mystery of the Lady Balloonist', the report went on, 'The young lady was dressed in the latest mode, certainly not equipped for a journey aloft. Mr Hurst, the balloonist, told us he did not know her name, but she spoke in the refined accents of the gentry. All those who witnessed the ascent were left speculating on her identity. We think she was perhaps an actress, someone known to Mr Hurst, paid to drum up business. If that is the case, it was a highly successful venture. The balloon went up and down many more times, with each passenger paying a guinea for the privilege, until nightfall brought it to a halt.'

Felix read it and smiled. They had not discovered who she was and for her sake he was thankful. It was not the sort of notoriety a young lady ought to attract in her first Season. But, oh, he admired her courage. Her shivering had not been entirely caused by cold, but when he suggested looking down at the ground so far beneath them, she had done so, even pointed things out and asked questions. Many a chit in those circumstances would have sat down and screwed up her eyes and refused to open them until they were safely down again.

It was purely fortuitous that he had been coming along the carriageway in a cab when their way was impeded by crowds of people on foot. Standing on the cab step to see what it was all about, he had been astonished to see Lady Esme Vernley approach the balloonist, amid cheers from the onlookers. Then it was a matter of racing the others to the basket. Had he meant to persuade her not to go? He was not at all sure. In any case, he had told Lady Trent the truth: the basket had left the ground as soon as he was on board. And, oh, how he had enjoyed the experience, standing side by side with the liveliest, the bravest, the loveliest young lady he had ever had the pleasure of meeting.

He knew perfectly well what Lady Trent had meant about keeping her feet on the ground. She would be accompanied and watched everywhere from now on and he might not enjoy another such encounter. But perhaps it was for the best. He was becoming far to wrapped up in her.

Esme never saw Felix in the park again, but she did encounter him several times in the homes of Rosemary's friends when they went calling or attended evening functions. Courtesy forbade Rosemary to ignore him, so she would pass the time of day politely when they met in a group and that meant Esme could speak to him, too. But they were never alone and never mentioned the balloon flight, both realising they might be overheard and the secret would be out. It was most frustrating and he never again even hinted at meeting in the park or anywhere else.

But that did not alter the fact that she was acutely aware of him whenever he was nearby. If he was talking to someone else, she longed for him to turn and notice her. If he happened to be speaking to her, she was so breathless she could hardly answer him and if the subject of his conversation was something like the weather or what the government was up to or the ongoing argument about the Great Exhibition, she wanted to turn it to a more personal level, to find out how he was feeling, why their earlier rapport seemed to have disappeared. She had not changed, except to try to heed Rosemary's advice and be a little more circumspect, a little cooler in her demeanour.

'Be proud,' Rosie had told her. 'You are the daughter of an earl, a Vernley, one of the oldest and most respected families in the kingdom and you can choose whomever you wish to marry, even without a dowry. But that does not mean you can behave like a hoyden.' She never missed an opportunity to lecture and Esme knew she was not going to be forgiven for that balloon ride.

She could not marry whom she wished because if she could she would choose someone like Lord Pendlebury and Rosemary considered him unsuitable. 'He is in trade,' she had said scornfully, repeating her earlier objection when Esme ventured to ask her what she had against him. 'A manufacturer of glass. Of all things! And his background is suspect.'

'Whatever do you mean?'

'His father made his fortune in India, trading with the natives, and was ennobled while out there, goodness knows what for. He amassed a fortune that enabled him to return home and buy an estate and live like a real aristocrat while his son roamed all over Europe and fell in with some very unsavoury characters.'

'How do you know this?'

'Rowan made inquiries.'

'Why?'

'A newcomer in our midst, whom no one knows, will always merit investigation. There are some blackguards about masquerading as gentlemen.'

'Oh, surely not Lord Pendlebury.'

'Why not Lord Pendlebury? Esme if you have developed a *tendre* for him on the strength of one highly improper episode, I suggest you stifle it. There are others more suitable....'

Esme did not comment on that, instead, she said, 'Whatever he has done in the past does not seem to have dented his popularity; he is everywhere we go.'

'A handsome face and an even handsomer fortune make some people blind.'

Rosemary's scathing opinion did nothing to change Esme's feelings towards the gentleman, unless it was to make her even more curious about him. Unsavoury characters— what unsavoury characters? He did not strike her as dissolute, though perhaps she was not knowledgeable enough to recognise that trait if she saw it. She could not believe a man with such a fine talent at his fingertips would use it for anything but good. She began to scan the newspapers looking for the result of the competition to design the Exhibition building, wanting him to win it, though that would hardly raise his standing in Rosemary's eyes. Rowan was still stubbornly against anything to do with the project, calling it an abomination to all right-thinking citizens.

He would have gone home to Larkhills, Felix told himself, except that he had made little progress with his work for Wellington, though in his spare time he dressed as a working man and haunted the taverns and meeting places of the low life of the city. His other reason, that Moorcroft had asked him to look out for Esme, was a sham. She did not need him; she had a perfectly good watchdog in Lady Trent. Esme's own conclusion that it was a lady keeping him in town, was nearer the truth, even if she did not know the lady was herself.

He battled with himself over it. His vow that he would never allow himself to be ensnared by a woman again was in grave danger of being broken. Lady Esme Vernley enchanted him, but he was only too aware of how false enchantment could be. In some hands it was almost a lethal weapon. It could attract in order to cut. He ought to keep clear of it. But though he tried, he found himself accepting invitations he never would have accepted before, simply because she might be there and he could get a glimpse of her, perhaps exchange a few words. His weakness annoyed him until he was face to face with her and drinking in the sight of her while apparently talking of nothing at all and then he was glad he had come.

It worried him that she seemed a little paler, a little less animated, and he guessed it was the repressive influence of her sister, whom he called the dragon, and he wanted to bring the old Esme back, the one who was ready for any adventure, who said straight out what she thought, who quizzed people because she wanted to know answers. The only question she had asked him lately had been a formal, 'How do you do?' How did he do? Abominably.

It became worse when the Season got under way and the grand houses of the West End were opened up for the aristocracy coming from their country homes. The round of party going, soirées, pleasure outings increased, to the evident satisfaction of the dragon. He watched as Esme was pushed in front of every young blade with a title and a moderate fortune and wanted to scream at her not to be bullied into accepting any of them. He was, he realised, losing his battle to remain aloof.

He consoled himself by drawing her, trying to recreate her figure, her oval face, her wayward curls, her small, expressive hands, but that was equally frustrating. He could not get it right whether she was walking, riding or sitting decorously with her hands in her lap. Paper was a flat medium—she needed substance, something three-dimensional. A sculpture, perhaps. But in London he did not have the materials for making one.

Esme and Rosemary hardly had an evening at home, unless they were entertaining, themselves. Everywhere they went, they met the same people and before long Rosemary was pointing out more young gentlemen she considered suitable husbands, whom Esme could safely encourage. Esme was polite to them, smiled at them, danced with them, but when she compared them with Felix Pendlebury, she found them sadly lacking. Not one was as handsome, not one as talented, not one could make her heart beat faster, or make her laugh in quite the same way he did. Laughter was a spontaneous and joyful sound when shared with Felix, a mere politeness when acknowledging the inane joke of any other young man. She no longer thought of him as Lord Pendlebury. None of her new acquaintances merited a Christian name in her head.

She dreamed of him, she dreamed of being in his arms, of being kissed by him and though she tried to imagine the sensation, she had only her reading of the latest novels to go by and was not sure she could trust them to be accurate. The very fact that she wanted it to happen must surely signify something was going on in her heart that needed clarification. She could not ask Rosemary and Miss Bannister insisted she knew nothing of such things being an elderly spinster. But she said it with a smile that seemed to indicate that she did know and she did understand.

Esme's spirits took an upward turn one day in early May when she and Miss Bannister were walking alongside the river at Chelsea, shading themselves from the sun under parasols. They had gone along the towpath as a change from the park and to give Esme fresh impetus to illustrate her letters to her parents which were full of where she had been, whom she had met, the latest gossip and fashions. Mama liked to know all that and she appreciated the little drawings

Esme included. Naturally she had not been told of the balloon ride and Lord Pendlebury's name was not mentioned except in passing, when she wrote the names of people who were present at a particular gathering.

They came to a spot where an oak tree on the bank hung over the water and shaded the grass beneath it. Sitting on the ground with his back against the trunk of the tree was the man who filled her dreams. He had taken off his jacket, which lay discarded beside him with his hat on top of it. His shirtsleeves were rolled up and though there was a pad of paper on his knee and a pencil in his hand, he did not appear to be doing anything with either. His eyes were half closed, a blond curl fell over his brow. A man in repose or a man with a great deal on his mind? She was not sure.

Their feet made no sound on the grass as they approached and they were on to him before Esme's shadow fell over him and he became aware he was not alone. He opened his eyes and began to scramble to his feet, but she stopped him. 'Please do not get up, my lord. You look so comfortable there.' And then she surprised him by dropping down beside him.

'My lady. Miss Bannister.' Having deliberately avoided the park in case he should meet her and have all his self-control fly away, fate had taken a hand. She was here, sitting beside him, her wide pink gingham skirts spread around her, a smile of delight on her face. The fight went out of him. He gave in, surrendered to her charm, discounting the possible consequences. 'What a delightful surprise.'

'Yes, isn't it?' She looked from him to Miss Bannister who was standing over them, uncertain how to proceed. She could not bring herself to sit on the ground, knowing it would bring on her aches and pains and it would be a struggle to rise again.

But she could not stand there like a sentinel. 'I shall go and sit on that log over there,' she said, indicating a fallen tree a few yards away. 'When I am rested, we shall resume our walk.'

'She is a dear,' Esme told him when the old lady was out of earshot. 'She should have been retired ages ago, but I think she would fade away if she did. She persuaded Mama to let her maid me, though she is a very educated lady and instructed us all as children. Lucy, Rosemary, me and young Johnny.' She smiled suddenly and the last vestige of his vow crumbled to dust. 'I have to take account of her age and infirmity and we stop frequently when out walking.'

'She is tactful,' he observed.

'Yes. So we may speak freely.'

'Don't you always do that?'

She laughed. 'Yes, and perhaps when I ought not to. Do you often come this way?'

'Occasionally, when I want to be alone to think.'

'Oh, and I have interrupted you. I am sorry.'

'I cannot think of anyone I would rather have interrupt me. A man would have to be made of stone to prefer his own company to yours.'

She was delighted by the compliment. 'That is kind of you. I have been looking for an announcement that would tell me you had won the competition for the Exhibition building. Has it been judged?'

'Not yet.'

'I saw a picture of one of the designs in the *Illustrated London News* yesterday.'

'Do you like it?'

'No, I do not. It looks to me like a cross between a brick-built cathedral and a railway station. Dark and forbidding on the one hand and all bustle and noise on the other.'

He laughed. 'I could not have described it better.'

'Why did they choose it?'

'Because they did not like any that were submitted to them.'

'Not even yours?'

'I haven't finished it yet.'

'So what are you drawing now?' She indicated his pad. He held it out to her. 'But it's me! It is me, isn't it?'

'Yes.'

'But why me?'

'Why not you?' He answered her question with another. 'I began it when I met you in the park, but I don't seem able to finish it. Just when I think I have it right, some feature, an expression, a line even, eludes me and it lacks something.'

'Animation, I expect. A drawing does not live and breathe, but I would say you have got as near to it as anyone could.'

'But now the real thing is beside me and I am content just to look.'

'My lord, I do believe you are flirting with me.'

'No, I am sincere.'

'No one has ever told me anything like that before.'

'Not even your new *beaux?* Whenever I see you in company, you are surrounded by eager young men.'

'That is because my father is an earl.'

'You do not think they are sincere in their compliments?'

'No, they are either too awkward or too glib, or they have been rehearsing for days, probably prompted by their mamas. They must be very foolish if they think I am taken in by that.'

'You do not think my motives might be the same?'

'No, I do not. You have never shown the slightest sign of toadying to me. I think perhaps because you are older...'

'Older?' He laughed. 'Do you think of me as old, so old you are in no danger from me?'

'I don't know how old you are and it makes no difference. I know I am safe with you or I would not be sitting here beside you, perfectly at ease.'

'Are you at ease?' he queried, looking into her face.

She was very far from easy. Under his scrutiny, she found herself trembling inside and out. Hurriedly she closed her parasol and put it on the grass beside her so that she could hide her hands in the folds of her skirt. 'Yes, of course.' The words were a hoarse whisper, which was all she could manage.

'I think perhaps that is a little fib.'

'What makes you say that?'

'I feel it, too.'

'W-what?'

'A feeling of helplessness, a feeling that I am not in control of my own destiny, that I have been bewitched by a pretty face and an innocent heart. It is innocent, isn't it?'

'I don't know what you mean.'

'No, and I am glad of it. Do not let anyone spoil it, stay as you are.'

'I shall grow old.'

'Like me?' His laugh was genuine. 'Never. Never in a million years.'

'You are not old and I never said you were.'

'I am twenty-seven and I have seen a great deal more of the world than you have. I have met some strange people in my time who have made me wary of becoming too close to anyone.'

His words seemed to confirm something of what Rosemary had told her. 'Then I was right, someone has made you sad. I saw it in your eyes when we first met, though lately it has disappeared and I thought you were perhaps getting over it.'

'You are very perceptive, my lady, though do not read too much into that.'

'Was she very beautiful?'

'She?'

'The lady.'

'There is no lady.'

'Then I think it is you telling fibs.'

He decided the conversation was straying on to dangerous ground and hurriedly changed the subject. 'You have your sketching things with you.'

'Yes. I thought I might draw the river traffic as a change from horses.' She was glad of the change of subject because she had a feeling that introducing the mysterious lady had been a mistake. He was not over it, whatever it was, and though she longed to comfort him, she was sensible enough to realise even to try would be presumptuous.

'Let me see.'

She handed over her pad. 'I started it the other day, but I couldn't get the water right. It looks so flat and lifeless when there is obviously movement there, even if it is just below the surface.'

So much went on below the surface, he thought, pretending to study what she had done. Memories, emotions, past deeds were all there, unseen, governing what happened on the outside, the way people behaved, the way they related to others. It would be rare indeed for someone to enter into a relationship without the clutter of a past. He believed Esme could and, in that, she must be very nearly unique. Unless he was deceiving himself. Again.

'It is all down to light and shade,' he said. 'This is how you do it. Use small strokes, to suggest what is there, the faint ripple, the unseen surge, light and shade. The eye of the observer will do the rest.'

'I see. How clever you are. I don't care what you say, you are a true artist. Have you ever exhibited any of your work?'

'No.'

'Then you should. Why not submit something for the Exhibition?'

'I do not think it is intended to show art as such. There are galleries and museums for that. The Exhibition is meant to display inventions and manufacture, the products of the working man.'

'You are a working man and art is your product.'

He laughed. 'I do not think the selection committee would agree with you. But you have given me an idea. I might manufacture something in glass.'

'And I shall look forward to seeing it.'

Miss Bannister had decided she had left her charge alone long enough and was advancing across the grass. He gave Esme back her pad and pencil and stood up, retrieving his coat and slipping into it. By the time the old lady joined them, he had helped Esme to her feet and handed her the parasol before putting on his hat. They walked a little way together.

'Do you go to Lady Aviemore's ball?' Esme asked him. 'She is calling it an Exhibition Ball because she is hoping to raise money for it.'

'Yes, I know. Most of the fund-raising committee have been invited and as I am one of their number, I shall put in an appearance. Do you go?'

'Oh, yes. Rowan—I mean Lord Trent, of course, is annoyed with Rosemary for accepting, but she says she cannot afford to alienate Lady Aviemore by refusing. She says everyone who is anyone will be there and I shall meet new faces.'

'She means gentlemen prospects, I suppose.'

'I suppose so, though there are bound to be other ladies there and perhaps I shall make friends with them.'

'Lady Trent takes her responsibility for you very seriously, doesn't she?'

'Oh, yes. Mama is not always in good health and she could not come with me, so Rosemary feels duty bound to do her best for me.'

'And you, being a dutiful daughter and sister, fall in with everything.' It was said with a grin.

'I try, but sometimes it is not easy.'

'Why not? Do you not like any of the young gentlemen?'

'Oh, they are pleasant enough to pass the time of day with, but I have not met one with whom I should like to spend the rest of my life.'

'Not a single one?' he queried.

'No one that Rosie approves of.'

'Esme!' Miss Bannister felt it was time she interrupted.

Esme laughed. 'I was only going to say that perhaps they feel the same about me, and if I were not who I am and if they were not being urged into paying attention to me by their mamas, they would not give me a second thought.'

'Then they are idiots,' he said firmly.

She gave a joyful laugh, which made him turn to look at her and smile, though he said no more. They parted on the corner of the King's Road and he did not see her again until the evening of the ball and by then the past was beginning to catch up with him.

Chapter Four

Having no room large enough to hold her ball, Lady Aviemore had taken over Willis's Assembly Rooms in King Street, and it was thence Rosemary took Esme on the last Saturday in May. Rowan, true to his principles, declined to attend.

Knowing Felix was going to be there, Esme took a great deal of trouble choosing her gown. It had a blue silk bodice and a velvet skirt hung over so many petticoats, one of which was stiffened with horsehair, that it ballooned out around her like a bell. The neck was boat-shaped, partially filled in with coffee-coloured lace, which also formed the flounces from the elbow of the narrow sleeves. Because the task was beyond Miss Bannister, Rosemary's own hairdresser came an hour before they were due to set out and somehow managed to tame her unruly locks into coils that he pinned up to the back of her head and fastened with a tiny coronet of flowers.

'Beautiful,' said Miss Bannister when Esme had slipped into her shoes and was ready to leave.

'Very good,' said Rosie when she went downstairs. 'The carriage is waiting, so let us be off.'

Esme had been looking forward to the ball ever since she had learned Felix would be there and all day she had been in a fever of excitement. Surely, surely he would ask her to dance? And surely, if she was very good and danced with all the other young men who asked her, Rosemary would not forbid it. If there was one thing Rosemary could not abide, it was a public scene.

The only thing the ballroom had in its favour was its size. It could accommodate seventeen hundred, so Esme was told, but if it had ever done so they must have been squeezed in cheek by jowl. Her ladyship had done her best to make it festive by importing a great deal of greenery, which was swathed round its pillars into which exotic flowers had been pinned. The floor had been polished and the candelabra cleaned, so that the room was full of light. There was a good orchestra to play for dancing, and refreshments in an adjoining room. Another room was set out for cards for those who did not care to dance. And all for the princely sum of ten guineas a ticket, the profits to go to the Exhibition fund.

Rosemary soon found a group of friends who invited them to join them and before long Esme was dancing. She was polite to her partners, answered their compliments with a deprecating smile, laughed at their jokes and tried not to appear distracted. But the man she was really waiting for was Felix.

He arrived about a half hour later, making quite a stir because she was not the only one hoping to spend a few minutes with him. For every bachelor hunting a bride, there were three young ladies hoping to catch the eye of a gentleman, and one in particular. Esme, who was dancing with

Toby Salford at the time, almost stumbled, but quickly recovered herself. Felix was here, and though he was surrounded by beautiful women in extravagant ball gowns, dripping with jewels, she was hopeful that he would seek her out.

It seemed for a time that he would not. Two dances later and he had still not spoken to her. She was aware of him, of course, aware of his tall slim figure in a black tailcoat, black trousers, enlivened with a purple waistcoat with silver embroidery and a lilac-coloured cravat. He made all the other men look dowdy. He danced with Captain Merton's sister, Caroline, a redhead in cerise taffeta with a neckline so low it was almost indecent. At least that was what Rosemary had said on seeing her. Esme was being partnered with Bertie Wincombe, a spotty adolescent whose only virtue, according to Rosemary, was that he was the Earl of Wincombe's heir.

The two couples passed each other on the floor, though Esme had made up her mind not to let her attention stray from her partner, she could not help herself and looked round as they executed a turn that brought her facing Felix. He was looking over the shoulder of his partner directly at her. And then he winked. She giggled.

'I beg your pardon,' the young Lord Wincombe said. 'Did I say something amusing?'

'Sorry?'

'I said I hoped those who are so set against the Exhibition could see the company tonight—they might realise they could not win.'

'Were you referring to my sister's husband, my lord?' It was said sweetly.

'Lord, no. Is he against it? I had no idea. But you are here. And your sister.'

'We are here to enjoy the dancing. And I do not have to agree with my brother-in-law.'

'No.' The dance came to an end. He bowed, she curtsied and they strolled off the floor together. She had hardly taken her seat when Felix came for her, holding out his hand and smiling. 'Lady Esme, my dance, I think.'

She glanced swiftly at her sister, who gave an imperceptible nod, and then rose to take the hand and was led on to the floor for a waltz. They did not speak. She could not think of a single thing to say that would not betray the tumult of her emotions and he simply wanted to savour the feeling of holding her. She stood out from the crowd in every way. Her gown was exquisite, her hair a golden halo; her trim figure, swaying to the music, moulded itself to his hand and he wished he could draw her closer. But such a thing would be the height of impropriety and so he contented himself with looking down at her, happy that she was not at all afraid to look up into his face.

'Have you managed to finish your design for the Exhibition building?' she asked at last, though what she was really asking was if he had managed to forget the lady who had distracted him.

'No. I have decided against it.' He didn't know why they were talking about that competition. He had had no real expectation of winning it and, to be truthful, had only thought of entering it on a whim. He wanted to talk about her, ask her more about herself, discover if what he felt for her was reciprocated. But he would frighten her away if he did. 'I simply do not have the time or temperament to oversee such a large project. I will stick with what I know best.'

'Glass manufacture.'

'Among other things.'

'Have you decided what you are going to exhibit?'

'Yes, I think so.'

'Oh, tell me, what will it be?'

'It's a secret, but you shall see it when it's finished.'

'Before it goes on display?'

'Yes.' He smiled down at her. On the one hand she seemed hardly more than a charming, mischievous child, full of daring and curiosity, on the other a bright attractive woman with natural good manners and none of the disdainful air of the usual society lady. Sometimes *ingénue,* sometimes wise, she looked fragile, as if she would be easy to break, but she had proved herself stronger than she looked, a little like glass. It was that which had given him the idea. He would try to reproduce her fragility and strength in glass and make it something of great beauty.

She wanted the dance to go on for ever, to go round and round in his arms, to feel his fingers curling over hers, the pressure of his other hand on her back, until they fell down exhausted. Now and again she was aware that his leg was very close to hers as they turned and it gave her a *frisson* of excitement. Was she, could she, be falling in love with him? Was this longing to be closer to him…desire?

'Oh, my God!' The words seemed to be torn from him. She wondered if he had somehow divined her thoughts and they had filled him with dismay. He had certainly gone very rigid, as if someone had thrown cold water over him.

She risked a glance up into his face. He was staring over her shoulder at something or someone she could not see. 'What is it?' she asked.

'Nothing.' He smiled down at her. 'Someone just walked over my grave.'

'Don't say things like that, please don't.'

The dance ended and he offered his arm to escort her back to her seat, but before they had taken many steps, their way was barred. 'Felix, *mon cher,* fancy meeting you 'ere. All the while we have been apart I 'ave imagined you at your 'ome in…what is it called? Lark'ills, I remember now.' The English was good, but the accent unmistakably French.

She was, Esme was bound to admit, a raven-haired beauty with flashing dark eyes. She was dressed in a dark red gown with a many-tiered skirt. Its neckline was so low that the top of her breasts were exposed. She wore a heavy ruby necklace and several rings flashed on her expressive hands as she waved them to indicate the company.

'Juliette.' Felix spoke her name quietly, but it was not difficult for Esme to detect the undercurrents to the encounter. He was decidedly agitated.

The woman looked Esme up and down. 'Will you not introduce us to your charming companion?'

He pulled himself together. 'Lady Esme Vernley, may I present Mademoiselle Juliette Lefavre. And this—' he stopped, indicating her companion '—this is my cousin, Mr Victor Ashbury.'

'How extraordinary,' Esme said. 'Mr Ashbury is known to me, but I had no idea he was your cousin.' She had met the young man at Luffenham Park when he was one of a party her father had invited for a shooting weekend. He came with Viscount Gorridge, a close friend of her father, and the Viscount's son, Edward, whom Lucy had been expected to marry, but nothing had come if it and she had married Myles instead. She had not seen either Mr Ashbury or Mr Gorridge since then.

Felix looked startled, as if he could not believe such a thing was possible. 'Forgive me, Lady Esme, if I hurry away.

Something has cropped up that I must see to.' He bowed briefly and hurried off towards the door.

Juliette laughed. 'It is I who 'ave cropped up and *le pauvre* is overcome. Victor, look after Lady Esme, *s'il vous plaît*. I must go to him.' And she was gone, too.

Victor grinned sheepishly. 'Shall we dance?' he asked as the orchestra began a country dance.

Esme allowed herself to be led back onto the floor, in such a state of nerves she hardly knew what she was doing. It had happened so suddenly, just when she thought she and Felix were getting close. She did not doubt for a moment that this was the lady who had kept him in London. But why, if he had been waiting for her, had he been so taken aback to see her? The reason was not important, she told herself as she danced woodenly beside Mr Ashbury. What was important was that she, Lady Esme Vernley, was of no consequence to him at all and she had been deceiving herself.

'Felix, do not run away from me.'

It was no good pretending he had not heard her, her siren voice was right behind him. He turned to confront her. 'I am not running away. I have an urgent appointment.'

'So urgent, you left your partner standing. That was not at all chivalrous of you.'

'What do you know of chivalry?'

'As little as you, *mon cher.*'

'Why do you persist in calling me "your dear"? I am not dear to you and suspect I never was. And what are you doing in London? And how did you come to meet Victor?'

She linked her arm in his to walk beside him. 'So many questions, Felix. I have one for you. Why did you run away from me?'

'I told you, I have an urgent appointment.'

'I did not mean tonight. Two years ago. I could have explained—'

'Explained your treachery? I think not.'

'Yes, I could. There was never anyone else but you for me, but I had to save Papa…'

'By going to bed with that traitor, Peaucille.'

He had never been able to understand why the daughter of a Comte should ally herself so strongly to the revolutionaries and Peaucille in particular. He was a hothead, prepared to get his way by violence, and he incited the lower orders to stop at nothing. Did she really believe in their cause or was it simply a rebellion against parental authority? The Comte was one of the old school, a dictator to his family and employees, but it was a benevolent dictatorship. She must have known that and yet she listened to Peaucille's ranting and had left home to go to live with him. The Comte had taken it hard, as he had himself, considering he had proposed marriage to her; though nothing had been officially announced, he had believed they had an understanding. How wrong he had been!

'You would have done better to have stayed by his side instead of breaking his heart.' He did not add, 'And mine', which he might have done at the time because now he realised his heart had not been broken; he was surprisingly heart-whole, although with the beautiful and spirited Lady Esme in town he wondered for how much longer.

'It was a question of ideals. Jacques Peaucille was no traitor; it was necessary for him to do as he did. The revolution succeeded.'

'So why aren't you with him now?'

'He was one of the first to be killed in the uprising.'

'And your father? What of him?'

'He died six months ago.'

'I am sorry for that. I liked him.'

'I know that or you would have come over to the Revolutionary Party with me. You always said you sympathised with the aims of the workers.'

'So I did and still do—it is the methods employed by the mob leaders I could not stomach. It looked to becoming the Terror all over again.'

'It is over now. The old monarchy is no more and we have a new Napoleon, but I am all alone in the world.'

He gave a harsh laugh. 'And so you thought of me?'

'I 'ave never stopped thinking of you. And you 'ave thought often of me, *n'est-ce pas?*'

'Only to wish to God I had never met you.'

She laughed. 'Ah, that is better than not thinking of me at all.'

'Go away, Juliette. I have nothing more to say to you.'

'You will change your mind.'

'Never!'

He hailed a cab. 'Where are you staying?'

'I am a guest of Mrs Ashbury,' she said. 'She 'ave a 'ouse in Clarges Street.'

'I did not know you knew her.'

'I did not before I come to England. 'Er nephew, Mr Gorridge, wrote and asked 'er to invite me.'

'Edward?'

'Yes, Edward. He was kind to me after Papa died and, when 'e 'eard I wanted to come to London, 'e wrote to 'is Aunt Sophie. Victor met me at Dover.'

'Did you know she was also my aunt?'

'Yes, Edward told me.'

'Why didn't he come himself?'

'Oh, 'e 'ad business in Paris.'

He helped her into the cab and directed the driver to the address in Clarges Street, but he made no move to accompany her.

'Felix, come with me, I want to talk to you.'

'No, Juliette, we have done talking.'

'Then let us kiss and make up, we do not need speech for that.'

He did not answer, but nodded to the cabbie, who whipped up his horse and carried her away.

He considered going back to the ball, but he was so unsettled he knew it would be difficult to act naturally and Esme was perceptive enough to know something was wrong. He needed to calm down before facing her again and apologising for his abrupt departure. Damn Juliette, damn the past, damn the revolution, damn his cousins and everything that came between him and the real love of his life. He could admit it now. Compared with Esme, Juliette was nothing and he had agonised over her betrayal for no good reason.

Why had she come back into his life now, just when he had begun to see a rosy future with Esme and the only obstacle was the dragon woman who could be overcome in time? The fact that Juliette professed to be alone, had lost both lover and father, would hardly account for it. She was handsome enough and clever enough to find herself a new meal ticket without much trouble. Edward or Victor? He ought to be able to dismiss her, but he found he could not. Something was not right.

He walked for hours, reliving the past, rehearsing what he would say to Esme, worrying that she might not understand. His personal concerns allowed little space in his head for thinking about his place in society and less for wondering about the effect Juliette's arrival would have on his standing with the commissioners for the Exhibition and the Duke of Wellington in particular.

This was brought to the forefront of his mind the following morning when a messenger arrived from Apsley House, asking him to call on the Duke that afternoon. The ageing Duke was still revered by almost everyone and, as Ranger of the Parks, was responsible for ensuring the security of the site and of those involved with every aspect of the Exhibition, be they workmen, exhibitors or visitors. He was especially concerned with the safety of the Queen, the Prince Consort and the Royal family.

He had been brought out of retirement two years before when the uprisings all over Europe and particularly in France, had threatened to spread to Britain and coincided with the Chartists holding a mass rally on Kennington Common. Extra troops had been brought to the capital and thousands of special constables recruited to guard public buildings. The Queen, on the advice of her ministers, left London. In the end the rally had fizzled out in the rain and those marchers who turned up were peaceful. It was fear of the resurgence of what someone had dubbed 'those of the pink persuasion' that caused so much feeling against the Exhibition.

'Pendlebury, glad you could come,' the Duke greeted him. 'We are faced with a new threat. Our ambassador in Paris has written to Lord Palmerston that he has heard certain characters of the Revolutionary Party intend to use the Exhibition as a means of promoting unrest among the thousands of British workers expected in town. The Prince will not have troops billeted in the Park because he says it would be against the spirit of the Exhibition, so we must be doubly vigilant.'

'Do you know who these characters are, your Grace?'

'None specifically, but there are many foreigners entering the country even now. They come as visitors to our shores, but their intent is not peaceful.'

'We cannot watch them all, my lord Duke.'

'No, but you have contacts in France, I believe. The name Lefavre has been mentioned.'

'Lefavre!' he exclaimed in dismay, wondering if the Duke knew his connection with the family. 'His daughter told me he had died. She has recently arrived in London.'

'It is not the Comte who concerns me. You are acquainted with his daughter?'

'Yes.' It was said guardedly.

'Then I ask you to do all you can to find out what she knows, particularly in relation to a certain Frenchman called Maillet.'

The last thing he wanted to do was to have anything to do with Juliette and he wanted to refuse, had almost decided to find some excuse for doing so, when the Duke added, 'The safety of the realm depends upon being able to nip trouble in the bud. We, in these islands, must be able to sleep peacefully in our beds. And as Prince Albert has set his heart on inviting the world and his wife to London, we must do our best to protect the populace, not least of whom is her Majesty and her consort.'

Felix nodded and bowed his way out.

Esme was miserable. She and Felix had been getting along so well; she had even begun to hope that Rosemary was softening towards him because she had stopped grumbling about him and did not snub him when they met in company. As he was so obviously accepted by all their friends, her sister really could have nothing against him except prejudice and that might be overcome. But she had been deceiving herself; the man had only been playing with her, amusing himself until his lady love arrived.

He was constantly in the Frenchwoman's company. Esme had seen them laughing together, dancing together, riding in the park, taking carriage rides, attending soirées. Poor Victor's nose had been properly put out of joint. As had hers. And Rosemary was crowing that she had known all along that he was a queer fish.

'Forget him,' Miss Bannister said, when she found her crying into her pillow one evening. She was supposed to be dressing to go to a concert with Rosemary and Rowan, but had made no move to take off her afternoon dress. 'He is not worth your tears.'

'Why, Banny, why did it happen? Am I too plain? Am I too young? Or boring? Miss Lefavre is beautiful and she is more his age and I do not think she can bore him or he would not spend so much time in her company. And she is very popular with the gentlemen. They are always crowding round her laughing. I wish I could be like her.'

'Never wish that, child. You are you and worth a dozen of her; if he cannot see that then he is blind.'

Esme rubbed the tears from her eyes and sat up. 'Perhaps I should try and open his eyes.'

'Now, miss, if you are thinking of more mischief, I beg you to think before you act. The consequences could ruin your reputation and with it your chance of finding a husband.'

'Why, Banny?' she asked in surprise. 'What did you think I had in mind?'

'I don't know, but when I see that gleam in your eye it reminds me of the times you fell into scrapes when you were little and the day you came home after going up in that balloon. I nearly had a seizure when Lady Trent came back and told me what had happened.'

'You are not to speak of that. No one knows it was me.'

'I know that and my lips are sealed, but you are a grown woman and should behave like one. If the man does not want you, for whatever reason, look elsewhere for a husband.'

Esme did not answer, simply because her head was buzzing. It was foolish to sit and mope when it was not in her nature to mope. She had to do something. Faint heart never won fair lady, and it never won a handsome man, either. But how to go about it, she had no idea.

The conundrum occupied her all through the concert. How could she make him see her, not as an amusing companion, but as a wife? She was so absorbed she did not even notice he was in the audience until the interval when everyone moved from their seats to go into the next room for refreshments. She suddenly found herself within three feet of him.

'Good evening, Lady Trent, Lady Esme, my lord.' This last addressed to Rowan who managed a grunted 'Pendlebury' in acknowledgement.

Esme looked into his face, trying to see if there had been any change in his countenance, if his eyes betrayed the fact that he had cooled towards her, but they were searching her face, just as they had done the first time he had seen her. They were as warm and intent as they had been then, except there was now no sign of amusement there. She had resented that at first, thinking he was laughing at her, but now she would have given anything to see evidence of it in his eyes. She began to hope that she could regain what had been lost. She smiled. 'Lord Pendlebury, are you enjoying the concert?'

'Very much.' The sight of her smiling face twisted his gut into knots. He wanted to grab her into his arms and kiss her until she was breathless. He might have been tempted to try if they had not been in a crowded room and if she had not been accompanied by the dragon and her husband. But even the dragon was less of a threat than Juliette, who stood behind him, waiting to be presented to Viscount and Viscountess Trent.

'Your friend is waiting for you,' Esme said, as her sister and brother-in-law avoided the civility by proceeding into the dining room, expecting Esme to follow.

He wanted to tell her the truth, longed to tell her Juliette was not his friend and if he had his way he would never see her or speak to her again, but he had been sworn to secrecy. If he told Esme he was acting on the Duke of Wellington's orders and she let slip what he had said, however innocently, the consequences could be disastrous. 'Yes.'

'I wish you a pleasant evening, my lord.'

He hesitated wondering what he could say to detain her, to let her know that his evening would be far from pleasant, that pandering to Juliette and pretending to have forgiven her for her betrayal was the last thing he wanted to do. How he had ever thought himself in love with her, he could not imagine. If he could only obtain the information the Duke wanted, then he could put an end to the whole sorry business. He smiled a little wryly. 'Good night, my lady.'

Esme watched the Frenchwoman drag him off and then followed her sister, but the encounter had told her one thing. Lord Felix Pendlebury was not happy. She wanted to smooth his brow and take away that forlorn look and make him smile again, but she could not compete with an old love that had never quite gone away.

Esme was out riding with Rosemary one afternoon when they came upon Mr Ashbury, also riding, and stopped to speak to him. He had no title and so Rosemary did not consider him as a husband for Esme, for which Esme was much relieved. She did not like the man; there was something slimy about him. She could not blame Miss Lefavre for preferring Felix. He greeted them politely, talked of the weather, spoke of Lady Aviemore's ball, which had raised a considerable sum for the Exhibition. 'It looks as though it will be going ahead,' he said. 'Money is coming in thick and fast.'

'More's the pity,' Rosemary told him. 'We have always been against it.'

'I can see you would find the upheaval almost on your doorstep somewhat of a nuisance,' he said. 'But it will disappoint those planning to visit these shores from abroad and those hoping to profit from it. There are always two sides to a coin.'

'Quite.'

'You are not with Lord Pendlebury today, Mr Ashbury?' This from Esme, who really wanted to know if Felix was with Juliette.

'No, but I shall see him this evening. We are going to the Adelphi to see *Esmeralda*.' He smiled suddenly. 'Is that your true name, Lady Esme?'

'No, I have always been plain Esme.'

'Esme, yes,' he said gallantly. 'But plain, decidedly not.'

She blushed. 'Thank you.'

'Do you have a message you wish me to give Lord Pendlebury?'

'No, no,' she said quickly. 'It was only that you are so much in his company, I wondered if he had gone away.'

'No, he would not go while the inducements to stay are so compelling.'

'You refer to Miss Lefavre?'

'Who else? We are constantly a three.' He paused, suddenly brightening. 'Would you consider coming to the theatre with me, my lady, and making up a four? We have taken a box.'

'We are engaged for tonight, Mr Ashbury,' Rosemary said quickly. 'Another time, perhaps. Now, if you will excuse us, the horses are becoming restless.'

He touched his hat and they parted.

'I did not know we were engaged for tonight,' Esme commented as they rode on.

'Rowan and I are dining with Colonel Sibthorp.' The Colonel was a Member of Parliament and one of the most vociferous voices to be heard against the Exhibition. 'I have to go to support Rowan. I am sure you can amuse yourself for once.'

'Of course I can. Don't give me another thought.'

It was as well that her sister did not notice the gleam in her eye, which Miss Bannister knew presaged mischief, or she would have been alarmed.

While Rosemary was dressing to go out, Esme wrote a note to Mr Ashbury, telling him that she found she could accompany him to the theatre after all, and if he would like to call for her at half past seven, she would be ready. She sent a footman to deliver it to his lodgings. Then she made some alterations to one of the gowns Lucy had given her. It was a black taffeta with huge puffed sleeves, over narrow beige lace undersleeves. The same lace was used to make a shawl collar to fill in the neckline. In no time the lace had been ripped out and the gown hung back in her wardrobe. Then she went down to dine with Miss Bannister, demure in watered silk, buttoned up to the neck.

Rosemary and Rowan came to say goodbye as they finished eating. 'You'll be all right, won't you?' Rosemary asked her.

'Of course I will. I have Banny for company.'

As soon as they had gone, Esme jumped up. 'Come on, Banny, help me to dress and then put on your best bib and tucker, we are going out.' She did not wait for a reply, but hurried from the room to put action to words.

'Esme, what do you mean, we are going out?' Miss Bannister demanded, toiling up the stairs behind her. 'I never heard Lady Trent mention it.'

'No, she was too busy getting herself ready. I believe it is an important evening for her.' She began stripping off her gown as she spoke. 'Come on, we mustn't be late.'

'But you can't go out alone, child, you know you can't.'

'I am not going alone. You are coming with me and we are to be escorted by Mr Ashbury.' She fetched the black dress and pulled it over her head. 'Do it up for me, please,' she said, presenting her back to the governess.

'Where are we going?'

'To the theatre. The Adelphi. We are going to see *Esmeralda*. Mr Ashbury asked me this afternoon when we were out riding.'

'And your sister agreed?'

'She did not exactly disagree.' She sat down at her dressing table. 'How shall I do my hair?'

Miss Bannister, looking in the mirror at her charge, was taken aback by what she saw. 'Esme, you cannot go out like that. It is not becoming. You are showing far too much... chest.'

Esme did indeed feel a little naked, but having decided on her course of action, she was not going to back out and there was no time to replace the lace. 'I shall wear the silk shawl Rosemary bought me, the one with all the lovely colours in it, and take a fan.'

'I am not at all happy about this, Esme.'

'It is not for you to be happy or unhappy,' Esme told her tartly and then regretted her words when she saw the look of shock and hurt on the old lady's face. 'Oh, Banny, don't look so downpin. I did not mean to be unkind, but I intend to go and if you do not come with me I shall go without a chaperon.'

'You would not be so daring.'

'Try me.'

'Why? Whatever has got into your head?'

'I cannot let him go, Banny, I just cannot. You could not tell me what desire was like and Rosemary wouldn't, but I think I have found out for myself. I do not want any of those silly young men Rosemary has paraded before me, I want him, and him alone.'

'Mr Ashbury?' Miss Bannister queried in surprise.

'No, of course not. You know perfectly well I meant Lord Pendlebury.'

'If you are planning to make him jealous, you might find yourself hoist on your own petard.'

'It's worth a try and I've got to do something. A little rouge, I think, and some kohl on my eyes.'

'No, Esme! I positively forbid that. Besides, his lordship would not like it. He will be disgusted with you.'

'He likes it on Ma'amselle Lefavre.'

'She is French. And how do you know he does?'

'He goes out and about with her.'

'That doesn't mean he would like to see you done up like a strumpet. If you put any of that on your face, I shall most definitely not let you go.'

Esme grinned, knowing her strategy had worked. She had no intention of painting her face, but it had diverted Banny from the main issue and she had more or less agreed to accompany her, which was just as well; she would never have dared go without her.

Both were ready when a footman came to tell them that Mr Ashbury had arrived. Esme threw her shawl about her shoulders and picked up her fan and, with Miss Bannister behind her, went to join her escort, who had hired a carriage to convey them to the theatre. He was obviously very pleased with himself and bowed and smiled and paid her compliment after compliment until she told him rather sharply to desist.

'I am coming with you to help you recover the affections of Ma'amselle Lefavre,' she said, 'nothing more, so there is no need to fawn all over me.'

Deflated, he handed her into the carriage. The journey to the Strand did not take many minutes, but by the time they drew up outside the theatre, Esme's heart was beating so fast she could hardly breathe. She knew perfectly well that what she was doing went beyond the bounds of acceptable behaviour and could well result in her being sent home to Luffenham in disgrace. She might have asked Mr Ashbury to take her back to Trent House if she hadn't, at that moment, seen Felix escorting the Frenchwoman into the theatre ahead of them. It renewed her determination. Felix must be prevented from making a terrible mistake.

* * *

Felix was already seated next to Juliette when they arrived in the box. He looked up as Victor entered. 'You are late, the curtain is about to go up,' he said. 'Where have you been?'

'Calling for my companion for the evening.' He stood aside to allow Esme and Miss Bannister to enter the box.

'Lady Esme!' Felix's face was a picture of shock and incredulity as he rose to his feet. 'What are you doing here?'

It was difficult, but she managed a confident smile. 'Come to see the play. Mr Ashbury was kind enough to invite me. Do sit down again. The curtain is rising.' And with that, she took a chair next to his and allowed her shawl to slip a little off her shoulders.

He subsided beside her. 'Just what do you think you are playing at?' he hissed, noticing the bare flesh above the neck of the gown. It excited his senses at the same time as it shocked him to the core. How could she? How could that sweet, innocent girl whom he loved to distraction behave so brazenly?

'I am not playing at anything,' she whispered back, and waved her fan at the stage. 'They are.'

'Where is Lady Trent? I cannot believe she allowed this.'

'Why not? I am chaperoned and I have known Mr Ashbury since I was a little girl.'

He turned to look at Miss Bannister, who had taken a seat immediately behind them. She shrugged her shoulders in a gesture of helplessness.

'Felix, do pay attention.' Juliette leaned towards him and tapped his arm with her fan. 'There will be time for conversation during the interval.'

He turned his attention to the stage, leaving Esme to study his profile. It was a strong profile, she had noticed that before, but now there was an angry twitch to the muscle in his jaw and his lips were clamped tightly together as if he were trying to stop himself saying something scathing. There was no doubt he was very angry and she wished with all her heart she had never embarked on this escapade. She would ask Mr Ashbury to take them home in the interval.

The play was a burlesque, but it did not raise a smile in either of them, though Mr Ashbury laughed uproariously. Juliette, Esme noticed, was not amused and kept leaning towards Felix and whispering. Not for a minute did he relax and when the curtain came down for the interval, he rose and took Esme's arm. 'Now, miss, you are going home.'

She wrenched herself away and remained seated. 'How dare you speak to me like that? You have no jurisdiction over what I do.'

'No, more's the pity, or I would put you over my knee and spank you.'

'Hold hard,' Victor put in. 'The lady is with me. She does not wish to go home. The play is only half done. Besides, I have ordered supper for us all at Rules for after the performance.'

'Oh, do sit down again, Felix,' Juliette added. 'Let us see the play in peace. Lady Esme is here now, so we might as well stay and see it through.'

Short of making a public scene, which was the last thing he wanted, he could not force her out of the box. He sat down again.

Esme was glad the lighting was not good or they would all have seen her tears. She had made a terrible mistake in coming and had been almost ready to let Felix take her home when Mr Ashbury had intervened. Now she must sit miserably through an indifferent play and pretend to enjoy it. Felix did not speak to her again.

* * *

The entertainment ended at last and they all rose to go. Esme longed for her bed, but Victor was intent on taking them all to supper. 'We cannot go,' Miss Bannister whispered to her as they walked side by side along the corridor to the stairs. Felix was talking in low tones to Victor and apparently ignoring her, ignoring Juliette, too. 'Do ask Mr Ashbury to take us home.'

They made their way out to the street where a line of cabs waited for hire. Felix hailed one. 'Juliette, my dear,' he said to her. 'You go on with Victor. I will join you later. I must see Lady Esme and her companion safely home.'

'Victor brought her, let him take her home.' Juliette was decidedly put out.

'I booked a table for supper,' Victor said. 'And I'm devilishly hungry.'

'Then go!' Felix, whom Esme had never heard raise his voice, was almost shouting. 'Enjoy your supper and leave me to set your foolishness to rights.'

'Oh, very well. Come, Juliette, you will eat with me, won't you?'

Juliette gave Felix a look of pure venom and allowed Victor to usher her into the cab. He climbed in beside her, leaving Esme, Miss Bannister and Felix standing on the pavement.

Felix put his hand under Esme's elbow and almost frog-marched her to the carriage and horses he had hired that had, at that moment, drawn up at the curb. 'In with you,' he said grimly.

Meekly, Esme obeyed. She was followed by Miss Bannister and then Felix gave his driver the direction and settled himself on the opposite seat. He did not speak for fully a minute after they set off, and then he sighed heavily. 'Just what were you thinking of, my lady? What did you hope to achieve?' He did not sound angry now, simply puzzled and hurt.

'It worked,' she said lightly, determined to make him smile again.

'What worked?'

'Why, sending Mr Ashbury off with Ma'amselle Lefavre. He was so unhappy that she had abandoned him for you. Now they are together again and will make up their quarrel, whatever it was, and be happy together again.'

He tilted his head back and laughed aloud. 'And what, in your scheme, was I supposed to do? Stand by and do nothing?'

'Why, see the error of your ways and go back to being what you were before.'

'What was I before?' He was genuinely puzzled.

'A fine gentleman, someone society accepted. Even my sister was coming round to the idea that just because you own a manufactory doesn't mean you are not a gentleman in her sense of the word. Since *ma'amselle* came on the scene, you have abandoned your old friends.' It was the nearest she dared come to telling him the truth.

'I do believe you are a little jealous.'

'I am not!'

He smiled. 'There is no need, you know. I could tell you—' He stopped suddenly. 'No, best not.'

'Tell me what?'

'Nothing.'

'Oh, you are infuriating.'

He turned and addressed himself to Miss Bannister. 'I am surprised at you, ma'am.' Her eyes were closed and her chest was rising and falling rhythmically. He smiled wryly. 'She is not much use as watchdog, is she?'

'You must not talk about Banny like that. She is paid to do as she is told. And refusing to come with me would not have changed my mind. I cannot see what all the fuss is about. It isn't as if I was out alone. I had an escort and a chaperon, all very proper.'

'Proper!' His voice, though a whisper, was scathing. 'You call that proper?' He waved his hand at her gown. She realised the shawl had fallen off and she was revealing too much of what Miss Bannister had delicately called her chest. Hastily, she pulled the shawl back into place. 'You are asking to be molested and the molester would excuse himself by saying you invited it.'

'Just let him try.'

Before she could do more than make a squeak of protest, he had dragged her across to sit beside him and pulled her round to kiss her savagely. She struggled for a moment, then gave in. What he was doing to her was having the most extraordinary effect. A trickling sensation ran down her throat and into her stomach where it spread across her hips and thighs and into her groin. It felt like a kind of opening out, like a bud opens into full flower and reveals the stamens and sweet nectar within, ready for the exploring bee. The pressure of his lips on hers increased as he gently eased open her mouth. It was exquisite torture.

She was not the only one to think it was torture. Felix was so roused, he hardly knew what he was doing. He had been wanting to kiss her for a long time, almost since their first meeting, but not like this, not brutally and in anger. The fact that the anger was directed against himself did not help. She should have been struggling, beating against him with her fists, crying out for help, biting him, anything to make him stop. If she had done that he would instantly have stopped and apologised, but she was compliant, her lips soft against his, and his anger evaporated. Did she understand what she was doing to him, what she was capable of doing to any man who called himself a man? It made him afraid for her. And for himself. He was lost.

A grunt from the other corner of the carriage brought him to his senses and he released her. It was a moment before she recovered sufficiently to return to her seat. Miss Bannister slept on. 'Are you saying I invited that?' she hissed.

'You said, as I recall, "Let him try."'

'You did not have to take me at my word.'

'Why not? Do you never mean what you say?'

'I hate you.'

There was no answer to that and they drew up outside Trent House without speaking again when the sudden cessation of movement woke Miss Bannister with a start.

He opened the carriage door and jumped down to help both ladies alight. 'Will your sister be at home?'

'No, there is no need for you to wait,' Esme told him. 'You must be anxious to rejoin your friends. I am sorry to have put you to so much inconvenience.' And before he could say another word, she had turned and made for the front door, which was opened by a footman as she approached. Miss Bannister, with a smile of sympathy for him, followed.

He got back in the vehicle and directed his coachman to Bruton Street. Rejoining Victor and Juliette was the last thing on his mind.

Chapter Five

'Esme, I need to speak to you urgently,' Rosemary said, coming upon her sister sitting on a bench in the garden with a book in her lap, though she wasn't reading it. She was dreaming of Felix, reliving that kiss and wondering if it would ever be repeated. Why had she said she hated him? She did not hate him, she loved him. She had done some foolish things in the past, not the least of which was making a spectacle of herself by accepting a challenge to go up in a balloon, but last night's folly had gone beyond that. No wonder he had treated her like a strumpet. That was the word Banny had used, wasn't it? She was glad they had arrived home before Rosemary; by the time her sister came in, she was in bed and pretending to be asleep.

Now she looked up to see her advancing across the lawn towards her and her heart sank. 'What about?'

'I have just come from meeting Mrs Ashbury in Mudie's library. I was shocked, shocked to the core, by what she told me. She got it from her son and I cannot think why he would invent such a tale.'

'Oh.'

'You might well say "oh." I don't know what could have got into you. You know perfectly well I declined Mr Ashbury's invitation on your behalf. I do not, and have never thought, he was a suitable escort for you and I was right. No right-thinking gentleman would take you to a burlesque....'

'I did not know it was a burlesque.' Esme sighed. 'I did not enjoy it very much.'

'Why did you go? And how did it happen that Mr Ashbury did not bring you home?'

'He went to have supper with Ma'amoiselle Lefavre. It worked out well in the end, because he only asked me to make her jealous. He thought she was spending too much time with Lord Pendlebury.'

'And that is another gentleman you should be steering clear of.'

'It was he who brought me home, Rosie.'

'So I gather. I wonder he was able to tear himself away from his paramour. I trust he behaved himself....'

She felt herself colouring, but answered swiftly before her usual honesty made her tell the truth. 'Of course he did. Miss Bannister was with us.'

'Much use she is. If I had my way, I would have pensioned her off years ago. I am surprised at Papa keeping her on, but I suppose Mama felt sorry for her.'

'She may have done, but Papa lets Banny stay because she does not cost wages, only her keep and a little pin money. She is happy with that because Luffenham is her home and she has nowhere else to go.'

'That may be, but you are wandering from the point. I am responsible for you, and if you cannot conform, then I must inform Papa.'

'Oh, please don't do that. Papa will make me go home and surely that will cause more of a scandal? I will be good, I promise. I won't stir from the house unless you are by my side.'

'I blame Lord Pendlebury, filling your head with nonsense. You would never have dreamed up such an escapade on your own.'

'It was not his lordship's fault, he had nothing to do with it. But for him, I think I might have been in a real scrape.'

'Be that as it may, I was obliged to tell Mrs Ashbury I had agreed you could go.'

'Thank you, Rosie.'

'The trouble is that now she is preening herself that I consider her odious son a suitable escort for you. It is up to you to discourage him.'

'Oh, I shall enjoy doing that. He thinks more of his stomach than his duty as an escort.'

'And the same goes for Lord Pendlebury.'

'Oh, no, for he was not in the least concerned about missing his supper. You should thank him for bringing me home.'

'Rowan has undertaken to do so.'

Rowan's idea of thanking Felix was to give him a very public dressing-down. Felix was enjoying a quiet drink and a perusal of a newspaper in Brooks's, when Viscount Trent approached him. 'Pendlebury I want a word with you.'

'Certainly, my lord. Take a seat. A glass of something?'

'No. I will not drink with you. I simply wish to let you know that I consider your behaviour and that of Mr Ashbury reprehensible.'

'In what connection?'

'You know very well in what connection. You may have a title and call yourself a gentleman, but no gentleman that I know of would lure a young and innocent girl away from the protection of her family and—'

'And what, my lord?' Felix's voice was deceptively quiet.

'Prey on her ignorance. She did not know that the entertainment offered by the Adelphi is not such as a well-nurtured young lady should see.'

'It is a perfectly respectable theatre.'

'I do not think she should be going to a theatre at all. The opera, perhaps, or Shakespeare, not common burlesque.'

'I agree, my lord, I did not take her there, I certainly did not lure her there.'

'You will keep away from her, do you hear? I do not like the company you keep and I do not want her associating with them through you. Do I make myself clear?'

Felix assumed he meant Juliette; the man had a morbid suspicion of all foreigners. 'Perfectly clear.'

Having established that, Viscount Trent turned on his heel and left him. Felix finished his drink, folded the newspaper and put it on the table in front of him and walked out of the building. It was done calmly and deliberately for the benefit of others in the club who had heard the exchange. He would not let them see how put out he had been.

He walked home and climbed the stairs to the top of the house where an attic room had been made into a studio. Here he picked up a series of sketches he had made of Esme. There were several drawn at different angles, front, back and sides. It was from this he would make a three-dimensional model. He sat down and studied them. They were not perfect, but he knew he would be given no opportunity to improve the sketches from life, and perhaps it was time he made himself scarce for a short while. He had learned nothing of any insurrection from Juliette and he doubted if she knew anything. He would suggest to the Duke that he might learn more talking to some of the people in the industrial towns of the north, and then could go home and work on his model of Esme.

If Esme had not been Rowan's guest and beholden to him for her board and clothes and if she had not been sure that Rosemary was doing her best for her, according to her own standards, she would have fallen out with both of them. It was true she had been foolish to go to the theatre and she was prepared to be punished for it, but it was no reason to blame Felix who was entirely innocent. If anyone was at fault besides herself it was Victor Ashbury. Rosemary had conceded he had behaved badly, but as she was convinced he had acted at the behest of Lord Pendlebury, she was not inclined to blame him. 'You asked him to call for you,' she had told Esme. 'His mother says he would never have done so otherwise, and he was prepared to bring you home safe and sound, except that Lord Pendlebury took over as if he had a right to do so. That is what I find so unforgivable. He was once affianced to that Frenchwoman and, for all I know, still is.'

That hurt. How could a man, engaged to one woman, kiss another like he had kissed her, arousing in her feelings so strong that even thinking about that kiss brought them all back and she could not sit still or even converse sensibly. She had to go out, go for a walk or a ride, anything to be active until they subsided. She did not see him on any of these outings, nor at the many social functions she subsequently attended with Rosemary. He had disappeared.

* * *

'What are you doing?'

Felix looked up as his mother entered the workshop he had built for himself in the grounds of his home. It was here he worked on his inventions and designed items to be made in glass, here he dabbled in painting, here he made models in clay. It was what he was doing now, working from the drawings he had done of Esme.

'Making a clay model.'

'A sculpture?' She came and stood over him. Dressed in widow's black, which she had donned two years before on the death of his father, she was a plump woman whose hair had gone prematurely grey, but she had the smooth complexion of a girl and clear blue eyes that missed very little.

'No, it is a model for a glass figure.' He leaned back to look at it. Fourteen inches high, the subject was dressed in a robe whose folds clung to her figure and swirled about her bare feet, which peeped out from beneath its hem. Her hair was loose and topped with a wreath of leaves and flowers. One hand was lifted to the back of her neck under the hair, while the other hung by her side, holding a posy of flowers, blooms facing downwards.

She studied it along with him. 'Very beautiful. Is she a real person?'

'Lady Esme Vernley.'

'Vernley. Isn't that the Earl of Luffenham's family name?'

'Yes, she is his youngest daughter. I met her in London. She is being brought out by her sister, Viscountess Trent.'

'And she caught your eye. I am not surprised; she is lovely. Did you see much of her?'

'A little.' He laughed. 'Don't make something of nothing, Mama. I have not found favour with the Trents.'

'Why ever not?'

'I am a manufacturer for one thing and for another I support the Great Exhibition and Viscount Trent is wholly opposed to it.'

'But did you not explain that your manufacturing is hardly more than a pastime and that you have a large estate to run? And as for the Exhibition, that is surely not a good reason for denying you the chance to pay your addresses to the young lady?'

'Perhaps not. But I never said I wanted to.'

'You don't have to.' She chuckled, indicating his model. 'Only someone in love with the subject could have fashioned anything so exquisite.'

'It is only a lump of clay, Mama. I have yet to make it in glass and I'm not at all sure that I can.'

'How will you do it?'

'Cover it in molten metal and when that has cooled, melt out the clay. The metal, in two pieces, will become the mould.' He was busy with a tiny knife as he spoke, working on the folds of the dress. 'You have seen me blowing glass?'

'Yes, of course.'

'It will be blown inside the mould. First I will wet the inside of the mould, then blow a cylinder and insert it in the cavity at the bottom and by blowing and turning at the same time it will assume the shape of the inside of the mould. The water will become steam and stop the glass coming into contact with the metal. When it has cooled, I have to remove the mould without breaking the glass and then I should have my Crystal Girl. That's the theory, anyway. I have yet to put it into practice.'

'Then what will you do with it?'

'Submit it to the selection committee for the Exhibition.

If it is successful, I could teach the process to the more skilled of the operatives at the factory and we could market them.'

'Hundreds and hundreds of Lady Esmes, surely not?'

'No, of course not. There can only be one of those, two or three at the most, but we could make other figures—animals, birds, things like that.'

'I see.' She was thoughtful. 'Felix, if this is anything like the real person and easily recognised, you cannot exhibit it without the permission of the lady herself and the Earl.'

'I'll worry about that when I make one worth showing.'

'So long as you do. Now, you have been out here long enough and dinner will be in a half hour, so come indoors and change. You are filthy.'

He looked down at his clay-bespattered overall. 'I'll be there in a moment.' She left him to wash his hands in the bowl on a side table, tidy his work away in a cupboard and take off the overall, before following her into the house.

Immediately on coming north he had visited the Pendlebury works in Birmingham, which were run by a very competent manager and hardly needed his presence except that he liked to involve himself in what was going on, especially the design of any new products. He had wanted to talk to some of the operatives to find out if they had heard anything about any uprisings or troublesome foreigners. Having satisfied himself on that score, he had come home to work on his Crystal Girl. Since then, he had been so engrossed, watching the figure of Esme grow under his fingers; he had had little time for anything else.

He did not want to think about anything else, because if he let his thoughts stray they only led to his predicament: how to satisfy the Duke of Wellington and thereby rid himself of

Juliette and how to reverse Viscount Trent's aversion to him and obtain Esme's forgiveness for acting so brutally on the night he took her home from the theatre. He hadn't seen her since, but their parting had been cool enough for him to realise she was angry with him.

It was strange in a way because, when he had kissed her, she had not been angry, not angry enough to struggle or cry out. It would not have taken very much to wake Miss Bannister, but she had not even tried. He could have sworn she had been almost as aroused as he was. If they had not been in a moving coach and if Miss Bannister had not been present, he would have been carried away past all reason. He ought to try and make amends with the living, breathing girl before even thinking of making her in clay and metal and glass. From wanting to stay away, he suddenly could not wait to get back.

But in that resolve he was thwarted. The very next morning, Lady Pendlebury received notification of the sudden death of Viscount Gorridge. 'He had a seizure three days ago,' she told Felix, as she read the letter from her sister, the Viscountess. 'The doctors tried to revive him, but couldn't. She was so shocked that she has only now been able to write with the news. The funeral is to be at the end of next week to allow time for Edward to return from the Continent. We will have to go. I must comfort my sister and you must attend the funeral.'

'Of course. Poor Aunt Arabella. She was devoted to him, wasn't she?'

'Yes, he was a good husband, though she could not shift him when it came to sending Edward abroad.'

'What was all that about? I never did hear the details.'

'Oh, it was all very sordid. Bella was convinced the silly girl was making it up or exaggerating. Edward said he only attempted to give her a peck on the cheek; he was, after all, supposed to be courting her and both families had agreed to the marriage.'

'Who are you talking about?'

'Why, one of the Luffenham girls. Lucinda, the eldest.'

'Lucinda,' he mused. 'She married Myles Moorcroft. I met him in London. I liked him, we got on famously.'

'Well, I don't know about that. I know she accused Edward of attempting to rape her and the evidence must have been telling because Gorridge believed it and sent him abroad to save him from prosecution. He hasn't been home since, but now, of course, he will inherit.'

'I remember Edward as something of a gambler. I had to bail him out on one occasion when the dunners were after him and he would not go to his father for relief. Six or seven years ago, I think it was. I thought that was why he had gone abroad.'

'Have you met Mrs Moorcroft?'

'Lady Moorcroft,' he corrected her, reminding her that an earl's daughter kept her title on marriage. 'No, she wasn't in town. One of the children had a cold, I was told. I wonder if it's because of what happened to her sister that Lady Trent seems so against me.'

'It had nothing to do with you. You are not a bit like Edward. And if Mr Moorcroft does not allow it to influence him, why should she?'

'I don't know. It was just a thought. When do you want to go to Gorryham?'

'Tomorrow, if it is convenient for you.'

'Of course.'

* * *

Linwood Park was a house in mourning. The curtains were almost completely drawn at the windows and black crepe ribbons swathed the pillars to the front door. Felix had stayed there once or twice as a child and remembered it as a sparkling, happy house, wanting for nothing money could buy. It was still sumptuous, still beautifully furnished, but all the pictures of the deceased were swathed in black; the female servants were in black dresses and the menservants in black trousers, with black armbands. His aunt greeted them, dressed from head to toe in black, her normally jolly face blotched by recent tears. As soon as she saw her sister, she flung herself into her arms and began to sob again.

'Oh, Fanny, I don't know what I am going to do without him. He was always my prop, I never had to worry about a thing and now there is nothing but worry. I wish Edward would come home.'

'No doubt he is on his way and will get here as soon as he can,' her sister soothed her. 'In the meantime, is there anything Felix can do for you?'

She mopped her eyes and looked up at him. 'Oh, Felix, I did not notice you there.' She moved forward and reached up to peck him on the cheek. 'Thank you for coming, but I am forgetting myself. Come into the drawing room and I will order refreshments. The staff are all at sixes and sevens and most of them unable to do a thing for weeping…'

'We can't have that,' Fanny said. 'I'll go and see to them. You go into the drawing room and tell Felix what he can do for you.' She bustled off in the direction of the kitchens.

'You could talk to the parson for me,' Lady Gorridge said as they seated themselves in what—in normal circumstances—was a bright, sunny room. Now, lit only by candlelight, it was so gloomy they could hardly see each other. 'He wants to know about funeral arrangements and how can I do that before Edward comes?'

'Of course, Aunt, I'll do what I can.'

'It was so sudden, you know,' she went on. 'He had no time to prepare himself. We did not even say goodbye.' She began to weep again.

He moved over and put his arm about her shaking shoulders. He knew it would be useless to tell her to stop crying, so he said nothing until she stopped of her own accord. 'I keep doing that, you know. Just when I think I am under control, I'm off again.'

His mother returned, much to his relief. She was followed by a parlour maid and a footman with the tea things. It was his mother who took charge, his mother who organised the servants, who told the cook what to prepare for dinner, who instructed the chambermaids to prepare rooms for guests, for there would more coming. It was his mother's bracing practicality that brought his aunt out of her bouts of weeping in order to answer her questions.

That was how they had learned that the Viscount had been about to go riding and was in the stables talking to one of the grooms when he suddenly collapsed. Two burly men had carried him into the house and one of the best horsemen sent off on the fastest mount to fetch the doctor, but it was all too late. His lordship never spoke again.

'Do you have any idea what brought it on?'

'None at all. He hadn't even been ill. Oh, what am I going to say to Edward?'

'He knows why he has been sent for, doesn't he?'

'Oh, yes. We had been hoping his father would relent and allow him to come home and make his peace. He had written

to him only recently on the subject and I had been praying…'
She stopped to control more tears.

Edward, in unrelieved black—black tail suit, black waist-coat, black neckcloth—arrived the day before the funeral, accompanied by Mrs Ashbury, the Viscountess's other sister and Victor. 'Hope you don't mind,' Felix told the new Viscount after offering his condolences. 'We didn't know if you would be home in time and your mother was fretting, so I have gone ahead with the arrangements for the funeral.'

'No, glad you did,' Edward said, while his mother sobbed on his chest. 'It was a rough crossing or I'd have been here sooner. I stopped with Aunt Sophie and Victor last night and we came on first thing this morning.'

Felix was glad to hand everything over to his cousin. Edward was pale and sombre, not at all like the wild young man Felix had known years before, but that was hardly surprising considering the circumstances. But was he capable of attempting rape? Perhaps all he had done was kiss the lady with too much passion, as he, Felix, had kissed Esme. Esme could just as easily have cried rape. If she knew what had happened to her sister, no wonder she had been angry. Was that why she had said, 'Let him try'? If she had complained, he could have been exiled like his cousin. The risk he had taken horrified him.

There were hundreds of people at the funeral because Viscount Gorridge was a well-liked man, a respected employer and a fair landlord. Among the many people who arrived were Myles Moorcroft and the Earl of Luffenham, which surprised Felix, considering what Edward was supposed to have done. Even more surprising was the fact that they returned to the house afterwards at Lady Gorridge's request.

Felix studied the Earl surreptitiously. If he was to obtain the Earl's permission to make and exhibit the little statue of Esme, he needed to know what kind of man he was dealing with. The white-haired Earl was upright in his bearing, stern of countenance and very correct in the way he addressed everyone. He was a man who knew his rank and would not let other people forget it. Myles introduced Felix.

'Ah, Pendlebury,' he said. 'Knew your father, many years ago. Good man. Take after him, do you?'

'I try, my lord. May I present my mother, Lady Gorridge's sister.'

The introductions made, he left his mother chatting to the Earl about his father and wandered out into the hall, which was crowded with people who had come to pay their respects to the widow and the new Viscount who, having accepted them, had left the room. It was difficult to imagine Edward with that illustrious title. Having nothing in common with the throng, Felix passed between them and mounted the stairs, intending to go to his room and prepare to leave, but he stopped when he heard Edward's voice coming from Lady Gorridge's boudoir, whose door was slightly ajar.

'Why did you have to invite him to the house, Mama? After what he did…'

'The Earl of Luffenham was a great friend of your father's, Edward…'

'So great a friend, Papa believed him before me.'

'Oh, darling, can you not put that behind you? It was so long ago and best forgotten.'

'Not by me, it isn't. And, by all accounts, not by my father. If he had put it behind him, he would not have left the estate in the hands of trustees, as if he did not trust me to run it properly.' To the listener in the hall he sounded furious.

It is only until you reach thirty-five, Edward, and you still have the title. They can't take that from you. And your father did stipulate that if you married and settled down befor that, the trustees could allow you to take over sooner.'

'Oh, I intend to do that, never fear.'

'No more gambling and loose women? You will settle down and marry a nice girl and give me grandchildren? It is a pity it could not have happened before your father—' she choked on a sob '—before he was so cruelly taken from us.'

'I could not marry while I was kept abroad, Mama, could I? There were Frenchwomen in plenty...'

'Oh, no, I did not mean those. I meant a sound English girl of good family.'

'And where am I to find one of those?'

'If you really do mean to turn over a new leaf and you want to prove it to the world, you could do worse than marry Luffenham's youngest. She has the pedigree and is young and healthy and, I believe, on the look-out for a husband.'

'Luffenham's daughter! Are you seriously suggesting I should marry her?'

'Why not, if you are sincere in wanting to make good? The trustees would certainly view that in a favourable light.'

There was a pause and then Felix heard him murmur, 'Why not, indeed.'

'She is in London now, I believe, staying with her sister.'

'Not Lucy?'

'No, Rosemary. She is Viscountess Trent now, you know. But you need to make haste, the season is already in full swing and Lady Esme will almost certainly be attracting potential husbands.'

'I am in mourning.'

'I know, but I think marrying and settling down so that you can take over your duties on the estate is more important. I am sure your father would have agreed.'

Felix changed his mind about going to his room and went to find his mother and tell her what he had overheard. 'I've got to get back to London,' he said. 'Esme is vulnerable…'

'Of course you must,' she agreed. 'You go, I'll stay here with Bella for a few days. I think she may need me.'

He returned downstairs and was in the hall, checking *Bradshaw's Railway Guide* when Myles approached him. 'Leaving, Pendlebury?'

'Yes, I have to return to London.'

'I am going myself. There's a train to Leicester in little over half an hour, we could travel together if you are ready to go.'

'I have to find my aunt and say my farewells, then we can be off.'

His aunt had returned to her guests and was bravely circulating among them, thanking them for coming. He waited until she spotted him and then explained that he had to leave, but his mother would stay and keep her company for a while.

'Thank you, Felix, for all your help.'

'It was the least I could do. Edward will take over now.'

'Yes, indeed. I have been urging him to find himself a wife and I believe he means to go to London soon for that purpose.'

'Won't he be in mourning?'

'Only half mourning. I am sure it was what his father would have wished.' She paused. 'Edward has been out of the country so long, he will find it strange. People will have forgotten he existed.'

'Oh, I do not think so, Aunt. Word will soon spread.'

'Well, I hope it is good and not scandal.'

'Oh, do you think it might be?' he asked, affecting innocence.

'I am not sure I altogether trust Victor. He always used to lead Edward into trouble when they were boys.' She smiled wanly. 'Do not tell your Aunt Sophie I said that or we should quarrel.'

'I wouldn't dream of it.'

'But you were always a steadying influence. Can I ask you to look out for Edward if you are going to town?'

'He isn't going yet, is he?'

'In a few days. He won't mind leaving me if your mother is here to bear me company.'

'But, Aunt, he is a grown man, older than I am, I could not influence what he does.'

'I know, but just say you will keep an eye on him for me.'

'Oh, I will do that, never fear.' It was said grimly, but she did not seem to notice that as she thanked him and kissed his cheek.

He passed his Aunt Sophie on the way out and bade her a hurried goodbye, saying he had a train to catch.

'Your mother tells me you are going back to London,' she called after him. 'No doubt we shall see you there.'

He waved his hand in acknowledgement and rejoined Myles, waiting for him by the door.

It was only two miles to the station and, as neither had much luggage, they decided to walk. It was no more than a wayside halt, built for the convenience of those who lived at Linwood Park and the village of Gorryham. 'I built the line,' Myles told him. 'From Peterborough to Leicester. It's all part of the wider network now.'

'Is that how you came to know Viscount Gorridge?'

'Yes. The Earl, too. He did not approve of me at first, because I liked to work with my men and I'm not a member of one of the old families, but he has mellowed in his old age.'

'It is a pity Viscount Trent has not followed his example.'

Myles grinned. 'Yes, he is a bit of a stick in the mud, but he means well.'

They did not have long to wait for the train and were soon settled in a first-class carriage and talking about the progress of the Exhibition. 'I don't doubt enough funds will be raised,' Myles said. 'Gorridge contributed generously before he died and his example has persuaded others.'

'What do you think of Edward?'

'I try not to think of him at all.' It was said firmly, discouraging more questions.

Felix changed the subject. 'Have you seen any of the designs submitted for the Exhibition building?'

'No, but I've been told there have been hundreds, some professionally done, others just scribbled on any old bits of paper, none so far seem to have impressed the judges. I recall you were submitting one yourself.'

'I did think about it, but to be honest I do not have the time or inclination to oversee so large a project.'

'Will you tender for the glass?'

'No, my manufactory is only a small concern, mainly for decorative products. And in any case, I am too close to the organizers—it might be construed as a conflict of interest.'

'I've been thinking of putting in for the steel,' Myles told him with a chuckle. 'Girders are not so very different from railway lines, are they?'

'No. I wish you luck.' He paused. 'I have been talking to my operatives and they are keen to see the Exhibition. It will be no little expense for them, what with the travelling, over-night accommodation and the entrance fee, even when it is reduced to a shilling. They will need to start saving up now, if they are to have enough. I have suggested forming a savings club and have agreed to be its treasurer.'

'I believe other industrial concerns are doing the same thing.'

'I need to arrange the best rates. You could help by discounting the rail fare on your lines.'

'I would be prepared to do that if sufficient numbers are interested. Let me know.'

'Indeed, I will.'

It was only a short journey to Leicester and a half hour later they were drawing into the station. 'Come home with me and dine with us,' Myles suggested as they stepped down on to the platform and Felix discovered he had a long wait for the next train to Rugby where he would have another wait while the London–Birmingham engine was coupled up before they could proceed to London. It would be late when he arrived. 'Stay the night. I'd like you to meet my wife. You can catch the train in the morning. It will have you at Euston soon after midday.'

Felix admitted to himself that he was curious to meet the third of the Vernley sisters and happily accepted.

In spite of having no prior warning, Lucy welcomed him warmly. 'My husband has often spoken of you,' she told him. 'It is a pleasure to meet you. You will have to take pot luck, but I am sure Cook will rise to the occasion.'

'Thank you, my lady.'

She was a more mature version of Esme, he decided. She

was several inches taller and her hair was slightly darker, but their features were very similar and when she smiled, it was almost as if Esme was smiling out at him. Rosemary, he concluded, was the odd one out with her starchy ways, more like her father, the Earl.

'You do not have a personal servant with you?'

'No, my lady. I long ago decided to dispense with a valet. If a man cannot, at the age of twenty-seven, dress himself, then there is something wrong with him.'

'That's what Myles always says. I'll have a room made ready for you. If you give your bag to a footman, he will carry it up for you. I'm sure you could do with some refreshment after your journey.'

'Sweetheart, it was only a half hour in a train and a few minutes in a carriage,' Myles said, laughing. 'And we were fed right royally at Linwood Park.'

'I am sure you were. Lady Gorridge was always an excellent hostess, but a cup of tea is always welcome, is that not so, Lord Pendlebury?'

'Indeed, it is.'

'Come into the drawing room then.' She instructed a waiting servant to bring in tea things and led the way.

The room in which he found himself was bright and comfortably furnished and certainly lived in. A book and a carelessly folded newspaper lay on a side table and there was a board game on the table in the middle of the room. The sound of young voices came from beneath it. 'Out of there, you two.' Myles's voice brought two tousled heads out from under the chenille cloth.

'Papa! You're home.' A boy of about five and a little girl, two years younger, scrambled out and hurled themselves at their father.

He picked them up, one on each arm. 'We have visitors, children. This is Lord Pendlebury, come to see if you have been good. Say how do you do.'

He put them down. The boy approached Felix boldly and held out his hand. 'How do you do? I'm Harry.'

Felix shook it solemnly. 'How do you do, Harry?'

'This is Vicky.' The boy pointed to his sister, who had her thumb in her mouth. 'She is shy.'

'Hallo, Vicky. You aren't shy, are you?'

She shook her head but did not speak.

'Off you go back to Miss Lovatt,' Myles told them, as a servant brought in the tea things and Lucy hurriedly removed the book and paper so that the tray could be set down at her side.

'Well,' Lucy said, after they were all seated and she had dispensed the tea. 'How was Linwood Park?'

'Shrouded in black crepe,' Myles said. 'But otherwise unchanged.'

'And was the new Viscount there?'

'Yes.'

'As odious as ever, I suppose.'

'My dear,' Myles said. 'Be careful what you say, Lord Pendlebury is his cousin.'

She turned towards Felix. 'I did not know. You have my condolences, my lord.'

He laughed. 'I was never very close to him, my lady, though our mothers are sisters. He has lived abroad for several years.'

'Do you know why?'

He hesitated. 'I believe he was involved in a scandal. I assumed it was gambling…'

'That may have been the root cause of it, but I shall say no more. It does not bear repeating.'

'My lady, I overheard his mother advising him to marry and settle down,' he said, realising that what she said seemed to bear out what his mother had told him. It emboldened him to go on. 'She recommended him to pay his addresses to Lady Esme.'

'Esme! He'd never do that. Papa would not hear of it for a start and I would never speak to Esme again if she was so foolish as to accept him.'

'When I left Linwood, Edward was in close conversation with the Earl,' Myles said. 'I heard him say he was deeply sorry for his past behaviour and was fully resolved to turn over a new leaf and be a model of propriety.'

'He is up to something.' She turned to Felix. 'I am sorry to speak so ill of a member of your family, my lord, but if he has designs on my sister... Oh, dear, I wish I could warn her to be on her guard.'

'I will endeavour to do that, my lady.'

'Are you acquainted with Esme?'

'Yes. I find her—' he hesitated '—delightful.'

Myles laughed. 'I think it is more than that, Lucy. When I left London his lordship was doing his best to engage her attention and she was certainly interested.'

She turned to Felix. 'Oh, if only you would protect her.'

He smiled a little wryly. 'I have been given the task of protecting Edward from Victor and Victor from Edward and both of them from a certain French lady and now I must watch over Lady Esme.'

'You do not mind, do you?'

'Not in the least, you do not have to ask, I would have done it anyway. The big problem is Lady Trent and her husband. I have been forbidden to see or speak to Es...Lady Esme.'

She noticed the slip of the tongue and smiled. 'Why, whatever have you done?'

He decided to tell them all that had happened, from the balloon ride to the visit to the theatre, but he did not think it would do his cause any good to confess to kissing Esme. 'No one knows the identity of the intrepid young lady balloonist,' he told them. 'It must, for everyone's sake, remain a secret. And I do not think there was anyone at the theatre who recognised her, but I am banned from Trent House because of it.'

The tale made them laugh, though he could see nothing amusing about it. 'That wasn't your fault,' Lucy told him. 'Esme was always one for mischief and never stopped to consider the consequences, but I am surprised at Rosemary blaming you.'

'No doubt she is guided by her husband and he is an implacable opponent of the Exhibition, so we were on opposite sides right from the start. And they were reluctant to attach any blame to Lady Esme. Nor would I want them to.'

'I have a good mind to write to Rosemary....'

'Oh, no, please do not do that. I must fight my own battles.'

A footman came to tell them a room had been prepared for Lord Pendlebury and a jug of hot water taken up for him to wash and change for dinner and the conversation was dropped.

The rest of his visit went by very pleasantly. The dinner was superb, the conversation afterwards was stimulating, ranging as it did from the Exhibition, the state of the railways, questions about glass manufacture and politics to whether he perceived a threat from foreign insurgents ostensibly coming to see what the Exhibition had to offer, to which his answer was guarded. He went to bed that night in the knowledge that he had made two staunch friends on whom he could rely and it made him feel a little better about everything.

The next morning, Myles took him to the station in his gig to catch the early morning train for London. He was looking forward to renewing his acquaintance with Esme and making her understand that he had kissed her because he loved her. And, given her permission, would do it again. And again, and as many times as breath would allow.

Esme had missed him and she wished she had not pretended to be so angry with him, when she was not angry but confused. Banny, of course, said it was all her own fault. If she had been patient, her sister might have overcome her prejudice and allowed him to call, instead of which he had been banned and taken himself off somewhere more congenial. 'He could not defend himself without blaming you,' she told her charge. 'And no gentleman worthy of the name would do that.' Esme did not need Miss Bannister to tell her that; her own good sense told her so.

She endured more of the Season's outings and events, going out and about with Rosemary and allowing Toby Salford to fawn all over her and Captain Merton to pay her extravagant compliments while treading on her toes in a dance. As for the pimply youth who was the Earl of Wincombe's heir, she could not abide him. Rosemary was in despair. And so was Esme, not because she would have to go back to Luffenham without so much as a hint of a betrothal, but because she had let the love of her life slip through her fingers. He had been interested in her, hadn't he? He had deliberately met her in the park and shown her how to draw a horse; he had said he was glad to be interrupted when they came upon him by the river; he had sketched her, raced others to be the one to go up in a balloon with her, danced a waltz with her and he had kissed her. Surely all of that had meant something? On the other hand, there was the Frenchwoman—Juliette, he had called her—who had disappeared about the same time as he had. The thought of them being together sent her nearly crazy.

Rosie hardly let her out of her sight, but there were times when a late night left her more than usually tired and she would stay in bed until noon. On those occasions, Miss Bannister accompanied Esme on a walk. Sometimes they went to Hyde Park and watched the riders, but the one she hoped to see was never there. Sometimes they went into Green Park or St James's, where nursemaids gathered with their aristocratic charges, among them Master John Trent. It made Esme wonder if she would ever have a child of her own. Sometimes they returned to the river. Everywhere she went, she found herself looking in vain for Felix.

But it was not out of doors she saw him again, but in Lady Bryson's crowded drawing room. Her heart began a sharp pitter-patter against her chest as he looked up from his conversation with Caroline Merton and caught sight of her. Dressed in a light brown jacket and trousers and a yellow waistcoat above which was a neatly tied dark blue cravat, he did not look any different from the last time she had seen him. He was still as handsome, his greeny-brown eyes just as searching, his mouth… Oh, that mouth. It had covered hers, had made her melt with longing and desire and she could not forget it. Even the memory made her grow hot. She watched, almost mesmerised, as he excused himself and made his way through the throng to stand in front of her.

'Lady Esme, how do you do?' he asked formally, though

formality was the last thing he had in mind. He wanted to ask her why the brightness had gone from her blue eyes as if someone had snuffed out a candle inside her and why her smile did not light up her face as it once did.

'I am well. And you?'

'I, too, am well.'

Neither could think of anything else to say, though their heads were filled with unspoken words: words of love, questions, explanations, promises, none of which could be uttered in a crowded room. 'What have you been doing with yourself?' he asked at last.

'Oh, nothing out of the ordinary. What about you?'

'I have been home to visit my mother and to do some work in my laboratory.'

'Oh, I thought…'

'What?'

She could not tell him she thought he had been with Juliette Lefavre. 'It doesn't matter. I have been looking for the result of the competition for the Exhibition building in the newspapers and hoped you might have won it.'

'Oh, that.' It was said dismissively. 'I decided not to enter, after all.'

'Why not?'

'I needed more time to get it right and somehow I could not put my mind to it. I preferred to work on my exhibit.'

'Is that what you were doing in your laboratory?

'Yes.'

'Is it finished?'

'Not yet—I had to leave it and go to Viscount Gorridge's funeral.'

'We saw the notice of his passing in the paper. I did not know you knew him.'

'The Viscountess is my mother's sister.'

'Oh, I see. The late Viscount Gorridge was a great friend of Papa's, you know.'

'Yes, I met your father there.'

'Oh, did you?' She suddenly brightened. 'How was he?'

'He seemed in very good form. I met your sister, too.'

'Lucy? Surely she was not at the funeral?'

'No, but Myles was. He invited me to stop at his home overnight on my way back to London. She is a charming lady and made me very welcome.'

'Unlike Rosemary, you mean.'

'No doubt Lady Trent had her reasons.' He paused, smiling. 'I behaved abominably. And plead your forgiveness.'

'Oh.' Was he referring to that kiss? 'No need. You probably saved me from a worse fate.'

Someone's elbow pushed him in the back and he found himself almost on top of her. 'I beg your pardon, my lady. This is a little too much of a squeeze, but I need to talk to you.'

'You are talking to me.'

'Not the way I want to.'

'Esme!' Rosemary had finished her conversation with Lady Bryson and come looking for her, only to find her almost in the arms of the man who had been banned from speaking to her. 'Lord Pendlebury, you must excuse us. It is time to go, Esme. Come along.' And just to make sure she obeyed, grabbed her arm and almost dragged her away.

'Rosie, you are hurting me and everyone is looking.'

Rosemary let her go. 'Why do you encourage him, Esme?' The words were a whispered hiss. 'You know how I feel about him.'

'I know you have an illogical antipathy towards him and it isn't his fault. Would you have me cut him? How would that have looked to the rest of the company?' A footman opened the front door for them and they made their way onto the street where the Trent carriage waited to take them home.

'There is a way of making clear a man's attentions are not welcome without cutting him. Did the book I gave you not explain that?'

'Yes, but you see, I do not find his attentions unwelcome. I only wish I was the only one...'

'What do you mean?'

'I mean I wish he had eyes only for me. I believe I am in love with him.'

'Love!' Rosemary's voice was scathing. 'You have had your head turned, that is all.'

'How can you be so sure? Were you not in love with Rowan when he proposed to you?'

'That is beside the point. Rowan was eminently suitable.'

'Suitable! I hate that word. It is so stuffy. And cold. Anyway, why is Lord Pendlebury unsuitable?'

'He associates with some very strange people, dangerous people, foreigners like that Frenchwoman. Rowan says they mean mischief. He has it on good authority that they are coming from the Continent on purpose to cause trouble. It is the Chartists all over again, just when we thought they had been subdued.'

'I do not believe Lord Pendlebury would have anything to do with them.'

'No, you don't want to believe anything against him, that's your trouble. Do not be deceived by honeyed words and good looks, Esme. A handsome face can hide a black heart.'

'Oh, I am sure his heart is not black….'

'Rowan does know what he is talking about, I promise you. Lord Pendlebury is out to make trouble. And I do not want you to breathe a word of what I have said to anyone, do you hear, least of all Lord Pendlebury himself. It could be dangerous if he knows he is being suspected.'

Esme did not know what to think. Surely Rowan would not lie? And she knew with certainty that Rosemary never would. Her sister believed every word she said. Did that mean it was true? Her confusion turned to worry. 'Why didn't you tell me this before now?'

'I hoped I wouldn't have to. When Lord Pendlebury left town, we hoped that was the end of it, but now he is back and you must be protected or you will find yourself tarred with the same brush. Not only will you not find a husband, whether you fancy yourself in love or not, you will be a social outcast.'

It was too much to take in. Esme sank back against the upholstered seat of the carriage and felt as though her heart were breaking. Was she such a bad judge of character that a villain could pull the wool over her eyes and make her love him? Could she ever trust her own judgement again?

'Oh, do cheer up,' Rosemary told her, seeing the tears rolling down her cheeks. 'Felix Pendlebury is not the only fish in the sea. And you have your ball to look forward to.'

'I don't want a ball.'

'Yes, you do. I have decided to hold it on the sixteenth of July, the last one of the season.'

Esme, scrabbling in her pocket for her handkerchief, gave a bitter laugh. 'The last throw of the dice, is that it? If you cannot foist me off on someone by then, you will have to send me home an old maid.'

'Don't be silly, Esme. You are only twenty, how can it be the last throw of the dice? And I do not care for the gambling allusion. It is not a gamble.'

'Oh, but it is,' Esme said, blowing her nose. 'The whole of life is a gamble, certainly choosing a husband is, and I am not very good at it.'

'Oh, I am swiftly losing all patience with you. The ball will be the high point of the season, the best one yet for music and decorations and food and drink. Everyone will be there. Rowan has said I need spare no expense.'

'Then I am truly grateful to him,' she said dully. 'I will do my best not to let you down.'

Impulsively Rosemary leaned over and kissed her sister's cheek. 'I knew you would see reason.'

Esme rubbed her cheek thoughtfully. She had never known Rosie to do that before and perhaps Myles had been right when he told her to be guided by her sister. But, oh, how her heart ached.

Chapter Six

Esme came home from a walk to the library with Miss Bannister two days later to find her sister entertaining Viscount Gorridge. He was sitting in the drawing room, his top hat on the floor beside him, drinking tea.

He rose when she entered. 'Lady Esme, how do you do?'

'Very well, my lord.' She was wary of him. He was dressed in a black suit and wore a black cravat wound twice about his neck and tied in a small knot. His dark hair was sleeked down on either side of a central parting. He had small dark eyes and they seemed to be scanning her in a way which made her feel as if her blue gingham gown and her two petticoats were transparent. 'May I offer my condolences on your bereavement.'

'Thank you. It was a great loss. I had been planning to come home from France in any case to help with the estate and was looking forward to working beside my father, but it was not to be.' He gave a sigh verging on the melodramatic. 'But there, we must accept the setbacks the Lord sends us, must we not?'

'His lordship is staying in London and called to pay his respects,' Rosemary added.

Esme wondered why he should take the trouble. Although Papa had remained friends with the late Viscount, she always understood Edward's name was not to be mentioned, certainly not in Lucy's hearing. Esme herself had been too young to be privy to what had happened, but it must have been very dreadful for his father to send him abroad. Had he taken liberties with her sister, liberties like forcibly kissing her? Felix had done that, but she would not have dreamed of telling anyone. Perhaps the difference was that Lucy had not loved Edward in the way she loved Felix. She stopped her errant thoughts. After what Rosie had told her, Felix was not to be thought of.

'I would not have left my mother at such a time,' he added, as if he had guessed the question that was on her tongue to ask. 'But I had business with the family lawyers and Mama wanted me to come while she has Lady Pendlebury to keep her company. I have opened up my house in Upper Brook Street and expect to do a little simple entertaining….'

'Entertaining, my lord?' she queried.

'Nothing elaborate, it would not be appropriate, but I have been out of the country so long, I am sadly behindhand with what is going on and who is in town. And so I thought of Lady Trent.' He smiled at Rosemary and then at Esme. 'And hearing that you, Lady Esme, were staying with your sister, I hoped I could prevail upon you both, and Lord Trent, of course, to attend a little evening gathering at Gorridge House three days from now.'

'I think we can manage that,' Rosemary said.

'I would be grateful if you would also advise me whom else to invite. Who is in town, that I should know? I wish it to be known that I have returned to the fold a better and wiser man than the one who left these shores over six years ago. You do understand, my dear Lady Trent?'

'Perfectly. May I suggest, Lady Aviemore, Lady Bryson, Lady Mountjoy, all of whom have sons and daughters and who have great influence on the social scene. Of the young men, you could ask Toby Salford, Captain Merton, Bertie Wincombe, James Bryson.'

'And young ladies? Besides Lady Esme, I mean.'

Esme listened in astonishment as her sister reeled off several names. It was evident Rosemary meant to be as cooperative as she could and it made Esme wonder what her father and Lucy might say to that.

She tackled her sister as soon as he had taken his leave. 'Rosie, what was all that about? You know Papa will not have Edward Gorridge's name mentioned.'

'Papa has changed his mind. Lord Gorridge told me he had spoken to Papa after his father's funeral and they are friends again. He assured me that the business with Lucy was all a mistake on her part, but he holds no grudges and agreed to live abroad to save her embarrassment.'

'Do you believe that?'

'I think so. At any rate I am prepared to give him the benefit of the doubt. I always did say Lucy made a fuss about nothing. He did no more than kiss her a little too passionately. I do not think she would have minded in the least, if she had not fallen for Myles.'

'If we go to his soirée, we will be telling the world all is forgiven and forgotten and he may safely be accepted in society.'

'Why not? He is a single man, with a title and a vast fortune and Linwood Park is a magnificent mansion. Any girl would be a fool to turn down the chance to be mistress of it.

For that alone his lordship would be accepted, but he came to us first and we will have the edge on everyone else.'

Esme laughed. 'Rosie, are you matchmaking?'

'Well, I can't see it will do any harm. You haven't found anyone else, have you?'

'Rosie, you know—'

'If you are still thinking of Lord Pendlebury, put him out of your mind. He is ineligible. Lord Gorridge met him in France and he more or less confirmed what Rowan told me, that Lord Pendlebury was involved with the troubles in France.'

'What exactly did he say?'

'He would not elaborate. He said Felix was his cousin and they had always been close as children, but lately had drifted apart, but the man was family and he would not have a word said against him and if I repeated what he had told me, he would deny it absolutely.'

'You have just told me.'

'Only what you need to know, but it goes no further, do you hear?'

'Yes, I hear.' She could not imagine why her sister thought she would want to spread rumours about Felix or anyone else. It was not in her nature, but it seemed the evidence was piling up against him.

Given only three days' notice, it was extraordinary how many people had accepted Viscount Gorridge's invitation. His drawing room was full to bursting when Rosemary and Esme arrived. Wearing a slate-grey suit with a black cravat, he hurried forward to make them welcome. 'Lady Trent, Lady Esme, you have come. I was beginning to think my guests of honour had forgotten.'

'Oh, no, my lord,' Rosemary assured him. 'The traffic was more than usually thick, my coachman had to force a way through.'

'You know everyone, don't you?' He waved a well-manicured hand at his guests.

'Oh, yes.' She caught sight of Lady Aviemore. 'I must go and speak to her ladyship.' And with that she darted away, leaving Esme facing Edward.

'I am so glad you could come,' he said. 'If you had not, the whole evening would have been spoiled.'

'Surely not?'

'I mean it. Ever since I saw you again three days ago, I have not been able to get you out of my mind. You have grown up into a lovely woman. I must say you outshine both your sisters and they are judged to be beautiful.'

'You are flattering me.'

'No, indeed not. It is no more than the truth. How long are you staying in town?'

'A little while yet. Rosemary is holding a ball to honour my coming-out and I shall certainly not go back to Luffenham before that.'

'Then perhaps we shall see something of each other. Can I prevail upon you to take a carriage ride in the park with me? The family landau has been stored in the mews ever since Mama was last in town. I can soon have it brought out and made ready. And I can hire horses from Tattersalls.'

'Please don't do that especially for me.'

'Why not? It would give me so much pleasure. And if I am to be in town for any length of time I shall need a vehicle. Do say you will come.'

'You will have to ask Rosemary.'

'Naturally I will.'

'Lady Esme.'

She would have known that quiet voice anywhere and whipped round to face him. 'Oh, Lord Pendlebury, you startled me.'

'Go away, Felix,' Edward growled. 'Lady Esme and I were having a private conversation.'

'Then I beg your pardon.' His determination to be polite and stay cool made him sound hard and unfeeling when the exact opposite was the case. He was keyed up with feelings, which the sight of her so deep in conversation with his cousin had heightened to an almost unbearable extent. Remembering what her sister Lucy had told him would have made him worried for her even if he had not been head over heels in love with her. He wanted to tell her so and to do that he needed to speak to her alone. 'But you are neglecting your other guests, Edward. I notice some have not even been served refreshment. If you want to make your mark in society, you neglect these ladies at your peril.'

Edward reluctantly conceded the truth of this. 'If you will excuse me, Lady Esme, duty calls. Shall we say tomorrow at two o'clock?'

'If Rosemary agrees.'

'Will she?' Felix asked as soon as he had gone.

'I expect so.'

'What will she be agreeing to?'

'A carriage ride, though what business it is of yours, I do not know.'

The sharpness of her reply made him start back as if she had struck him. What was the matter with her? Five days ago she had seemed pleased to see him back. They had had a short friendly conversation which had been interrupted by her sister who had marched her off, but there was nothing out of the ordinary in that. Esme herself had been her own sweet self. He gathered himself to reply evenly. 'I am concerned for you.'

'Are you, indeed? If that is so, then will you please desist from addressing me.'

'Very well, I will take my leave. But before I go, allow me to warn you against putting your trust in wolves in sheep's clothing.'

'Please do not trouble yourself, my lord. I have already learned that lesson the hard way. Now, if you will excuse me…'

He bowed and left her. He managed to keep his temper until he had gained the street and then he kicked a stone so hard he hurt his foot. Hobbling, he continued on his way, cursing as he went.

Esme wished she could go away and hide, so that she could have a good cry. Felix had looked so hurt by her sharp retort that she began to doubt what her sister had told her, after all. Could it all be some terrible plot to discredit him? But why would anyone want to do that? And why did he associate with these dreadful men if he had no part in their plotting? The answer came to her like a thunderbolt. Juliette Lefavre. She had lured him into bad company. He must love her very much to turn his back on his country. The conclusion, far from making her feel better, served to depress her spirits even further.

She looked up as Lord Gorridge returned. 'It's all arranged,' he said. 'Lady Trent cannot accompany you, but Miss Bannister will be your chaperon. I will call for you at two and we will ride in Hyde Park. And then if you are agreeable we can take tea at Clarendon's.'

'I shall look forward to it.' It was said in a monotone, but he was so pleased with himself he did not notice her lack of enthusiasm. Riding in Hyde Park with a gentleman was tantamount to declaring she accepted that he was courting her. She felt sure Felix would interpret it that way.

'There is hope for you yet,' Rosemary said as they were going home in the carriage. 'He is definitely interested and if you know what is good for you, Esme, you will encourage him.'

'How?'

'Smile a little more. Give him some of that beaming countenance you wasted on Lord Pendlebury. Let him know you like his compliments, flatter him on his accomplishments.'

'I do not know what they are.'

'Then find out, you goose. Ask him. Take an interest. You did not have much trouble quizzing Lord Pendlebury, did you? You had his life history in a half hour.'

'But was it his life history? He told me only what he wanted me to know. How much did he keep back?'

'Ah, that is a good question. But I wish I had not mentioned him. It was a poor example of what I meant.'

'Rosie, I am not sure I want to encourage Viscount Gorridge.'

'Why ever not? You like him, don't you? He is handsome and has evidently set his heart on you, so think yourself lucky. Being Viscountess Gorridge and mistress of Linwood Park is not to be sneezed at.'

'Lucy sneezed at it.'

'Lucy was blinkered by her attachment to Myles Moorcroft.'

'I do believe you would have liked him for yourself.'

'Don't be silly. After Lucy turned him down he left the

country. And I do not, for a moment, regret marrying Rowan, so don't say anything like that again.'

'I'm sorry, I didn't mean… Oh, Rosie, I am so muddled. I thought I knew what I wanted. I thought I was sure, but now I do not know what to think.'

'Then don't. Accept Lord Gorridge's attentions and enjoy the prestige it gives you. The rest will follow.'

'And if it does not?'

'Oh, then I give up.' It was said with exasperation.

The carriage drew up outside the house and they left it to go indoors where Rosemary regaled her husband with everything that had happened. He had declined to accompany them, saying he was never comfortable in a roomful of women, all gossiping so loudly it was difficult to hear oneself think. 'He had half the *beau monde* there,' she told him when they came upon him reading a newspaper in the drawing room. 'But he had eyes only for Esme. I do believe she has made a hit.'

He folded his paper and smiled up at his sister-in-law. 'What do you think of that, Esme?'

'I'm not sure.'

'Perhaps being unsure is best. It does not do to tumble head over heels in love on too little acquaintance, as I am sure you have already learned. Let him take his time and you take yours.'

Wise advice, she conceded. Tomorrow she would be in Lord Gorridge's company for two hours, at least, and she could discover a great deal in that time—notably, could he make her forget Felix?

He arrived promptly at two o'clock. Esme kept him waiting five minutes before she joined him in the drawing room. She could not make up her mind what to wear and Miss Bannister was no help at all, going about the room with her lips pursed as if she would like to say something, but dare not. Esme, too agitated herself to wonder what was the matter with her, chose a day dress in figured muslin in two shades of blue and a straw bonnet decorated with silk flowers. Picking up her parasol, because the day was oppressively hot, she went downstairs to meet her fate. At least, that's what it felt like. She had promised Rosemary she would give Lord Gorridge a fair chance and so she would. It was not his fault she could not get Felix Pendlebury out of her head.

'What a delightful picture!' his lordship exclaimed as she entered the room. His suit was charcoal grey and his cravat black—as befitted his state of mourning—but his cheerful countenance was far from mournful. 'I shall be the envy of everyone we meet.'

'Lord Gorridge, good afternoon.'

'Oh, I forgot myself. Good afternoon, Lady Esme.' He bowed and from behind his back produced a small posy of flowers and presented them to her.

'Thank you, my lord. They are very pretty.'

'Pretty flowers for a pretty lady,' he said, ignoring Miss Bannister who had entered the room behind her. 'Shall we go? The carriage is outside.'

The landau was a grand affair, black as ebony and just as shiny with the Gorridge coat of arms emblazoned on the door. The hood was down and revealed seats with red velvet cushions. The horses, Esme noticed, were not up to the standard of the vehicle; they were thin and ill-groomed. 'I wish I could have brought my own horses down,' he told her as he handed her up. 'These were the best to be had at short notice, but next time I shall insist on the best.'

'Next time?' she queried, putting up her parasol, though the sun had gone behind a cloud.

He sat beside her with Miss Bannister in the facing seat and ordered the coachman to proceed. 'I hope this will be the first of many such outings, Lady Esme.'

'Oh.' She thought about this for a moment before asking, 'Are you not expected to return to Linwood Park very soon?'

'I think I can safely leave the estate in my manager's hands for a week or two and my mother will see to the house, as she has always done and will continue to do until I take home a wife.'

'Is that one of the reasons you have come to town, to find a wife?'

'It is time I settled down.' He laughed. 'So my mother tells me and, of course, she is right.'

'Then I wish you success in your quest.'

'I am heartened by that, my lady.'

They turned into the gates of Hyde Park and on to the carriageway, where the press of vehicles was such that the horses, which had been maintaining a steady trot, were reduced to a walk. 'I did not expect such a crush,' he said. 'London has become more congested since I was last here.'

'When was that?' Esme asked.

'The day I left for the Continent. Six years ago now.'

'Did you enjoy your time abroad, my lord?'

He turned sharply to look at her, but decided she was simply making conversation and he was going to have to answer many such questions now that he was back where he belonged. 'Sometimes I did, sometimes I longed for home.'

'You are home now, though in sad circumstances. I cannot conceive what it would be like to lose a father.'

'Sad though it is, it is the nature of things and we must

accept it. Life must go on and certainly it is up to me to continue running the estate so that I can pass it on to my son in the fullness of time.'

'In the same way as Johnny will take over from Papa one day, but I pray not soon.' She paused. 'Rosemary said you spoke to Papa at the funeral.'

'Yes, we had a little conversation. He was always my father's friend. We talked of him and my regret that I had no opportunity to see my father before he died.' It was said with every evidence of deep sorrow.

'Do you blame Papa for that?'

'No,' he said evenly. 'He acted according to his lights. I understood that. Though the whole affair was no more than a misunderstanding, I could not bear the embarrassment, not for myself but for my parents, and so I agreed to live abroad for a time. Plans were afoot for me to come back when I received the dreadful news that my father had passed away.'

'I am sorry for that, my lord.'

'Thank you. I sincerely hope, Lady Esme, you will not hold what happened against me. Your sister assures me you will not.'

'I am not sure I understand what *did* happen, but if you did something that was misconstrued and for which you are truly sorry, then of course I will not hold it against you.'

'That is all I ask.' He sounded relieved. 'Now, tell me about yourself. Are you enjoying your Season?'

'Yes, Rosemary has been very good to me and has made sure I have made many new friends.'

'Is there one in particular? A gentleman who has caught your eye, perhaps?'

'No,' she lied firmly.

'I am glad.'

'Glad, my lord?'

'Oh, please do not misunderstand me. I only meant I was glad you might be free to allow me to escort you occasionally. It will show that the rift between our two families has been healed.'

'Is that all?'

'Oh, dear, I am not expressing myself very well, am I?' His smile was full of apology. 'Of course that is not all, it is not even a tenth part of it. I am a little nervous.'

'Whatever have you to be nervous about?'

'Being with you, wanting to get to know you better, wanting your good opinion of me, which is very important to me on a personal level. It was foolish to use the Earl's clemency as a way to achieve that. I should know you are wise enough to make up your own mind about people.'

'I hope I am.' She ignored the sound Banny made. It was almost a snort.

'What other things have you been doing?'

'Oh, the usual parties and routs, picnics, walks, riding…'

'I remember the Luffenham ladies were all good horsewomen. I like to ride myself. Perhaps one day we could ride together.'

'I should like that,' she said, remembering Rosemary's instructions to encourage him. 'But riding in the park is not like hunting, I fear you will be disappointed.'

'With you at my side, how could I be?'

Was this mindless sort of conversation the way it was done? she asked herself. Was this how one chose a partner for life? It was so cold, stiff with politeness and fulsome compliments apparently learned by rote, while they sat side by side not even looking at each other. She needed to see into his eyes. You could tell a great deal from a person's eyes. She turned slightly so that she was half facing him. 'What do you think about the Great Exhibition?' she asked him.

'What do I think of it?' He sounded puzzled by the unexpected change in direction.

'Yes, do you think it is a good thing or a bad thing?'

'I cannot say. Why did you ask?'

'There has been so much controversy over it, those for and against. Some say it will encourage undesirable elements from abroad to come here and cause trouble.'

'Is that so?'

'Yes, you have lately been abroad, have you heard anything of it?'

If he thought there was anything behind her question, he did not show it. 'Nothing of any consequence, my lady. I had heard of the Exhibition, who could not, when it is in all the Continental newspapers and people debating what best to exhibit? But as for trouble... No, I am sure such a thing could not happen in England.'

'My brother-in-law, Viscount Trent, would be very pleased to hear you say that. Trent House is so very near the site.'

'I can understand his concern. It is a huge project and bound to cause some disruption to the normal life of the capital when they start building. Do you know when that will be?'

'No. I am not sure if the architect has even been chosen yet. I know those who are against it have not given up trying to stop it.'

'Do you think they will?'

'I don't know. Lord Trent hopes they will. There will be more to it than putting up the building, won't there? The inside will have to be laid out and arranged ready for the thousands of exhibits that are expected.' She paused as a picture of Felix flashed into her head, Felix smilingly telling her he was going to exhibit something in glass, which he would show to her first. How could a man talk of doing that when he planned to disrupt the whole thing? Perhaps Lord Gorridge was right and there was nothing in these rumours, but why had he said that when he had told Rosemary the very opposite? Oh, now she was more confused than ever. 'There will be wagons and carts coming and going all the time and when it is over, the whole thing has to be dismantled. Rowan says the normal life of the city will be ruined for years.'

'Then I am not surprised he is against it.'

'Yes, but on the other hand, it will be a wonderful way of showing the world what we can do, won't it?'

'Yes, indeed.'

She heard Miss Bannister, who was facing backwards, give a little gasp as a rider drew up level with them. When he did not attempt to overtake them, Esme swivelled round in her seat, to find Lord Pendlebury riding alongside. He smiled and swept off his hat. 'Good afternoon, my lady. Edward.'

If Esme thought she had her heart under control, she was wrong. It began beating twenty to the dozen and so loudly she felt sure everyone else could hear it. And it made breathing difficult, let alone speaking. Her 'Good afternoon, my lord' was a squeak.

'What are you doing here?' Edward demanded of him.

'I am out riding. It is something I like to do when I have the time.' He hoped his cheerfulness did not sound forced.

'Alone, Felix? Where is Ma'amselle Lefavre?'

'Do you know, I haven't the faintest idea.'

'I should go and find her, if I were you, before Victor carries her off.'

'Oh, I do not think he will do that,' he said easily. 'It is too hot for such strenuous exercise, and if Victor deplores anything it is exercise.'

'Oh, you will have your little joke.' He turned to Esme. 'Even when we were boys he always liked to score off me, as if we were bitter rivals when, of course, we were, and still are, the best of friends.'

Esme permitted herself a smile. From being deadly boring, the afternoon had suddenly become intriguing. The two men appeared to be friendly, but she detected undercurrents of animosity and the business of scoring off each other was more than a joke. 'I am glad you are friends,' she said, looking from one to the other. Felix was smiling, but his expressive eyes were glittering like steel and Edward was looking decidedly put out. Here was no evidence of friendship, but deadly enmity. If Lord Gorridge was right about Felix, then it was no wonder he was annoyed with the effrontery of his cousin. On the other hand, if Felix knew what was being said about him and it wasn't true, he had every right to be angry... 'Then you will look out for each other,' she finished lamely.

'Oh, most definitely,' Edward said. 'Lord Pendlebury bears watching.'

'Just what do you mean by that, Cousin?' Felix demanded.

'Why, nothing,' he said. 'Except that a certain Frenchwoman has sworn vengeance on anyone who takes you from her.' He turned to Esme. 'If his eyes should stray...' He shrugged his shoulders.

Felix laughed. 'Take no notice of him, my lady. If anyone needs watching—'

'Oh, do stop it, both of you,' she said. 'If you cannot leave off taunting each other, then I shall insist on being taken home.'

'There! See what you have done,' Edward said, addressing Felix. 'Go away and let us continue our ride in peace.'

'Lady Esme?' Felix looked directly at her, making her blush to the roots of her hair. It was impossible to be indifferent to him, impossible to tell herself that her brief infatuation for him was over and had never meant anything to either of them, impossible to deny the trembling in her body. You could not turn out love, like snuffing out a candle. She desired him. She desired to be held in his arms, to be kissed again until she was breathless. While he rode beside them, she could not think of anything else and her stomach churned like a whirlpool. She did not want to send him away, but she could not let him stay. His presence was too disturbing and she was afraid Lord Gorridge would detect it. Perhaps he already had and that was why he was baiting Felix.

'I think you should ride on, my lord,' she said, not daring to look into his face.

'Very well, my lady. Your wish is my command. Good day to you. Good day, Edward.' His moved slightly forward until he was abreast of Miss Bannister, then leaned over so that his face was very close to hers. 'Whatever you do,' he whispered, 'stay awake.'

She went very pink, but did not answer and he rode away. Esme watched his stiff back as he went farther and farther from her. He had known she would be in the park that afternoon and she did not doubt he had come on purpose to waylay them and the altercation with his cousin had been a strange one, as if they were talking in code. She wished she could decipher it.

'He was always a strange boy,' Edward said. 'Full of fancies. A dreamer. Sometimes I am not sure if he is able to tell fact from fiction.'

'We cannot all be doers, my lord. People of imagination have been known to achieve great things.'

'Yes.' He looked directly at Miss Bannister. 'What did he say to you, ma'am?'

The old lady looked flustered. 'I am afraid I did not hear him very clearly. I am a little hard of hearing.'

'It was nonsense, I have no doubt. Now, let us forget about him and enjoy the rest of our ride, then we will go and have tea at Clarendon's before I take you home.'

Felix rode on to the end of the carriageway, as sure as he could be that Esme was watching him, knowing also that she was bound to have realised he had come to the park on purpose to speak to her. He should have known it would not work, not with Edward listening to every word and interrupting with a mention of Juliette. Esme herself had had very little to say. It was more than he dare hope that she had taken to heart his warning to beware of wolves in sheep's clothing. He smiled suddenly, thinking of Miss Bannister's pink face; *she* had known what he meant.

If only he could uncover the plot—if there was a plot—he would be able to throw off all this secrecy and tell Esme the truth. This struggle between duty and desire was tearing him apart.

He was so absorbed he hardly noticed where he was going until he came to the boundary with Kensington Gardens and turned back. The road was as busy as ever, but there was no sign of the Gorridge carriage and the sky had suddenly become dark and menacing, presaging a storm. He put his horse over the rails and galloped across the grass to the Park Lane gate, trying to beat the rain. But everyone else had the same idea. Horses that had been ambling along were suddenly whipped into life, carriage hoods were hastily put up, umbrellas brought out, coat collars turned up. And the rain came in torrents. He was soaked before he reached his front door.

Esme, watching the storm through the front window of the Clarendon Hotel, wondered at the force of it. It was almost as dark as night, the rumble of thunder and sheet lightning were almost instantaneous and followed by torrential rain. Already the road was a quagmire of mud. Pedestrians were trying to avoid being splashed by the vehicles that hastened along it, rain dripping off the drivers' hats. Every doorway along the street sheltered someone. The poor crossing sweepers gave up in despair.

'We were only just in time,' she said, feeling sorry for the Gorridge coachman, who was endeavouring to put up the hood of the carriage and becoming soaked in the process. The horses looked even more bedraggled than they had before.

'Yes. It is just as well you sent Pendlebury on his way, or we should have been further delayed and caught out in it,' Edward said, as tea and cakes were placed on the table in front of them. 'Will you do the honours?'

She picked up the pot, pouring tea automatically, her mind back in the park. Did Felix think that telling him to go had been an act of dismissal? Had she hurt his feelings? She felt like running out in the rain and finding him to tell him she had not meant it. 'I wonder if he got wet.'

'Who?'

'Lord Pendlebury.'

'Depends where he was going. I noticed a cake stall near the corner of the park—perhaps he took shelter there.'

'Old Mrs Hicks's place,' she said. 'It is only a shack and

meant for people to buy fruit and cakes to take out on to the grass. I doubt many could squeeze into it.'

He put milk in his tea and stirred it vigorously as if he would like to stir Felix out of his life, certainly out of hers. 'Do not trouble yourself about him. He has been used to worse conditions than this. This is only a shower compared to the monsoons they have in India, where he was born.'

'Was he? I didn't know that.'

'There is a lot you do not know about him, my lady, but let us not talk of him. I can think of more interesting subjects for our discourse. When will you come riding with me? We could perhaps go out to Richmond and take a picnic.'

'I must ask my sister,' she answered without thinking. Her mind was elsewhere, hoping Felix would not take cold, wondering about his life in India, longing to see him again. It was no good; she could not think of him as a villain whatever Rosemary or anyone else said.

'I will talk to her about it,' he said. 'We could make up a party.'

'If the summer has not gone,' she said, looking at the rain streaming down the window. It had all but blocked out the view of the street.

'Oh, no, it is only June, after all. This will clear up and the air will feel much fresher. It has been far too oppressive of late.'

Oppressive. Yes, it had and not only because of the heat. She was sorely oppressed by conflicting emotions. The promise made to her sister weighed heavily on her, especially as she had just made up her mind that she would have to see Felix again and get to the bottom of the mystery surrounding him. Before that ill-fated expedition to the theatre, she had told Banny she would fight for him and that determination had suddenly been renewed. If he told her she meant nothing to him, that kissing her had been a jest to prove that he could, if he told her that he loved Juliette, it would break her heart but she would accept it.

How to bring about the encounter was the problem, considering she was always chaperoned and she never knew where he would be on any given day. And she had to see him alone. Only a few weeks before, she could be sure that if she walked in the park or along the river bank, she would come upon him; it was almost as if fate decreed it. But that had not happened since he came back from his trip north. Except today and today she had been with his cousin.

If she was quieter than usual Edward did not seem to notice and when the rain eased and they were able to return to the carriage, he took her home in high good humour, chatting about his proposed picnic, which he put to Rosemary as soon as they arrived.

'What a delightful idea,' she said, after offering him refreshment which he declined on the grounds that they had been confined at the Clarendon for fully an hour and had drunk two pots of tea and eaten two custard tarts. 'Which day did you have in mind?'

'I leave that to you, dear lady. My engagement book is at your disposal.'

'Before Esme's ball, I think, as I intend that to be the culmination of her season. You never know, we might have an announcement to make.' It was said archly and Esme squirmed with embarrassment.

'Rosie!' she protested.

'Oh, do not mind me,' Rosemary said. 'I am such a romantic at heart.' Which had Esme fidgeting even more.

Rosie, romantic! It was almost comical. 'I hope you will still be in town and able to attend, my lord.'

'Nothing would keep me away,' he said. Esme, who had been studying the arrangement of flowers in the empty grate, looked up suddenly and saw his smile. It made her shiver with apprehension. He took his leave soon after that.

He was back the next afternoon, impeccably attired and oozing charm, with some proposals for the picnic, which was soon assuming the proportions of a route march. 'I thought we could make up a party,' he said, addressing himself to Rosemary, although Esme was present, sitting demurely in the window seat of the drawing room looking out on the dripping trees in the garden across the street. The overnight rain had gone and the sun was shining, making the droplets of water sparkle on the leaves. The street had been washed clean of the collected ordure of horse droppings, mud and discarded refuse, which now lay in the gutter in heaps waiting for the dustcart to remove them. 'I thought of approaching the Ladies Aviemore, Bryson and Mountjoy to bring their daughters, and there is Toby Salford, Bertie Wincombe, Captain Merton and my cousin Victor Ashbury. That is if you agree, my lady.'

'Yes, of course. If they are free, that is. If you wish, I will make inquiries.'

'Thank you, my lady.'

'What about your other cousin, Lord Pendlebury, my lord?' Esme queried, turning from the window.

'What about him?'

'You said you were good friends. Surely you meant to ask him?'

'Certainly I will if you wish it,' he said, with only the

tiniest hesitation. 'But from the manner in which you sent him away the other day, I did not think he would be acceptable.'

'Why not?'

He sighed. 'I concluded Lady Trent had told you—'

'I did,' Rosemary said. 'Perhaps you would be good enough to repeat it. She might then believe it.'

'I hesitate to speak ill of a member of my family and one with whom I have always been on the friendliest of terms.'

'It is for Lady Esme's own good.'

Esme sat with her hands in her lap and said nothing. She was anxious to hear what Felix had done that was so dreadful and to make up her own mind about him.

'Then I will speak, but please make allowances for a young man's folly. He was, as I have said before, born in India and as a boy spent a great deal of time with Indian servants. His father saw no harm in it, but he was learning their ways, sympathising with them, even dressing like them. His mother became afraid he would turn native and persuaded his father to bring the family home to England. For a time he lived as any normal boy would, going to school and university and taking a Grand Tour.

'It was while he was in France that he became involved with the Revolutionary Party. In order to do their work, he inveigled himself into the social circle around Count Lefavre, who was loyal to the King and privy to the measures being taken to counter an uprising. He became engaged to the Count's daughter, Juliette. When the revolution began, he fled back to England, abandoning the lady. The revolutionaries killed her father...'

'She does not seem to have held it against him,' Esme put in. 'She is here in London and seen out and about with him.'

He smiled. 'She has a forgiving heart. And when the heart is involved…' He shrugged. 'No doubt he had a plausible excuse that she believed.'

'How do you know all this?'

'I was in France at the time and met him there. I did my best to persuade him out of his folly, but to no avail.'

'And now he is mixed up with the troublemakers again.' Rosemary put in. 'Here in England. Our way of life is threatened. The safety of the Royal family is threatened, and all because of that monstrous Exhibition.'

'I find it hard to believe,' Esme said.

'That is what makes it so dreadful,' Rosemary said. 'He looks the essence of what an English gentleman should be. But appearances can be deceptive.'

'No one else seems to believe ill of him,' Esme said. 'He is accepted in the highest social circles. Why has no one denounced him? Why have you said nothing except to us, Lord Gorridge?'

'I have been asked by someone very high up to keep silent. The authorities are watching him, hoping he will lead them to the ringleaders. I beg you to say nothing yourselves, either to him or anyone else because I have betrayed a confidence in telling you.'

'There!' Rosemary exclaimed. 'Now are you convinced?'

Esme was shaken to the core. It all sounded so plausible. Why did she find it so hard to credit? Because her heart was involved? Because he had kissed her and sent her whole body into such a tumult she had mistaken it for love? Was it possible to love a traitor? Juliette Lefavre evidently thought it was. She was so muddled, she could not find the voice to respond to her sister.

'Let us talk of happier things,' Edward said, his sombre

countenance suddenly brightening. Having delivered what he guessed was a bombshell, he was prepared to dismiss it. 'The picnic. Will Saturday week be convenient? We shall need several carriages for the ladies and the picnic hampers, but the gentlemen will no doubt ride…'

Esme sat and half listened as Lord Gorridge and her sister set about ordering her life for her. The picnic was only the beginning, there would be other outings involving his lordship, culminating in the ball, all carefully orchestrated to marry her off, preferably to Lord Gorridge himself. If she had known what would happen, she would never have come to London. But then she would never have met Felix, never felt his arms about her, never looked into his eyes, never tasted his lips, never felt desire trickling through her. Was the memory of that all she would be taking back to Luffenham with her? Could she possibly consider marrying anyone else when her heart and soul were elsewhere? Ought she to dismiss Felix Pendlebury from her mind once and for all? Myles had advised her to be guided by her sister? Did he know the truth? Did anyone, except Felix himself?

She was hardly aware that Lord Gorridge was taking his leave, bowing low over Rosemary's hand and then hers. Somehow she conjured up a smile and a few polite words and then he was gone. Before Rosemary could start to comment on the visit and the information he had disclosed, she excused herself and fled to her room.

Chapter Seven

Felix was not at all sure whether he was keeping an eye on Edward to please his aunt or because he was afraid Esme would accept him. The thought of the woman he loved being married to that man made his blood boil. And yet he was obliged to keep his feelings in check and maintain an urbane countenance.

It was not made easier by Juliette's assumption that he had accepted what she had told him about her affair with Peaucille and that he had forgiven her for it. As if he did not know that Peaucille was not the only one! Here, in London, there were others and it was these others he had been set to watch. Some were French, but there were Englishmen among them who were deliberately setting out to stir up discontent among the workers from the factories whose chimneys belched smoke, those whose living was made on or about the river and sweatshop employees, as well as those without work, who spent their evenings drinking and making plans to turn on their employers and anyone in authority. How much of it was simply the drink talking and how much they really meant to put into action, he could not be sure. He sympathised with their plight, but not their way of going about redressing their wrongs.

He tried remonstrating with Juliette, asking her why she mixed with these men, but she laughed, trying to tease him out of his sombre mood. 'Oh, Felix, *chéri,* you are jealous!'

'No.' They were talking in his Aunt Sophie's drawing room, though the lady herself was absent, as was Victor. 'I am concerned for your safety and reputation. Good God, Juliette, you are the daughter of a nobleman…'

'The nobility 'ave 'ad their day.'

'You forget that I am one.'

'No, I do not forget, but an aristo embracing the workers' cause would lend it credence, don't you think? You should follow the example of your cousin.'

'Victor was always a hothead.'

'Not only Victor. Edward.'

He had laughed. 'If you think Edward will give up his title, wealth and privileges to embrace a lost cause, then you are more naïve than I thought. He is enjoying being Viscount Gorridge too much to risk losing it. Why do you think he is toadying to every title and socialite in the capital?'

She laughed. 'Including Lady Esme Vernley. *Oui,* I 'ad noticed. But let us not talk of them, Felix. Let us talk about you. And me. If you want me to give up my friends, then I will do so, but I will need something from you. I will need protection.' She paused to make sure she had his full attention. 'A wedding band might do it. You do understand me, I 'ope.'

He understood perfectly well; she was not so committed to the cause of revolution as she pretended and he wondered what her associates might say or do when they realised that.

Was that what she meant by protection? One thing he was sure of—nothing on earth would persuade him to comply. 'I would not dream of putting you at risk, my dear,' he said, with a twisted smile. 'Let us think of some other way.'

She hid her anger well. 'You won't win her, you know.'

'Who?'

'Lady Esme. I think she would like being a viscountess, don't you? A viscount is better than a baron, *n'est-ce pas? Moi,* I am 'appy to be a baroness.'

'Then I wish you luck in finding your baron.' With that he turned on his heel and left the house, passing his aunt on the way.

'Going, Felix?' she queried.

'I am afraid I do not have time to stop, Aunt. Another time, perhaps.'

He left her staring after him and hurried down the street. He wasn't sure where he was going. The one place he longed to be was barred to him and so he walked the streets until hunger and thirst drove him into one of the seedier clubs on Monmouth Street. He had given up his hat and was striding across the foyer when he spotted Edward through the open door of one of the gaming rooms, sitting at a table with Victor and two men he did not know. One was dressed impeccably in a dove-grey suit and a lilac cravat. He had dark side whiskers and hair that Felix felt sure had been dyed to cover its grey streaks. He was the older of the two by several years. The other, red-faced and corpulent, favoured the checks of a countryman. There was a pack of cards spread across the table and a heap of coins in the middle which the dark man was scooping up, watched warily by Edward as if he would like to snatch it from him.

'Ah, Felix, the very man I want to see,' Edward called out to him.

He did not feel like talking to anyone, let alone his cousin, but politeness and curiosity won and he crossed the room to join them.

'Do you know Monsieur Philippe Maillet?' Edward indicated the man taking possession of the money. 'And Mr Patrick Connelly?'

Maillet! That was the name the Duke of Wellington had mentioned. He was careful to keep his voice neutral as he answered, 'No, I do not think I have had the pleasure.'

'Philippe, Patrick, my cousin Felix, Lord Pendlebury. Tell them, Felix, that I am good for a few thousand.'

Felix guessed his cousin had lost heavily. 'Why ask me to vouch for you? Is your word not as good as your bond?'

'Oh, it is, but unfortunately my friend Patrick needs to be paid immediately and I cannot lay my hands on that amount. The lawyers are taking their time winding up my father's estate and I'm short of the ready. You'll stand buff for me, won't you? You can have it back as soon as the lawyers are done.'

Felix was reminded of what he had overheard on the day of the late Viscount Gorridge's funeral. If Edward wanted money, he would have to go through his trustees. Or marry. Esme! His dearest Esme. He would impoverish himself before he let that happen. 'How much do you need?'

'Five thousand.'

'Five thousand!'

'Yes. Four for Patrick, five hundred for Philippe, less the fifteen guineas he scooped up from the table, the rest to keep me going for a week or two. I have an important social occasion to arrange.'

Felix turned to Connelly. 'If you meet me here tomorrow at two o'clock, I'll have a draft drawn on my bank.'

'Thank you,' the man said, rising. 'Good day to you, Gorridge. Mr Ashbury.'

He left, followed by the Frenchman, who walked with a slight limp. As soon as they were out of earshot, Felix turned to his cousin. 'Who are those men, Edward?'

Edward shrugged. 'Just a couple of gamesters I met through Ma'amselle Lefavre. I do not know them well.'

'Well enough to gamble with them.'

'Why not? Connelly has connections with a good Anglo-Irish family and Maillet is related to a French aristo. He told me he had an English mother, which is why he speaks such perfect English. I am eternally grateful to you for standing buff for me.'

'There are conditions to that.'

'Conditions. You said nothing of conditions when you agreed to stump up.'

'I did not want to embarrass you in front of strangers. I will pay your debts as long as you leave Lady Esme Vernley alone.'

Edward laughed. It was a high-pitched cackle, which made Felix want to smash his fist into the man's face. 'I do not see the joke,' he said coldly.

'No? I will not be allowed to leave Lady Esme alone, her sister will see to that. Lady Trent is determined to make her sister a Viscountess and the lady herself is more than willing, I can tell you. I believe the announcement will be made at Lady Esme's coming-out ball. If you want your money back, you will have to accept that.'

'I haven't given it to you yet.'

'Oh, you will, my dear cousin, you will. I know your reputation for keeping your word is something you value above everything. If my friends are thwarted, the word would soon spread—' He stopped in mid-sentence and shrugged his shoulders.

Felix turned on his heel and strode out. For the second time that day he walked the streets until, no nearer a solution, he returned home and went up to his studio, where he sat drinking cognac and staring at the sketches he had done of Esme. Was she really about to accept Edward Gorridge? Had he lost her? He ran his finger over the drawing he had made for his Crystal Girl, the outline of her head, the expressive eyes, the soft lips. He had once felt the real thing, the smooth flesh, the soft lips responding to the pressure of his own and discovered himself in love, and he was not prepared to give in without a fight. He smiled suddenly, emptied his glass down his throat and went to bed.

Esme saw Felix again sooner than she expected when she was out walking with Rosemary two days later and, strangely, it was in almost the identical spot she had seen him before, close by Annie Hicks's cake stall. Even more strangely, he was talking to an elderly gentleman she recognised immediately, from pictures she had seen of him, as the Duke of Wellington.

'Fancy him being friendly with the Duke,' Rosemary murmured.

'Why shouldn't he be? They are both on the Exhibition committee.'

'I wonder if the Duke knows.'

'Knows what?'

'About Lord Pendlebury's dubious activities.'

'Rosemary, I do hope you are not intending to make trouble. I am sure his Grace would not be speaking to him if there was anything at all dubious about him.'

'You heard what Viscount Gorridge said.'

'He might have a personal reason for that.'

Rosemary looked sharply at her. 'What reason?'

'I don't know. When they were together the other day, they were baiting each other and exchanging veiled insults. Lord Gorridge pretends they are friends, but that was not my understanding.'

'Oh, what can you know of men? You are only just out of the schoolroom, easily gulled. Besides, it is not only Lord Gorridge who says it. Rowan warned us ages ago. Why do you think he was so angry when you went off on your own to meet the man?'

Esme assumed she was talking about that disastrous visit to the theatre because, as far as she knew, her brother-in-law knew nothing of the balloon flight. 'You make it sound like an assignation and it was nothing of the sort.'

'Assignation or not, Lord Gorridge is bound to have heard about it from Mr Ashbury. You should be sincerely thankful that he does not appear to hold it against you.'

They were almost level with object of their discourse and already Esme was feeling the telltale *frisson* of excitement, but now she was wondering if it might be fear and not desire after all: fear of the unknown, fear of being drawn into a whirlpool of intrigue. 'Are you going to cut him?' she queried in an undertone.

'No, not while he is with the Duke.' She approached the Duke, smiling. 'My lord Duke, good morning.'

'Lady Trent, your obedient.' His Grace had always appreciated good-looking ladies, and he swept off his hat and bowed to her. 'Are you acquainted with Lord Pendlebury?' He indicated his companion, as if he intended to present him.

'Yes, indeed,' she said quickly, and favoured Felix with a very tiny inclination of her head before returning her attention to the Duke. 'May I present my sister, Lady Esme Vernley.'

Esme bent her knee. 'My lord Duke.'

He looked her up and down appreciatively. 'Enjoying a Season, are you?'

'Yes, your Grace.'

'Affianced yet?'

'No, your Grace.' She risked a glance at Felix and found him studying her face. He seemed to spend most of his time doing that whenever they met. Did it mean her thoughts and feelings and doubts were emblazoned there? Oh, she hoped not. She looked away quickly.

'We are holding a ball for my sister's coming-out on the sixteenth of July,' Rosemary put in. 'We would be honoured if you would attend.'

He chuckled. 'I might at that. Don't dance myself these days, but like to watch young people enjoying themselves, eh, Pendlebury?'

Felix smiled. The Duke undoubtedly thought he would be one of the guests, but unless something happened to change Lady Trent's opinion of him, he doubted if he would be invited. Esme would not look at him and he wondered why. It was not shyness—that young lady did not know the meaning of the word—more like evasiveness, a reluctance to meet his eye. Had her sister persuaded her against him? Or Edward. What had Edward been saying? Was she so easily swayed?

'It is much pleasanter walking out since the rain, don't you think?' the Duke went on, addressing Esme.

'Yes, your Grace.'

'Ride, do you?'

'Yes, your Grace. We come to the Park frequently, but we have been wondering whether that will be curtailed when the building begins.'

'They won't touch Rotten Row, m'dear, but as soon as they have decided on the form the building will take, there will be heavy wagons coming and going with construction materials. When that happens, they will put a fence all round the site and that might cause a little disturbance.'

'You could ride in Green Park,' Felix said. 'Mornings are best.'

'Yes, perhaps we will do that,' Esme said. Was that code for an assignation? She wanted to believe it was, but could not be sure. She was not sure of anything these days. Not sure of what to believe, not sure of her own feelings, not sure if she dared meet him. If what Lord Gorridge said was true, she should have nothing to do with him. But was it true?

It was Rosemary's turn to interrupt. 'Come, Esme,' she said. 'We must not keep the Duke and Lord Pendlebury.'

The two ladies took their leave and went on their way. Rosemary chatted about the encounter, saying that if the famous Duke came to her ball, it was bound to be a runaway success.

'Are you sure Rowan will be happy about it?' Esme asked. 'The Duke has always been a strong advocate of the Exhibition.'

'No, he is simply a loyal subject of the Queen and if her Majesty sees fit to indulge her Consort's whims, he goes along with it.'

'That's Rowan's opinion, is it?'

'I have no doubt he got it from someone close to the Duke.'

'Lord Pendlebury and the Duke seem to deal well together.'

'I believe the Duke was a friend of Pendlebury's father when they were both serving in India.'

'I wonder what his Grace makes of the rumours about Lord Pendlebury.'

'How should I know? He might not have heard them. After all, the story is not common knowledge and Lord Gorridge has sworn us to secrecy.'

'How could he not know? If Rowan does, then I'll wager the Duke does, and if that is so, he chooses not to pay it any heed…'

'Esme, he is a very old man. It would be easy to pull the wool over his eyes.'

Esme did not believe that. She was becoming more and more convinced there was more to it than appeared on the surface. The Duke would not consort with a traitor. She had to find out the truth. Felix had suggested riding in Green Park and he had been speaking to her when he said it. The message was there if she chose to read it. He would meet her in Green Park. Dare she go? The problem was how to manage it.

And then fate played a hand.

She came downstairs dressed for riding two mornings later to find Rosemary looking decidedly pale and in no condition to go out, much less mount a horse. Esme was instantly concerned and set aside her own wishes to drop to her knees beside the chaise longue on which her sister was reclining. 'Rosie, what has happened? Are you ill?'

'No, not ill, but I am afraid riding is out of the question. If you want to go, then I am sure a message to Lord Gorridge will bring him here at once to escort you and bring you safe home.'

A fleeting suspicion crossed Esme's mind that perhaps Rosie's illness was a ruse to send her off with the Viscount, and he was the last person she wanted with her if she contrived to come across Felix. 'I would not dream of going if you are not well. I can wait until you feel more the thing.'

Rosemary made an effort to laugh. 'Then you will have several months to wait.'

'Several months!' Then suddenly she understood. 'Oh, Rosie, you are going to have another child. Are you pleased?'

'Of course I am. I had a suspicion, and when I kept being sick in the morning, Rowan insisted on sending for Dr Peters...'

'Oh, so that was the gentleman who called yesterday afternoon.'

'Yes. He confirmed it. No more riding, I am afraid.'

'We could go for a walk instead.' It was not at all what she wanted; she was anxious to ride in Green Park. She had been hoping to go the day before, trusting to providence to find a way of speaking to him without Rosemary interrupting, but her sister had said she was expecting a visitor and the ride had been postponed, so she never knew if Felix had gone or not, nor if he would go again. The longer she left it, the less likelihood there was that he would keep going. He would probably assume she had not understood his hint or, having understood it, meant to ignore it.

'No, I do not feel up to anything this morning. But you are dressed for riding. You may go. Ask Croxon to instruct one of the grooms to follow for appearances' sake.'

'Are you sure?'

'Yes, but, Esme, do not do anything foolish, will you?'

'Foolish, Rosie?' Surely her sister had not understood the message? No, she decided, or she would not be suggesting she should go.

'Yes. Galloping, or riding at fences. The park is not a hunting field.'

'I know that, Rosie. I'll have a sedate walk and perhaps a little canter if there are not too many people about.'

'Off you go, then.'

She was dancing with impatience while Croxon saddled the mare that had been hired for her and arranged for his young son to escort her. 'I can't spare anyone else,' he said. 'His lordship hev ordered the carriage for this afternoon and it hev to be cleaned and polished and one of the horses hev to be took to be shod. Albert will see you come to no harm.'

'I am sure he will.'

The saddle was on, the young Albert saddled a cob for himself and she was on her way at last. She rode sedately, but inside she was in a fever of impatience. He would be there, wouldn't he? He would not give up after just one day, would he? Along Kensington Road and Knightsbridge to Hyde Park Corner she went, carefully picking her way through the traffic. Vehicles of all kinds, carriages and carts, with one horse, with two horses, with four, mixed with riders and pedestrians, hawkers, beggars and soldiers coming to and from the barracks. She passed Apsley House, wondering if the Duke of Wellington were inside; that led to wondering what he and Felix had said to each other. She did not go up Piccadilly, but turned into Green Park with Albert doggedly behind her.

There were several riders about, ladies with gentlemen escorts, gentlemen in twos and threes, walkers, children running about on the grass, dogs sniffing for rabbits and cows munching the grass. She rode on, keeping to the paths. There was no sign of Felix. Her spirits sank; she had missed him. She reined in and walked her horse forward, looking about her. No Lord Pendlebury. No Felix. The path ahead of her was busy, but not so crowded that she could not scan every rider—he was not there.

Her mare was becoming impatient with their slow pace and snorted and pranced, anxious to be off. She leaned forward and patted her neck. 'He is not here,' she whispered, sick with disappointment. Turning off the path, she put her mount into a canter across the grass. The move took her escort by surprise and he was slow to follow. Reaching a group of trees, she slipped from the saddle, threw her reins over a bush and walked on. What made her do it, she did not know. It was cool among the trees and she went deeper into their shade, taking off her hat and shaking out her hair. Almost crying with frustration and longing, she flung herself down by a tree and leaned back against its trunk, squeezing her eyes tight shut to stop the tears falling.

She had not been there long when she heard a footfall and assumed it was Albert. But if it was, he had no right to sit beside her. Her eyes flew open. 'Oh. It's you.'

'Whom did you expect?'

Felix was smiling at her, as if the sight of her trying to master her tears amused him. It stiffened her spine at the same time as it set her stomach churning. It was impossible to be indifferent to him. And now she realised she had not rehearsed in her mind what she was going to say to him, the questions she meant to ask. 'Albert.'

'You mean that slow-witted youth who has been following you like a faithful hound?'

'That's what he's paid to do.'

'And now I have paid him not to do it. He is minding all three horses and that will keep him occupied for a little while.'

'You had no right.'

'How else was I to have a private conversation with you?'

'Why do you want a private conversation with me?'

'Oh, Esme, you sweet innocent, why do you think?'

'If you are going to kiss me again—' She stopped, feeling her face growing hot. It was presumptuous of her to suppose that he had given that kiss a second's thought since it happened.

He laughed. 'There is that, of course, but first we must talk.'

'What about?'

'Everything. All that stands between us—'

'Like Ma'amselle Lefavre,' she interrupted before he could explain.

'Among other things.'

'You still love her…'

'No, I do not. I don't think I ever did.'

'Then why are you seen out and about with her? I have been told you are engaged to marry her.'

'Who told you that?'

'My sister. And Viscount Gorridge confirmed it.'

'I see.' It was not only her sister spreading the poison, it was his cousin. It was all part of the man's plan to discredit him and have Esme for himself. He told himself, untruthfully, that he could have borne it if there had been a genuine attachment there, but Edward was only concerned with laying his hands on his legacy. 'Then they were both misinformed.'

'You are not betrothed to her?'

'Certainly not.'

'Why don't you deny it then? Why let everyone think you are?'

'There is a very good reason for it, which I cannot tell you.'

'I am sure I do not want to know,' she said tartly. His words seemed to confirm what Lord Gorridge had told her and yet she still did not want to believe it. 'It is none of my business, except…'

'Except what?'

She took a deep breath. 'Except that I thought we were friends…'

'And friends trust each other?' he finished for her.

'Yes.'

'We are friends. One day I hope more than friends, so can you not trust me?'

Her heart was pounding. He was talking in riddles and she could not decipher what lay behind them. More than friends, he had said. That implied… Oh, she wished he would say straight out what he meant. 'Why all the secrecy? Trust works both ways, you know. If you cannot tell me why I have to trust you, then you do not trust me.'

'I would trust you with my life, but it is not my life I am thinking of.'

'Riddles! Riddles! Riddles!' she exclaimed in exasperation. 'You said we had to talk, but we haven't been talking, or if we have it makes no sense to me. Are you going to be more open or am I going to return to my horse and ride home?' She started to rise, but he seized her arm and pulled her back.

'Esme, stay. Please don't leave in anger.' He smiled suddenly. 'Perhaps I was wrong to say we should talk first. Perhaps actions speak louder than words.' He turned and cupped her face in his hands and gently put his lips to hers.

They were all there, the sensations she had felt before: the shivering, the urgent need to cling to him, to push herself as close to him as she could, to let him surround her, as if her body were melting into his, his into hers. She had no will of her own, it was sublimated to his. He took his hands from her face and put one at the back of her neck and drew her body closer with the other, as his kiss deepened. Everything about them faded, trees, grass, horses snuffling, a dog barking, a bird singing somewhere above them. She was only half aware of them through a haze of joyous passion.

It was when she moaned that he suddenly realised what he was doing and that what had been intended as a tender kiss had become much more than that and it was only a matter of seconds before he lost all control. He released her, breathing hard. 'I'm sorry.'

'Sorry?' She did not understand him. 'Is that all you can say?'

'What do you want me to say? Do you want me to humble myself and tell you I did not mean it, that I was tempted, carried away by your beauty, by your compliance, that I will never do such a thing again?'

'Is that the truth of it?' She sat up, trying to straighten her riding jacket, which had somehow come undone at her throat.

'Of course it is, except….'

'You were taking advantage of my trusting nature.'

'Ah, we are back to that.'

'Yes.'

'Esme, there is nothing I can tell you. I am not at liberty—'

'Then what has this meeting been about, if not to indulge your passions? Talk, you said.'

'I meant talk about us.' He paused and took her hand and noticed it was trembling. He had frightened the wits out of her, but she was proud and defiant. Esme Vernley had courage. 'Esme, I admit I was indulging myself in a way, but I was also trying to convince you of how much I love you.'

'You do?'

'Don't sound so surprised. You must have guessed.'

'Should I have done?'

'Perhaps not. But I am telling you now. You are my life, the only woman I have ever loved, the only one I will ever love. Without you, life would be bleak indeed. The sun would vanish, the grass would die, the flowers wither.' He rubbed his thumb gently over the back of her hand. 'I hoped, still hope and pray, that you feel something for me and that soon I shall be able to tell the world that we are to marry. Say yes, please.'

Now she was in a quandary of momentous proportions. She wanted to fling herself at him and say, 'Yes, yes, yes.' But how could she with so many questions unanswered?

'My lord…'

'Felix, please. We are alone.'

'We should not be alone. We should not be sitting here like this. It is highly improper.' Why was she prevaricating, talking about impropriety instead of answering the most important question she would ever be asked? Young she was, but she was not a simpering schoolgirl and she had already shown him she did not care about convention. She could see his impatience in his eyes.

'Be damned to that. You came here of your own free will, knowing I would come looking for you…'

'I did not.'

'Oh, come, Esme, be honest.'

'I came because—' She stopped suddenly, remembering she had promised she would tell no one, especially not Felix, about the story Lord Gorridge had told her and Rosemary. She had been hoping somehow to learn the truth without divulging what she knew.

'Because?' he prompted.

'Because you said it was a good place to ride.' It was a whisper.

'Ah, you understood after all. I wondered if you had when you did not appear yesterday.'

'You were here yesterday?'

'Of course. And would be here tomorrow and every day thereafter while I thought there was a chance you would come.'

'I nearly did not. It is not easy for an unmarried lady to ride alone.'

'I know and just now you have a very attentive escort.'

'Albert?'

He laughed. 'No, not Albert. I was referring to Viscount Gorridge.'

'Oh. He is not with me today.'

'Thank goodness for that! How did you manage to throw him off?'

It was good to hear her laugh; her voice had been watery, full of unshed tears until now. 'I didn't have to, though I think he was expecting to meet Rosemary and me in Hyde Park, we go most days, but today Rosemary was not well and left me to go alone.'

'And how will you explain your non-appearance?'

'I went and we missed each other. The park is very crowded.'

'Are you going to marry him?'

'A minute ago you were asking me to marry you. I cannot wed you both.' She was still shaking from that kiss.

'No, you can't, but I beg you, humbly beg you, not to let the prospect of being a viscountess influence your decision.'

'If you think I would do that, you must have a very poor opinion of me, my lord,' she snapped.

'I beg your pardon. I am only concerned that undue pressure is being put on you.'

'I am quite able to make up own mind, my lord. I must love the man I marry, his rank is not important. Just as my rank should mean nothing to him. I want to love him for the good man he is and him to love me for myself.'

'Which I do.'

'And he must have no secrets from me.'

'Back to that,' he said, with a heavy sigh. 'What makes you think I have secrets from you?'

'Don't you?'

'There are certain things going on that I am not at liberty to divulge at the moment, but—'

He was not allowed to finish. As far as she was concerned he had confirmed her worst fears. 'I hate you!' she said furiously, jumping to her feet. 'Go back to your paramour. I never want to speak to you again.' She grabbed her hat and ran back to her horse.

She was being helped into the saddle by Albert when he caught up with her. 'Esme! Damn you, woman, why won't you ever let me finish a sentence?'

'I do not care for your language, Lord Pendlebury.' Clicking her tongue at the mare, she kicked in her heel and the animal shot off across the grass as if she had been stung. Esme's hat flew off and landed at his feet. Slowly he bent to pick it up, wondering if she might return for it, but when she did not, he flung himself into his own saddle.

'Get after her!' he shouted to Albert. 'It's what you are paid for, isn't it? And don't let her go off alone again or I'll have your guts.' This last order was yelled at the terrified boy's departing back.

Felix went home, cradling the hat, a high-crowned affair with a sweeping green feather and a wisp of a veil. It smelled faintly of her perfume. He carried it up to his room where he put it on an old wig stand on his dressing table and then sat on his bed and gazed at it, as despondent as he had ever been in his whole life.

His talk with the Duke of Wellington had not given him the freedom he wanted. 'Need you, boy, need you,' his Grace had said when he endeavoured to explain his predicament. They had gone to Hyde Park to talk to Ann Hicks who had been running the cake and fruit stall by the Serpentine for years and lived in a nearby shack. She would have to move before building commenced, but was proving obstinate. Some members of the Commission wanted her ejected by force, but the Duke who, as Ranger of the Parks, had the ultimate responsibility, had been against that and had gone to talk to her himself. After a great deal of argument in which she accused the Exhibition people of depriving her of her living, she agreed to go quietly for just over ninety-two pounds, but not before the building started. The season was in full swing and she was doing a good trade. It was after she had gone back inside, muttering to herself but secretly pleased with her deal, that Felix had updated the Duke on what he had discovered so far and asked to be relieved of his onerous duty.

'I can't spare you,' the Duke had explained. 'I have had hundreds of letters from ordinary citizens about the security of the realm, asking me what I intend to do about the threat. Some say the Royal Navy should be stationed in the Irish Sea…'

'Why there?'

'Goodness knows. Perhaps they think trouble will come from that quarter. They talk of blockading the ports. Others suggest the whole of London should be cordoned off and troops drafted in to assist the police in examining everyone coming and going. Can you imagine it?'

Felix had smiled wearily at the image that created. 'Pandemonium.'

'Yes. Couldn't be done. London is not a village street—it is the greatest metropolis in the world. If troublemakers want to come in, they will find some way of doing it, and so I told the Prime Minister. He suggested enlisting the help of French and German police on the grounds that they will recognise malcontents from their own countries.' His scornful tone betrayed what he thought of that idea. 'I can provide for the safety of the populace without the help of Frenchies.' He had fought Napoleon for years and found it difficult not to think of the French as the enemy.

'So what is your answer?'

'Infiltration. I must use agents like yourself to forewarn me of trouble.'

'I haven't been able to uncover anything as yet. I have found Maillet, though so far have learned nothing against him.'

'Try harder.' The instruction was blunt and brooked no argument.

It was then that Rosemary and Esme had walked up and Esme had charmed the Duke, but not enough to let him off the hook. His idea of meeting her and asking her to trust him and telling her that all would be well in the end had failed miserably, and all he had to show for it was one battered hat with a crushed feather.

Esme had missed her hat before she reached the park gates, but nothing on earth could have persuaded her to return for it. She felt angry and humiliated and as miserable as anyone could be. She ought to be overflowing with happiness; he had, after all, kissed her, melted her insides, made her forget that the reason she wanted to talk to him was to find out if there were any truth in the rumours about him. Deep down inside her where her conscience resided she admitted she had wanted him to kiss her again. It was only to find out if what she felt was truly love, she told herself, as she slowed her horse to a walk and allowed Albert to catch up with her. It might have been fear or simply the *frisson* of excitement that came with doing something forbidden. It might possibly have been the same whoever kissed her; she had no way of knowing.

She could, she supposed, allow Edward Gorridge to kiss her and that might tell her. The trouble was, the mere thought of doing that was repugnant. There was Victor Ashbury, of course, and Captain Merton and any of the other young men she had met; the answer was the same. If they tried it, she would scream for help. She hadn't screamed when Felix kissed her. She had not even struggled. And when he had told her he loved her, using such romantic terms she had wanted to cry, she had been convinced he meant it and was ready to discount the evil that other people spread about him. A man that could say those words with such tenderness could not possibly be a villain. Why, then, was she so wretched?

Was it because he had refused to trust her? Because he admitted to having secrets? Everyone had secrets. Was it because he had declined to sever his connections with Ma'amselle Lefavre? Because he refused to deny he was betrothed to the woman? A man who could play fast and loose with two ladies at the same time was most definitely not to be trusted.

'Lady Esme.'

Startled at being addressed when she was so deep in thought, she looked up, half afraid it was Felix and they would go on where they left off, quarrelling with each other, she was almost relieved to see Lord Gorridge, who had just entered the park. He was riding a jet-black stallion. They both reined in a little to one side of the path to allow others to pass. 'Good morning, my lord,' she said, pulling herself together to speak pleasantly. 'Is that a new mount?'

'Yes, just purchased. What do you think of him?'

'He is magnificent. Have you named him?'

'Linwood Gorryham, Gorry for short. I thought I would try him out and, as Hyde Park is crowded with people going at the pace of a snail, I decided to come here. I had no idea you would be here. You are on your way out, I see.'

'Yes, but I am in no hurry. I will stay and watch you put him through his paces and then you may escort me home, if you wish.'

'Nothing would give me greater pleasure, my lady.'

She turned her horse, half expecting to see Felix riding up behind her, but there was no sign of him. He had obviously chosen a different exit. Her bravado, the need to show him she did not care by happily riding off with Lord Gorridge, suddenly evaporated, but it was too late to change her mind.

With Albert trailing, they rode side by side until they came to an open space where Edward left her in order to gallop as far and as hard as he could. She watched in admiration. He was a splendid rider and the horse was outstanding. She wondered idly how much it had cost him and then realised he was so rich the cost of anything he wanted was immaterial.

'Bravo!' she said, as he returned. 'You have a winner there. Do you intend to race him?'

'I might. We shall see.' They turned and began walking their horses side by side towards the exit. 'I intend to ride him to Richmond when we have our picnic. Will you go in one of the carriages or will you ride with me?'

'I hadn't thought about it.' That was true; her head had been too full of Felix to pay attention to the arrangements for the picnic.

'Then say you will. It will give me so much pleasure to have you at my side.'

'I am not sure the mare is up to it. She is only used to hacking in the parks.'

'Then I will buy you a decent mount.'

'Oh, no, I could not allow you to do that.'

'Why not?'

'It would be too costly a gift.'

'Not at all. What is money for, if not to spend, especially on someone for whom I have a great fondness?'

'My lord!'

'You are shocked that I have spoken so freely, I can see. I apologise if I am a little precipitate, but I say what is in my mind. I live in hope that you also have certain feelings for me and that between us there will come to be an understanding. I say no more for now, but ask you most humbly to think about that.'

Why did she want to laugh? It was not a laughing matter. Two proposals in as many hours must surely be out of the ordinary. And so differently couched. 'My lord, I don't know what to say,' she said solemnly.

'Simply say you will think seriously about what I have said.'

'I think I can promise to do that.'

They had arrived at Trent House, where she dismounted

and handed the mare over to Albert. 'You did well, Albert,' she said. 'You may tell your father that.' Blushing furiously, he set off for the mews at a trot, leading the horse. 'Will you come in for refreshment?' she asked Edward.

'Not today, if you will excuse me, Lady Esme. This animal needs rubbing down and—' he paused and smiled '—I have a horse to buy.' He pretended not to hear her protest as he rode away.

She went indoors, to be greeted by Rosemary coming into the hall from the drawing room. 'Was that Lord Gorridge I saw you with?'

'Yes, we met in the park.'

'Why did you not ask him in?'

'I did, but he declined. He said he had an errand that could not wait.'

'What a pity. I wanted to ask him something about the picnic.'

'No doubt he will be back.'

'You are looking very flushed. Has something happened?'

'What do you mean?'

'The Viscount, has he said something of his intentions?'

'Yes. He wants to buy me a horse.'

'A horse!' This was evidently not what she expected to hear. 'Why a horse?'

'So that I can ride beside him to the picnic and not go in the carriage.'

'Oh, Esme!'

'Yes, I know you are appalled. It is not done for young ladies to accept costly presents from gentlemen and so I told him.'

'It is permissible if the gentleman's intentions are serious. The world will know that you are his chosen one.'

'Ah, but I haven't chosen him.'

'No, of course not, you must wait to be asked.'

It was all too much and Esme fled upstairs to her room on the pretext of changing out of her riding habit. She dashed into her room and fell on the bed, laughing. Edward Gorridge was so pompous, he sounded like Mr Collins in Jane Austen's *Pride and Prejudice,* doing the lady a favour by asking her to marry him. Fondness, indeed!

Felix had not said fondness, Felix had said love. Felix had made her feel loved. It was only afterwards, when they quarreled, that she had doubted it. He would not ask her again. He would go back to his first love. And she was bereft. It was then, in the privacy of her room where no one could see or hear her, the laughter turned to tears.

Chapter Eight

The day of the picnic dawned warm and sunny. Rosemary who had been unsure of whether she should go, declared herself fit and well able to withstand the carriage ride. She bustled about urging Esme to make haste, that the carriage had been ordered for ten o'clock and Lord Gorridge was sure to be on the doorstep at the appointed time ready to escort them.

Esme had not seen him since the ride in the park and had no idea if he really had meant to buy her a horse. Perhaps it was all show, just to see how she would react, and she hoped he had taken her at her word that she could not accept such a gift. She was disabused of that idea when Croxon came to the back door and asked to speak to Lady Trent.

'What can he want?' she demanded. 'He was given his instructions yesterday. He can't have forgotten them.' She left the room, but was back in less than five minutes. 'He wanted to know if it was my wish that he put your saddle on the new mare,' she told Esme. 'It seems Lord Gorridge has been true to his word.'

'What did you tell him?'

'I told him yes, you were expecting to ride and to have it saddled and brought round with the carriage.'

'Oh, dear, I did not think his lordship would do it.'

'Well, he has, so hurry up and change. Put on your new habit. That one of Lucy's has seen better days.'

She went reluctantly. Miss Bannister, ready herself in stiff grey taffeta and a poke bonnet, was picking up Esme's shawl. 'It might be cooler by the time we return,' she said.

'I have to change, Banny. It seems I am to ride, after all.'

'Oh, I wish people would make up their minds,' the old lady said, abandoning the shawl to help her out of the light spotted muslin she was wearing. 'Does that mean I am not to go?'

'Of course you must go.' Esme knew the old lady had been looking forward to the outing; she missed the clean air of the countryside around Luffenham. 'Rosie might need you to help her.'

'Why change your plans so late in the day?'

'It was not my doing, Banny. Lord Gorridge has bought me a horse.'

'A horse! Oh, Esme, you have not accepted him, have you?'

'No, but it seems I must accept the mount, at least for today.'

'Same thing.'

'You do not sound very pleased.'

'It is not for me to be pleased or otherwise, my lady.'

It was said so stiffly that Esme laughed. 'You don't like Viscount Gorridge, do you?'

'It is not what I like that counts. Which habit are you going to wear?'

'The new one, Rosie says.'

'If you want my opinion, Miss Esme...' She paused, waiting.

'Go on.'

'You must not allow other people to make up your mind for you.'

'About what I should wear?'

'You know very well I did not mean that, but no matter. I have said all I am going to say.'

'Do you know something against Lord Gorridge?'

'Ask your sister.'

'Rosie?'

'No, Lady Lucinda. Does she know he is here in London and pursuing you?'

'I don't know. I wrote to her when I first arrived, but I have been so taken up with all our social engagements I have neglected my correspondence. I know there was some trouble between him and Lucy years ago, but he assures me it was all a misunderstanding and all is forgiven and forgotten.'

Miss Bannister's reply was a sniff, but Esme had no opportunity to press her because the sound of the front door knocker put an end to the conversation and both ladies went downstairs, where a footman was just admitting the Viscount.

He almost bounded into the hall, smiling broadly and doffing his tall riding hat. 'Lady Esme, good morning. It is going to be a lovely day. I see the new mount is saddled up and waiting and you are looking delectable in that habit.'

'Thank you, my lord, but I have not said I will accept the horse.'

'Oh, you will when you see her. She is a real beauty.'

Rosemary came out of the drawing room, pulling on lace gloves. She was followed by Rowan, who had elected to ride in the carriage with her. 'Good morning, Lord Gorridge. We are all ready.' She accepted her parasol from her maid and preceded everyone out of the house.

Esme gasped when she saw the mare. She was, as Edward had said, a real beauty, as black and glossy as the horse Edward had bought for himself, except that she had a white blaze on her nose and a white sock on her left foreleg. Esme walked forward and patted her neck.

'She is my stallion's half-sister,' he told her.

'Oh.' That seemed to make her embarrassment even worse. 'What is she called?'

'That's up to you. It ought to be Linwood something or other.'

'Blaze,' she said, stroking the mare's white nose.

'Linwood Blaze it is. Shall you mount up?' He bent to take her foot and lift her into her saddle.

The animal stood patiently while everyone else settled themselves in the carriage and then Edward mounted and they were off, walking the horses down Kensington High Road towards Hammersmith, following the carriage, whose pace was dictated by the traffic.

'How is she?' Edward asked after several minutes of silence.

'Excellent, but you know, my lord, I cannot accept her as a gift. It would not be seemly.'

'Oh, you ladies are so stiff with protocol, it is a wonder you manage to do anything, but if you will not take her as a gift, then I will keep her for you to ride whenever you want to. Will that satisfy the proprieties?'

'I don't know. I shall have to ask Rosemary.'

'If she was going to object, she would have done so at once, don't you think?' he queried. 'Now, let us forget about it for today. Enjoy riding her and we will talk of it again when you have answered my other question.'

'Other question?'

'The one I put to you on the way home from the park the other day. You promised to give it serious thought.'

'I am still pondering on the meaning of it.'

'Meaning? I thought I made it clear that I was offering you marriage.'

'You did not say so.'

'I certainly was not suggesting anything else.' He sounded affronted.

She should have told him immediately she would never consider marrying him, but to spend the rest of the day with a disappointed and perhaps irritable man was more than she was prepared to do. 'In that case, I will give the offer the careful consideration it deserves, but please do not expect an answer today.'

He did not seem to notice the deliberately ambiguous way she had framed her answer. 'Very well. Shall we say the day of your ball? It would be an appropriate time to make an announcement, don't you think?'

'You shall have your answer by then.'

They were passing through what had once been open fields with a few houses dotted along the road, but new housing and businesses had begun filling in the gaps and very soon, Esme realised, Hammersmith would soon become part of the great metropolis. It was not easy to talk because the road was busy and they were often forced into single file. In a way Esme was glad of the chance to be alone with her thoughts. She tried to imagine herself married to Edward Gorridge, being held in his arms, sleeping with him, sitting opposite him at breakfast, directing the army of servants at Linwood Park, and failed utterly. Images of someone else kept getting in the way. She wondered where he was, if he was thinking about their last encounter. She had not handled it at all well and had learned nothing at all, except that he did have a secret and that secret involved Ma'amselle Lefavre. She was tempted to ask Lord Gorridge if he knew anything about it, but decided against it. She had a notion that anything his lordship said would be biased.

It was when they stopped to rest the horses and allow them to drink at the trough by the river bank that they were joined by Mr Ashbury driving Juliette in a phaeton and Captain Merton and Bertie Wincombe on horseback. 'The other ladies have cried off,' Ashbury said. 'On account of the news.'

'What news?' Rosemary asked.

'About Sir Robert Peel. You must have heard he was thrown from his horse last Saturday?'

'Yes, indeed we did, but I cannot see why that should make their ladyships cancel today's outing, unless...' She paused. 'Oh, do not tell me the poor man has died of his injuries.'

'Yes, afraid so.'

'Oh, dear, how shocking. Rowan, what do you suppose we should do?'

'I ought to return,' he said. 'But that means taking the carriage and you would have to come with me.'

'Then we would all have to return. I cannot let Esme go on without me.'

'I do not mind in the least if you think we should,' Esme said.

'Oh, please do not deprive your sister of her outing,' Edward put in. 'She has been so looking forward to it and I have sent a couple of servants on ahead in a dogcart with all the picnic things. They will be expecting us.'

'My lord,' Victor said, addressing Viscount Trent. 'If you feel you must return, I would be pleased to offer you my phaeton if you would allow Miss Lefavre and me into your carriage with Lady Trent and Miss Bannister.'

Rowan looked dubious. 'What do you think, my dear?' he asked his wife.

'It would be a pity to cancel the picnic after Lord Gorridge has gone to so much trouble.'

'Very well.'

The exchange was made; Victor and Juliette settled themselves opposite Rosemary in the carriage and the little procession continued on its way. As they approached the bridge, they had a view of Richmond and the wooded area of Richmond Hill and a building standing on a prominence which Edward said was the famous Star and Garter hostelry, beloved of Mr Dickens. Having crossed the bridge and entered Richmond, they found the builders had been at work here too and it was rapidly growing into a small town. Moving on up the hill, they entered the Great Park at one in the afternoon, nearly an hour later than Edward had intended.

His servants were already in the spot he had chosen almost at the top of the hill, which gave a wonderful view of the countryside, woods and meadows and the river, winding its way towards London. The air was sweet and clean after the smoke-laden atmosphere of the town and everyone, dismounting or getting down from the carriage, filled their lungs with it and turned their faces to the cloudless sky.

'Everything is ready,' Edward said. 'I hope the ride has given you an appetite.' He waved his hand at the rugs spread on the ground beneath the shade of an oak tree and a white cloth loaded with food: pies, chickens, hams, salads and cakes. Nearby on a small folding table were set out bottles of wine and glasses.

The food, served by a footman in the Gorridge livery and a maid in a blue check dress and snowy apron, was delicious and everyone did it justice, except Esme, who had little appetite of late. Afterwards, while Lady Trent and Miss Bannister took their ease, the younger members of the party went for a walk. There were deer in the park which Esme had been told were tame enough to take food from her hand, and she took some crumbled pie for them. But they shied away when she approached them. 'We are too many,' she said, discarding the pie and hurrying to catch up with the others who had continued on their way.

They were walking round the ponds where anglers were fishing when Esme found herself beside Juliette. She felt she ought to make some conversation, but hardly knew how to begin when all she felt was curiosity about where Felix was and why the lady was being accompanied by Mr Ashbury.

'Are you enjoying your stay in England?' she asked at last.

'Yes. It is very different but I must learn your ways if I am to make my 'ome 'ere.'

'Are you? Going to live here permanently, I mean.'

'Yes. Felix cannot live abroad now he is the baron, can 'e?'

'Oh.' She paused to make a huge effort to gather herself. 'When is the wedding to be?'

'We 'ave not decided. Soon, I 'ope.'

'Then allow me to felicitate you.'

'Thank you, my lady. I 'ope soon to felicitate you, *n'est-ce pas?*'

'Oh, it is too soon for that,' she said, and hurried to join Captain Merton and Edward who were ambling ahead of her, but before she reached them her footsteps slowed. She was in no mood for conversation of any kind and wanted desperately to be alone. She turned along a second path that led into the trees, hoping no one would miss her. If she had ever looked forward to the outing, it was spoiled for her now. Felix was betrothed to Juliette and even if he wished he was not, he could not break off the engagement without a terrible scandal. Was that what he had been hinting at when he said there were things he could not tell her? As if she would think of marrying him after that! She had been right to be angry.

She stumbled on, her eyes so full of tears she could hardly see where she was going. She wanted comfort, but there was no comfort to be had. Rosemary would give her none; Rosemary had known what Lord Pendlebury was like from the first. It was a pity she hadn't believed her and had allowed herself to be ensnared.

'Lady Esme, where are you going?' Edward was calling after her.

She did not turn round and, if anything, her pace increased, but it was not enough to lose him. He caught her arm. 'Did you miss your way?'

Obliged to stop, she turned to her tear-streaked face towards him.

'Whatever is the matter? Oh, my dear, tell me what is wrong.' He took her into his arms and held her close. 'Whatever it is, I shall put it right for you. Trust me.'

If he had not said those two words, she would have succumbed, allowed herself to be comforted, but those two words, trust me, had reminded her of Felix. If he had not refused to tell her the truth about Juliette, she would have trusted him and that would have been a mistake. Almost had. She dared not risk it again. She scrubbed at her eyes and pulled away from him. 'Nothing's the matter. I caught my foot in a rabbit hole.'

'Let me look at it.'

'Certainly not!'

'Very well. Lean on me and I will escort you back to the carriage.' He was smiling, but it was not a smile she found agreeable; it reminded her of a cat with a bowl of cream. 'You know you can always lean on me.'

Caught in her own trap, she hobbled along with her hand on his shoulder and his arm about her waist. They emerged from the trees not far from the carriage. Rosemary, on seeing them, scrambled to her feet and went to meet them. 'Esme, what has happened?'

'Lady Esme caught her foot in a rabbit hole, my lady. Perhaps you should look at it.'

'Yes, take her to the carriage.'

He lifted her onto the seat and stood back as Rosemary stepped up behind her. 'Thank you, my lord,' Esme said, dismissing him.

'Now, let us have a look at that foot,' Rosemary said, as soon as he had gone

Esme kicked off her shoe and poked out a foot.

'There doesn't seem to be much wrong with it, Esme.'

'It's better now.'

'There never was anything wrong with it, was there?'

Esme had never been able to lie successfully and though she protested, Rosemary simply laughed. 'It was a ploy to get Lord Gorridge to help you along, wasn't it? Oh, Esme, you are so transparent. But never mind, I will not give you away. What did he say to you?'

'Nothing.'

'You mean he did not propose?'

'Oh, he did that before.'

'He did?' her sister queried in astonishment. 'When?'

'The other morning when we met in the park and again today when we set out.'

'And what did you say?'

'I said I would think about it and let him know before my ball.'

'Oh, good, then we can make the announcement then. It will be a fitting end to your season.'

'I have not said I will accept him.'

'But you will, I am sure you will. He has everything a lady could desire: looks, manners, wealth and a title. What more do you want?'

There were, she decided, different aspects to that word desire. 'I want my husband to love me.'

'That will come. He is a proud man and would not risk declaring himself in love in case you should reject him. He would not want to be humiliated as Lucy humiliated him, would he? Now, am I to say you are too injured to ride back and must ride in the coach or will you have made a miraculous recovery?'

Lord Gorridge's escort was better than enduring her sister's endless matchmaking and especially the presence of Ma'amselle Lefavre. 'I can ride.'

'Then as soon as the others come back, I think we should make a start. I'll send Lord Gorridge to hurry them along.'

The return was accomplished in less time than the outward journey because they did not stop either to rest or for Edward to point out landmarks and they arrived at Trent House at six in the evening. The ladies left the carriage and Edward helped Esme to dismount and kissed her hand. 'I wish you a speedy recovery,' he said, maintaining the fiction that she had hurt her foot. 'And hope to see you out and about again very soon.'

Rosemary was effusive in her thanks to him for arranging everything and apologetic that the others had not come and so much food had been wasted, but he shrugged it off as of no importance. Mr Ashbury's phaeton was brought round from the mews and everyone parted. Esme, leaning on Miss Bannister for support, followed Rosemary into the house and breathed a sigh of relief.

But the day's revelations were not over. When she went down to the drawing room in response to the dinner bell, she found Rowan telling Rosemary about Sir Robert's demise. 'The fatal injury was caused when his horse stumbled over him as he lay on the ground,' he said. 'Prince Albert is apparently most upset. Apart from his admiration for him as a politician, he was his principal ally for the Great Exhibition. There is talk of it being scrapped in deference to his memory.'

'So, we shall not have to endure the upheaval, after all,' Rosemary said. 'I wonder what will happen to all the money they have been collecting.'

'Presumably, it will have to be returned, whatever has not been spent on preliminaries, that is. I believe that has been considerable.'

'How can they return money collected in pennies and shillings from the workers?' Esme asked him. 'I don't suppose there is a record of who gave what. And they will be so disappointed. And what about all those people who are preparing exhibits and arranging for them to be transported?' She couldn't help it, her thoughts flew to Felix as she spoke. He was preparing an exhibit. Would she ever see it now? Did she want to? What would he make of all this talk of cancellation?

'They will have to find other ways of showing off their wares,' Rowan said.

'Myles will not be pleased, nor Lord Pendlebury. They both invested heavily.'

'Myles is rich enough not to be concerned. As for Pendlebury, he might very well be ruined.'

'Oh, no, surely not.'

'I have been told by the Commissioner of Police that a certain Patrick Connelly, a troublemaker they have been watching for some time, has been arrested and found in possession of a money draft made out to him on Lord Pendlebury's account. It is very damning, although it is being kept quiet for the moment in the hope he will lead them to others.'

Esme, who had been standing in the middle of the room, sank on to a sofa and stifled a cry by putting her fist to her mouth.

'I always did say he was queer fish,' Rosemary said, looking hard at Esme. 'And that silly French woman went on and on about how wonderful he was while we were coming home in the carriage, I had to tell her I had a headache and wanted it to be quiet. They are a pair made for each other, if you ask me.'

The butler came to tell them dinner was served. Esme let her sister and brother-in-law go in alone. She could not have eaten a bite without choking and excused herself, saying she felt unwell. 'I think I was in the sun too long this afternoon,' she said and fled to her room.

She found Miss Bannister tidying her day clothes away. 'Aren't you going in to dinner?' she asked.

'No. Oh, Banny, I am so miserable.' She flung herself on her bed and covered her face with her hands.

Miss Bannister sat beside her and pulled her hands down so that she could look into her tear-wet face. 'Tell Banny all about it.'

She had to tell someone and it all poured out, leaving Banny gasping with shock. 'Miss Esme, you should never have allowed him to kiss you.'

'I couldn't help it and, oh, Banny, it was so wonderful. I never felt anything like that before, all tingling and cherished. It wasn't sordid or repugnant or anything like that. I would never at that time have believed ill of him—' She stopped suddenly. 'It is strange, but the more people castigate him and blacken his character, the more I want to defend him. Is that very perverse of me?'

'It sounds as if you do not believe the rumours.'

'But that means someone is lying.'

'Yes.'

'But why?'

Miss Bannister shrugged. 'Why do people lie? Jealousy, perhaps, envy, hate, to divert attention from what they are up to themselves, to make themselves look better, for power, monetary gain, take your pick.'

'And Ma'amselle Lefavre—why would she say they were engaged if they were not? She made it perfectly clear to me that they were planning to marry.'

'Then you must either believe her or believe him.'

'I don't know what to believe.'

'I cannot tell you. You are a sensible girl, so trust your instinct.'

Her instinct was to believe Felix, but how trustworthy was her instinct? 'And if I say I believe Lord Pendlebury, then Rowan is not telling the truth and Ma'amselle Lefavre is a liar.'

'Lord Trent has only repeated what others have told him. As for that Frenchwoman—' She stopped.

'You rode in the coach with her, what did you think? And do not tell me it is not for you to think. You are my friend, you have looked after me all my life and if there is one person I do trust, besides Mama and Papa, it is you.'

'I could not take to her. There is something underhand about her. How a nice gentleman like Lord Pendlebury ever got into her clutches, I do not know.'

'Oh, Banny!' Esme's eyes were shining through the tears that still lay on her lashes. 'You have given me hope.'

'It is only my opinion, child, and perhaps I am not a good judge.'

'I have to find Lord Pendlebury...'

'Now, Miss Esme, I hope you are not going to do anything foolish and cause a scandal. It would not be fair on Lord Pendlebury when he is already fighting for his good name.'

The old lady's words subdued her. Talking to Felix again was not going to be so easy as it had been the first time. He would not want to talk to her after her parting words in the park and she was never without an escort. If it was not Rosemary, it was Viscount Gorridge. 'I know.' It was said with a sigh.

'You must rely on meeting him at some social occasion and somehow contrive to let him know you regret your quarrel. More than that you must not do.'

'But what social occasion? Will he still be acceptable in society?'

'It depends how far the rumours have spread. If Lord Trent has been told in confidence, it might not be so bad.'

'Then I shall encourage Rosemary to accept every invitation she possibly can, though if she is not feeling well... Oh, why is life so complicated?'

Miss Bannister patted her hand and stood up. 'Now, shall I go and ask for a little light supper to be sent up to you?'

'Yes, please. I'm starving.'

Felix was at Larkhills when he heard the news that Sir Robert had died. After his quarrel with Esme, he felt as low as he had ever felt in his life. She had seemed determined to misunderstand him. The trouble was that he could not explain and asking her to trust him was more than she seemed able to do. That had made him as angry as she was at the time, but on reflection he could not blame her; he had done nothing to deserve her trust. He could only pray that everything would be resolved before she fell into the trap Gorridge was setting for her. Everything pointed to Connelly and Maillet being the ones to stir up trouble, but when he had tried to warn Edward against associating with them, his cousin had laughed in his face. And then he had had the temerity to ask him for more money. 'Need to buy a horse,' he had said.

'You've had five thousand already.'

'That was to pay my debts. But this will be an investment. I'll pay you back with interest, as soon as my funds are released.'

'And when will that be?' He knew the answer to that, but wanted to hear it from the man's own lips.

'When a certain lady agrees to become my wife. My father was negotiating terms for the match just before he died.'

'You are talking of Lady Esme Vernley, I assume.'

'Yes, of course. Who else?'

'And has she agreed?'

'Not formally. That will take place on the evening of her ball.'

His cousin's expression of triumph was more than he could stomach. He had refused to give him another penny and taken himself off to Larkhills for a little peace and quiet and to work on the clay model of his figurine, prior to making the mould. He had worked hard on the features to reproduce Esme's youth and innocence, but at the same time convey a subtle hint of the eternal Eve. He would never be totally satisfied with it, but it was as good as he could make it and he had set about making several moulds. Two days before he had made the glass and blown his first model, which had broken. He made the next, which was passable, but not quite right. He tried again and again until he was satisfied.

'Perfect,' his mother said on being shown the final attempt. 'But it looks so fragile, as if you could break it in your fingers.'

'Like the original, it is stronger than it looks, but I'm going to make three to be safe. One I'll keep here, the others I'll take back to London with me.'

'She cannot fail to be enchanted.'

He doubted if Esme would be swayed by anything so trivial and had considered abandoning the whole idea, but working on it, making it as perfect as he could, had given him a little solace.

The day before he had made two more models and was just cleaning up after himself before going back into the house to change when his mother came to him, waving a newspaper. 'Felix, Sir Robert Peel has died of his injuries and this paper is saying the Great Exhibition will have to be cancelled.'

He took it from her and scanned the report. 'I had better get back. There's bound to be a debate and we can't let the opposition win.'

It was not until he arrived back in London that he heard about Patrick Connelly's arrest and the implication being put on it by the money draft found in the man's possession. It was just one more hurdle to be overcome.

Unsure how far the rumours had spread, he went about town as usual, though he avoided Gorridge House and the Ashbury residence where Juliette was still residing. If she knew he was back in town, she made no effort to contact him and he hoped she had at last realised she would get nowhere with him. He called on Lady Mountjoy with an invitation from his mother to visit her at Larkhills, wondering if he would be received, but she had either not heard the rumours or had chosen to discount them because she made him welcome. As luck would have it, Lady Aviemore arrived while he was there. Her ladyship, learning of the move to have the Exhibition cancelled, had deemed it necessary to rally all her friends to reinforce their support of the project and to send a united petition to the Prince Consort not to allow such a thing to happen. She had heard something to his detriment, but put it down to malicious gossip on the part of those who wanted to put an end to the Exhibition. 'Come to my soirée on Wednesday evening,' she told him. 'That will show them you are a loyal subject of her Majesty.' She dug him in the side with the point of her parasol and laughed. 'You will have the ladies of the *ton* on your side at any rate.'

Wincing a little, he thanked her and promised to be there. It was one hurdle overcome. The next was to convince Esme, but he had seen nothing of her, though he walked regularly in the park, hoping to catch a glimpse of her.

Rosemary had not been at all well since the picnic and had hardly been out of the house, which had meant Esme did not go out either, so she did not see Felix. She filled her time with running errands for her sister and reading the newspapers and journals that Rowan had delivered daily, looking for mention of Lord Pendlebury, either to confirm or deny the latest rumours, but there was nothing. What was worse, Lord Gorridge was never off the doorstep. He arrived bearing flowers for Rosemary and for Esme; he begged to be allowed to run errands for them, to help with the arrangements for the ball, anything to keep him in the forefront of their minds. His visits stopped abruptly when Myles and Lucy arrived.

They had been going to come for Esme's ball in any case, but had decided to travel down a couple of weeks early. Myles wanted to do what he could to see the Exhibition come to fruition. He was not a member of Parliament and not a peer so, unlike Felix, he could not speak in the Lords, but he did have some influence in the business community, which he intended to use.

When Esme told Lucy that Viscount Gorridge was a constant visitor, Lucy lost no time in telling Rosemary what she thought of her for allowing him to call, at all. 'He is a charlatan, a liar and a lecher,' she said. 'And how you can bring yourself to receive him, I do not know. And as for encouraging him to lust after Esme—'

'Lust after Esme! How can you say that?' Rosemary said. The three sisters were talking in Rosemary's boudoir where she spent much of her time since learning of her pregnancy. 'You have not been here and have not seen him. He has never put a foot wrong and, whatever happened in the past, he has repented of it.'

'He said it was all a misunderstanding,' Esme put in. 'And that all had been forgiven and forgotten.'

'Not by me,' Lucy said. 'And not by him, I'll wager. He's up to something.'

'Nonsense. Esme is quite a catch.'

'Yes, she is, and that's what worries me.'

'What exactly did happen?' Esme demanded. 'Rosemary said he tried to kiss you too passionately and you were about to be engaged anyway.'

'I never was. I had rejected him and he tried to force the issue. He tried to rape me, Esme. Do you know what that means?'

'No, not exactly,' Esme said doubtfully. 'But I believe it is very terrible.'

'It is. If he had succeeded, he would have ruined me for life. No other man would have considered marrying me and that was what he'd hoped for.'

'Yes, but exactly what did he do?'

'I found him in one of the glasshouses at Luffenham with a girl from the railway works. They were both naked. He sent the girl packing and turned on me. He tore my clothes off and flung me on the ground… No, I cannot go on.'

'No, you should not,' Rosemary said. 'You are poisoning Esme's mind against him. You were keeping him on tenterhooks and the girl seduced him. Men are easy prey to girls like that. You should not have reacted so violently, crying rape when none was intended. As a result, he spent six years in exile. He has expressed remorse, so it is not kind of you to drag it all up again.'

'I did not drag it up. Esme asked and she has a right to know.'

'He is devoted to her, as you will see for yourself when you see them together, and even if you did not want to be mistress of Linwood, perhaps Esme is not so stupid.'

'Esme?' Lucy appealed to her.

Esme looked from one to the other. She had been shocked by Lucy's revelation and it made her see Lord Gorridge in an entirely different light. But why, if he knew Lucy hated him so much, was he paying court to her? There was another mystery here and she wanted to solve it. It had nothing to do with wanting to be a Viscountess and mistress of Linwood Park because she had no intention of agreeing to marry him; it was nothing more than curiosity. 'I wish you would not quarrel over it,' she told her sisters. 'I am being pulled both ways and it is a very uncomfortable feeling, I can tell you. Will you not let me make up my own mind?'

'Very well,' Lucy said icily. 'But if you marry that man, I shall never visit you and he will never be welcomed into my home.'

Esme began to laugh hysterically. 'And I suppose if I were by some miracle to marry Felix Pendlebury, Rosemary will never visit me and he will be barred from Trent House as he is now.'

'Marry Pendlebury!' Rosemary exclaimed. 'Whatever put that idea into your head, you foolish girl?'

'I can dream, can't I?'

'That's all it is, a dream. He will undoubtedly be tried for incitement to treason.'

'Treason!' Lucy exclaimed. 'Why do you say that?'

'He has been supplying the dissidents with money to pursue their treasonable objectives.'

'You must be mistaken. Myles would have known about it and told me.'

'It is not generally known. I think the authorities are trying to hush it up to prevent general panic.'

'I find that very hard to believe.'

'Why do you say that? You have never met the man.'

'Indeed, I have. He has visited us in Leicester and I found him very agreeable.'

'Oh, that was because he is another like Myles, a man who likes to get his hands dirty.'

'Please, please stop!' Esme cried, clapping her hands over her ears. 'I don't want to hear another word about either gentlemen and if this bickering goes on any longer I shall ask to go home to Luffenham.'

'But you can't,' wailed Rosemary. 'There's your ball. The invitations have gone out and the arrangements are far advanced.'

'It would be easy to say you were not up to it,' Esme said.

'How can I? I am not ready to retire from society yet. It is too early…'

'No, Esme, you had better stay,' Lucy said. 'We don't want a scandal, do we? Remember, you are a Vernley and hold your head up. You don't have to accept anyone. There doesn't have to be an engagement or an announcement.'

And that was how the matter was left and the arrangements for the ball continued, though Esme was far from enthusiastic. If only she had not quarrelled with Felix, if only he could be invited to the ball, then it would be different. She would be looking forward to it in a fever of impatience. But it was not only Rosemary who was a barrier to that, it was Juliette Lefavre. What was the truth of that?

Lucy took a great deal of the work from Rosemary's shoulders and it was Lucy who accompanied Esme on shopping expeditions and walks and rides in the park. It was to Lucy, that Esme confessed her abiding love for Lord Pendlebury and her conviction that there must be a plot to discredit him because she could not possibly love a man who was wicked. It was his obduracy in not telling her of it that she found so hard to bear. 'If only I could discover the truth,' she told her sister, as they strolled along the path through Hyde Park, after a visit to the shops in Regent Street. 'I might be able to do something to help him.'

'Ask him.'

'I tried, but he would not tell me and we quarrelled. I would give anything to tell him I did not mean to doubt him.'

'It looks as though you will have your wish,' Lucy said, smiling. 'Here he is.'

Felix had spotted them and was walking purposefully towards them. Esme only had time to notice his grey suit and black cravat and that his dear face looked troubled, the gleam of amusement gone from his eyes, before he was on them and doffing his black top hat. 'Ladies, good morning.'

'Good morning, my lord,' Lucy said cheerfully, digging Esme in the ribs with her elbow to bring her out of the reverie in which she seemed to be indulging.

It was difficult to get the words out but she managed it. 'Good morning, my lord.'

'How do you do, ladies?' he said, addressing them both, but looking at Esme. Her general complexion was paler than he remembered it, but there were two high spots of colour on her cheeks. Was she remembering their quarrel, as he was? Had she regretted a single word she had said to him?

'We are both well.' It was Lucy who replied.

'I am on my way back from looking at the site of the Exhibition.'

'Is it still to take place?' Esme queried. 'I had heard it was to be cancelled.'

'It is to go before Parliament next week and I want to make sure I have all the facts before I get to my feet.'

'You will speak in its favour, I expect,' Lucy put in, while Felix and Esme continued to look at each other like two hungry urchins with a meal held tantalisingly just out of their reach. They had unfinished business to transact but it could only be done in private and the opportunity was simply not there. And so they maintained a stiff politeness that would have been amusing if it had not been so heartrending.

'Of course.'

'You are going to speak?' Esme asked in surprise. 'I thought... Oh, dear...'

He gave her a twisted smile, realising she had heard the rumours, but then how could she not considering Edward would have made sure she knew of them? 'Still doubting me, Lady Esme?'

'No, no, not at all,' she said quickly. 'I never doubted you, but other people might not be so charitable.'

'I am glad of your confidence.' His smile was wide. 'As for others, they will be answered.'

'We saw that picture in the *News* on Saturday,' Lucy said, looking from one to the other and wishing she could knock their heads together. 'The one Mr Paxton submitted.'

None of the designs entered in the competition for the Exhibition building had found favour and the Commission were on the point of going ahead with their own design when a drawing was published in *Illustrated London News* that had everyone talking. Over eighteen hundred feet long and four hundred feet wide, with a dome high enough to enclose the huge elms, it would be made almost entirely of glass held together by iron girders. 'It will blow down at the first gust of wind,' Rowan had said contemptuously when he saw it.

'I believe Mr Paxton is employed by the Duke of Devonshire to look after his gardens at Chatsworth,' Lucy went on. 'According to the report he designed the great conservatories there for his Grace's exotic plants.'

'Yes, so I understand.'

'Do you like it?' Esme asked him. 'I recall your own design used glass as the principal building material.'

'So it did, but it was not on such a grand scale and as I explained, I did not submit it because I do not have the time to devote to its construction.'

'You told me you were more interested in making your exhibit.'

'Yes, among other things.'

'Is it finished?'

'Yes, as far as my poor talent is able to finish it.'

'You made it with your own hand? I thought it would be something from your manufactory.'

'This I made myself in my own laboratory.'

'You said you would show it to me.'

'I will, but other things have to be resolved first.'

'Oh, you make me so cross!'

He smiled and Lucy laughed. Esme turned on her. 'It is not a laughing matter.'

'No, of course not,' she said, then to Felix, 'My lord, what shall we do with her?'

'I do not know about you, Lady Lucinda, but I should like to put her across my knee and spank her. And after that I should like—' He stopped speaking, searching Esme's face for a flicker of that liveliness he had first seen in her, the ability to laugh at herself, the exuberance. It lit her face for a moment, then faded. 'No, that would make her even more cross.'

'I do not think you had better tell us the rest, my lord,' Lucy said, smiling indulgently. 'Or I shall be obliged to end the conversation and take my sister away.'

'Oh, please do not do that. I will behave. Let us talk of other things. Are you on your way home?'

'Yes. We have been shopping.'

'Then may I escort you?' He turned and faced the way they had been going and held out both arms. With one each side of him, they proceeded down the path, he in a plain brown suit of clothes and a cream cravat, and the two ladies in silk dresses: Lucy in green and Esme in pale blue which, in his opinion, matched her eyes. All three received envious glances from others in the park. They were, in the eyes of Annie Hicks, who watched them from the door of her stall, Quality with a capital letter, and as such did not have to worry about filling their bellies or clothing their limbs or keeping a roof over their heads as she did. The young gentleman had been present when she agreed to her compensation. Was it worth telling him it was not nearly enough and she wanted more?

Esme's hand was tucked into Felix's elbow and he squeezed it gently. It was enough to set her quivering, just as she always did when she was anywhere near him. He seemed so at ease, as if the rumours being circulated about him did not trouble him in the least, just as if they had not quarrelled, as if she had not told him she hated him and never wanted to see him again. Nothing could have been further from the truth.

'My lord, do you go to Lady Aviemore's soirée?' she asked him, wanting to learn if he was being ostracised.

'I shall certainly put in an appearance. Do you go?'

'Lucy and Myles are going to take me. I do not think Rosemary will go.'

He smiled. 'No, I did not think she would. Are you out of favour for accepting?'

She gave a little chuckle, the first he had heard from her for some time. 'She has never been able to stand up to Lucy.

And, of course, with Myles to back her, even Rowan will say nothing, though he glowers a lot.'

'Then I shall look forward to seeing you there,' he said, squeezing her arm again.

At the park gate he took his leave and she went the rest of the way treading on air.

Chapter Nine

Felix was in his study, working on the speech he meant to make in the Lords, when a messenger brought him a note from Myles, asking if he and Lady Lucinda could call later that afternoon. It gave no indication of why they wanted to see him, but he supposed it might have something to do with Esme. Perhaps she would accompany them, though the letter gave no indication of it. He hastily penned a reply saying he would be delighted and then sent for his housekeeper to make sure she would have refreshments prepared. After that, he could not put his mind to his speech and went from room to room picking things up and putting them down again, unable to settle to anything.

He did his best to hide his disappointment when Esme did not arrive with her sister and brother-in-law. After greeting them and making them welcome, he sent for tea and cakes and ushered them into the drawing room. When the tea tray came, he asked Lucy if she would do the honours. 'At the moment this is a bachelor establishment,' he said. 'I rarely entertain ladies for tea. In fact, I do not think I ever have, though my mother enjoys it when she is in town.'

Lucy sat at the table to pour the tea, while the men took armchairs on either side of the hearth. 'I learned from Esme that you are still not welcome at Trent House,' she said, handing Felix a cup of tea. 'And so we decided there was nothing for it but to come and see you.'

'And very welcome you are.'

'We heard the sad news of Sir Robert's passing and came down at once,' Myles put in, standing up to take his tea from Lucy. 'According to reports I have read, his death is giving the opposition fresh impetus.'

'Yes. Did you know Colonel Sibthorp has put down a motion calling for a setting up of a select committee to reconsider the whole idea?'

'Yes. It is one of the reasons I am keen to do my bit to keep the momentum going. I am sure Sir Robert would not have wanted it abandoned. I would value your views. Personally I think the arrangements are too far advanced to cancel and if this design of Paxton's is passed, it will be a step nearer fruition.'

'Did you know the building is being called the Crystal Palace by Punch?' Lucy put in. 'It rolls off the tongue so much better than the Great Exhibition of the Industry of All Nations, don't you think?'

'Yes. It seems to have caught the imagination of the public and that perhaps is a help. I plan to use it when I speak against the Colonel's motion when it reaches the Lords.' It was common politeness to pursue the subject introduced by his guests, but what he really wanted to hear was how Esme was. 'The money is nearly all there and I believe there has been a good response from all over the world to requests for people to send exhibits. Even the entrance fees have been decided and the ordinary people are all looking forward to visiting it, saving up their pennies towards the cost. Trains have been laid on for them and lists of cheap accommodation are being prepared so that they are not left to sleep on the streets. It would be a crime to cancel it now.'

'I agree. My railwaymen are particularly keen and I have booked space myself to show one of my new locomotives. It might have to be transported from the rail depot in pieces and assembled on the spot, but it can be done.'

'My exhibit is not on such an enormous scale,' Felix said, with a laugh. 'In fact it is only fourteen inches high. I have it with me. Would you like to see it? I would value your opinion.'

'I don't know anything about glass manufacture, but I will be honoured.'

Felix went to his bedroom and fetched a box containing the figurine from a cupboard where he had put it when he arrived back in London. While they watched, he sat at the table opposite Lucy, took it from its case and carefully undid the yards of material he had wrapped about it and stood it on the table. 'There! That is my Crystal Girl. What do you think of her?'

'Why, it's Esme!' Lucy exclaimed.

'You recognise her?'

'Of course. You have captured her exactly.'

'Thank you, my lady.'

'Did you know about the new name for the Exhibition when you named her?'

'No, it is coincidence. She has always been my Crystal Girl.'

'I am sure it will be much admired. Is that what you promised to show Esme?'

'Yes. I wanted to know what you felt about it. Would she object?'

'I don't see how she could. It's exquisite.'

'She doesn't know what it is yet and I cannot display it without her consent or the consent of the Earl and I am not sure I can obtain either. Esme… We quarrelled, you see, and she is always so jealously guarded, I cannot get near her to try to explain.'

'You spoke to her yesterday.'

'Indeed, I did, and it was a pleasure to think she might have forgiven me, and I thank you for allowing it, but it was not like a private conversation.'

'You said you would not show it to her until other things had been resolved. Would that perhaps have something to do with Ma'amselle Lefavre? That is her name, is it not? She told Esme you were engaged to be married. Is it true?'

'No, although there was a time, several years ago, when it might have come to pass, but she suddenly went off with someone else. He died and so did her father and she came to England, hoping to renew my interest.'

'And succeeded?'

'No, she did not.' He was emphatic. 'I told Esme so, but I could not give her any assurance that I would not see Juliette again.'

'Then you cannot blame Esme. You see, Lord Gorridge told her you were helping the Revolutionaries in France in forty-eight and that's how you met Ma'amselle Lefavre and became engaged to her, but when the uprising began, you left her and fled back to England. She has only now been able to follow you.'

'He said that? No wonder she was angry, but why did she not tell me what he said?'

'I think she wanted you to tell her yourself without any prompting.'

'But I could not.' He paused and took a deep breath. 'I had better tell you the whole, in strict confidence, that is, and you shall judge as you see fit.' He went on to tell them everything that had happened. 'I am in a cleft stick. I cannot tell Esme about my work for the Duke and her mind has been poisoned by others. I am afraid she will not listen to me. And, forgive me, Lady Lucinda, Lady Trent is your sister, but she is almost throwing Lady Esme at Viscount Gorridge, who is being altogether too accommodating.'

'Why don't you approach our father?' Lucy said after a moment's thought. 'I would be extremely surprised if he would condone a match between Esme and Edward Gorridge. Tell him everything. Get his permission to approach Esme. Rosemary can do nothing then, though you will still have to deal with Lord Gorridge and your other problems.'

'That's sound advice,' Myles said. 'I doubt the Earl has heard all the gossip, which I am sure is confined to a certain section of London society, and there is no need for you to tell him you have been denied entry to Trent House.'

'Thank you.' He carefully wrapped the figurine again. 'I should like say how much I appreciate the trust you have put in me. It is comforting to know I have at least two allies.'

'Oh, more than that, I am sure,' Lucy said. 'There is Esme…'

'Ah, there's the rub. How can I ask her to share the life of someone so tainted by gossip, even if my problems were resolved?'

'I was given to understand you already had,' Lucy said with a smile.

'I tried, but the rumours have become worse since Mr Connelly was arrested. The money draft found on him was mine. I gave it to him to pay Edward's gambling debts, but Edward refuses to go to the police and corroborate it.'

'I see what you mean about a cleft stick,' Myles put in. 'But surely the Duke of Wellington has it in his power to exonerate you?'

'No doubt he will do so in his own good time—I only pray it will be before Esme commits herself to Gorridge, or anyone else.'

'She won't do that,' Lucy assured him. 'She loves you.'

'Loves me!' he exclaimed, the weariness suddenly leaving his voice and becoming animated. 'Are you sure?'

'She says she does and I have no reason to think she does not mean it. Her problem is Ma'amselle Lefavre.'

'Then I will have to deal with it. Please, I beg of you, treat all I have said in confidence, tell no one, not even Esme. I must resolve that problem myself.'

His visitors assured him they would say nothing and soon afterwards took their leave. As soon as they had gone he began pacing the room, backwards and forwards. Esme loved him. His sweet Crystal Girl loved him. He did not doubt that Lady Lucinda, if not Myles, had come to him with the express purpose of telling him so. But he wanted to hear it from Esme's own lips and he could not ask her until she had been convinced that Juliette Lefavre meant nothing to him. Suddenly making up his mind, he went into the hall, grabbed his hat from a side table and left the house.

Clarges Street was only a short walk away and did not give him time to have second thoughts. It would perhaps have been better for everyone if she had not been at home when he arrived, he might have calmed down and approached her in a different way. Instead he went in all guns blazing.

Mrs Ashbury, he was told by the footman who admitted him, was not at home and neither was Mr Ashbury.

'Miss Lefavre?'

'I believe she is in the garden, my lord.'

'I'll find her,' he said. 'No need to announce me.'

As far as the man was concerned, Lord Pendlebury was an acceptable visitor, nephew to the house's owner, so he did not demur and went back to cleaning the silver, leaving Felix to stride through the house and make his way into the small garden at the rear where he found Juliette sitting on a bench beneath a cherry tree, with a book on her lap.

She jumped up when she saw him, letting the book fall to the ground. 'Felix,' she cried in delight. 'Madame Ashbury and Victor 'ave gone visiting and you 'ave come to bear me company in my loneliness.'

'No, I have not.' He stooped and retrieved the book, putting it on the seat where she had been sitting. 'I came to ask you—no, to *demand* to know why you told Lady Esme Vernley we are to be married.'

'But, *mon cher*, would you have me deny it when she asked me most particularly if it was true? I could not tell the lies.'

'It is most certainly not true and I do not know why you should think it is. I would not marry you if you were the last woman on earth.'

She laughed harshly. 'I might be the only one who will 'ave you by the time the gossips 'ave done with you.'

'Gossip that you have promoted, you and that evil cousin of mine. If you want to stay in this country, I suggest you do something to repair the damage. No, I do not suggest it, I require it.'

'Oh, Felix, you are so funny.' Her laughter had a bitter edge to it. 'When the revolution comes, it will all go into the melting pot and we shall see who gives the orders then.'

'It won't happen, not in England.'

'We shall see.'

'Yes, we will. And you will find yourself on a boat back to France and those evil associates of yours imprisoned. One of them already is.'

'The man was—'ow do you say?—expendable.'

'Go back to France, Juliette. There is nothing for you here.'

'Oh, yes, there is. Now, if you value your good name, you will leave before Mrs Ashbury returns and I tell her you 'ave ruined me.'

'You wouldn't?' It was a rhetorical question; he knew the answer. As if to reinforce it, she put her hand to the neckline of her dress and began to tug at it, though not enough to tear it. He stared at her as if she were mad, bowed formally and turned to go. Furious, she picked up her book and threw it at him. The corner of it caught his cheek. He turned his back on her and left, dabbing at the cut with his handkerchief. 'You will regret that, Felix Pendlebury!' she shouted after him. If she had not been his enemy before, she certainly was now, and far from resolving matters, he had exacerbated them.

Esme dressed with particular care to go to Lady Aviemore's soirée. She was going to see Felix and with luck might contrive to have a little private conversation with him. She was as excited as a small child, when given the present she had most longed for. 'What shall I wear?' she asked Miss Bannister. 'I must look my best.'

'You always look well, Miss Esme. What about the white spotted muslin?'

'No, that makes me look pale. The striped silk.'

The stripes, in two shades of blue and one of cream, were used lengthwise on the sleeves and the bodice, which finished in a point at the tiny waist, and in alternate diagonal panels in the full skirt. A small row of ribbon bows went down the front from neck to hem, otherwise it was unadorned. A tiny headdress of lace and ribbons sat on the back of her head, hardly concealing the rich gold of her hair, which Miss Bannister had tamed into smooth curls with combs and pins. Impatient to be off, she slipped into her shoes, picked up a tiny reticule and a fan and went downstairs to join Lucy and Myles.

If anything, Lady Aviemore's salon was even more crowded than it had been before and the sound of everyone talking at once reached their ears as soon as the door was opened to admit them. 'My goodness, Babel!' Myles exclaimed, as they made their way into the room.

'I cannot see him,' Esme whispered to Lucy.

'Patience, sweetheart,' Lucy admonished. 'If he is here, he will find us.'

They moved farther into the room and were immediately swallowed up by the throng, many of whom knew Myles and Lucy and were anxious to ensure their support for the project. Esme, a little outside their conversation, looked about her for the man who filled her heart and all her thoughts. Even then she did not see him until he spoke her name just behind her left ear and she whirled round to face him. 'Oh, you startled me, coming up behind me like that.'

He smiled. 'I beg your pardon, Lady Esme. Are you well?'

'Yes, thank you.' She was shaking like an aspen and her knees were feeling decidedly wobbly. 'Are you?'

'Yes, but all the better for seeing you.'

'You must not say things like that.'

'Why not?'

'You know why. It is flirting, and men who are betrothed should not flirt.'

'Not even with their prospective brides?' It was said with a quirky smile and his head turned slightly to one side.

She was not amused. 'But that is Ma'amselle Lefavre. She said you and she were to be married—'

'She lied.'

'She did?'

He looked down into her face, noting that the animation had returned to it and her eyes sparkled. Her lips were slightly apart and he longed to crush them beneath his own. 'Yes. Oh, we cannot talk here, it is too crowded. I must speak to you privately.' He looked about him. Everyone was busy with their own conversations, mostly in very loud voices; they did not appear to be interested in Felix and Esme, cocooned in their own little world. He took her hand. 'Come with me.'

She pulled away. 'No, I cannot. We will be missed.'

'Very well. I am going into the garden for a breath of fresh air. If you have a crumb of pity for me, join me in a little while. I will not keep you long.' He bowed formally and she watched him make his way from the room. It was a slow progression, because he had to keep stopping to speak to people on the way, who wanted to know his views on the Exhibition and whether he would speak against the Colonel's motion. He disappeared through the door at last but when, after a minute or two, she moved to follow him, she found her way blocked by Edward Gorridge.

'My lord, you startled me. I did not know you would be here.'

'It seems everyone is here,' he said. 'Her ladyship is no mean hostess.'

He would not move aside and she was forced out of politeness to speak to him, though, remembering what Lucy had told her, she was wary. 'Yes, she is very popular.'

'I trust you have recovered from your injury?'

'Yes, thank you, my lord.'

'I am sorry our trip to Richmond was not as enjoyable as I had hoped it would be. I planned to arrive at least an hour earlier so that we could ride together and you could put Blaze through her paces before we sat down to eat.'

'That wasn't your fault.'

'I am glad you think that. I would find it unbearable if you thought ill of me.'

His words made her look sharply into his face, but his dark eyes gave nothing away of what was going on in his head. 'Thought ill of you, my lord? What reason could I have for doing that?'

'I trust you would have no reason,' he said. 'Except there are some who cannot forgive, however much a man might repent his folly, and I feared they would turn you against me.'

'I will make up my own mind,' she said, itching to get away, but unwilling to let him see her impatience.

'By that I must suppose you have not yet decided to put me out of my misery and consent to marry me.'

'You do not look miserable to me.'

'Ah, that is because I live in hope.' He smiled, an oily smile that almost made her shudder. She found herself thinking of what Lucy had told her and if Lucy had seen him arrive. She did not want a scene, but had no idea what to say to him. She was saved having to reply when he went on, 'Can I prevail upon you to come riding with me tomorrow morning? We could go to Green Park and you could give Blaze her head there.'

'My lord, you know I cannot accept her.'

'I understand but, as I said, I live in hope and will leave her in the mews in case you change your mind.'

'My lord, I think I should tell you now that I have decided—'

'Ah, Gorridge, just the man I want to see.' The voice was loud and insistent.

They both turned to see a rather fat man in a brown check suit pushing his way through the throng towards them. She heard Edward curse under his breath, just before the man reached them. 'Go away, Philippe, can't you see I am busy?'

'You are for ever busy, Gorridge. I think perhaps you have been avoiding me and that will not do, will not do at all.'

It sounded like a threat to Esme and she looked from one to the other in puzzlement.

'I beg your pardon, Lady Esme.' Gorridge said. 'May I present Monsieur Philippe Maillet, an acquaintance of mine from my days in France. Maillet, Lady Esme Vernley.'

The man bowed perfunctorily. 'My lady, I am pleased to make your acquaintance. My friend Gorridge has been singing your praises and now I know why.' His English was so perfect he could easily have been mistaken for a native.

Esme said, 'How do you do?' before turning back to Edward. 'I will leave you to speak to your friend, Lord Gorridge. Please excuse me.'

As she moved away she heard Edward say, 'What do you want, Philippe? Couldn't you see I was engaged? Now I do not know if the lady will ride with me or not.'

'This is important. Connelly will spill the beans if something is not done to stop him.'

She would have liked to stop and hear the rest of the conversation, but was more intent on leaving the room unobserved and finding her way into the garden. Oh, let him have waited, she prayed, as she walked swiftly across the lawn, looking for him. If I don't talk to him tonight, when will I have another opportunity before my ball?

He was down at the very end of the garden, concealed from the house by shrubbery, pacing the two or three steps from the path to an arbour and back again. He turned when he heard her footsteps. She started to run towards him and then stopped in confusion. What was she thinking of? Nothing had been settled between them—running to him like an eager bride was not the way to approach him. She slowed and walked sedately to a seat in the arbour and sat down. Honeysuckle wound round its wooden supports and filled the air with its perfume. It was quiet there, the only sound the trickling of water somewhere out of sight and the distant barking of a dog.

'Esme, you came, I was beginning to think you had changed your mind.'

'I'm sorry I was so long,' she said. She was almost breathless, as if she had run all the way down the garden and not just a couple of paces. 'Viscount Gorridge waylaid me and I could not get away from him.'

He came and sat beside her, turning so that he was half facing her. 'I would not have expected him to attend a function like this. What did he have to say?'

'Just politeness, nothing of any consequence.'

'Did he follow you?'

'No, because he was accosted by a friend of his, a Monsieur Philippe something or other, and I left them talking.'

'Maillet?'

'That's it. The name sounds French, but he speaks perfect English.'

'I believe he had an English mother.' He picked up her hand, which was nervously pleating her skirt along the line of the stripes. 'Never mind about him now. We must talk.'

'The last time you said that...'

He laughed. 'Yes, I remember I said actions speak louder than words.'

Colour flooded her cheeks at the memory of his kisses. 'I...I didn't mean that, I meant the substance of what you said.'

'As I recall, there was little substance to our conversation.'

'Asking me to marry you has no substance, then?' she demanded sharply. 'Do you make a habit of proposing to young ladies on the slightest acquaintance, no matter that you are planning to marry someone else?'

'No, I do not. In the first place, I would not have said our acquaintanceship was slight, would you? And in the second, I have already told you there is no one else; if a certain lady told you there was, she lied.'

'Convince me.'

'That is precisely why I asked to speak to you.' He paused. 'How can I convince you?'

'Deny it.'

'I do.'

'I mean, make her admit she lied.'

'That would hardly be chivalrous, would it? I have spoken to her and she knows that she was wrong. In doing so, I am afraid I have made an enemy. "Hell hath no fury like a woman scorned." Isn't that what they say?'

'Does that worry you?'

'No, of course not.' It was said firmly enough to convince her in spite of his own misgivings. 'What worries me a great deal more is what you think of me.'

'I think—' She stopped. 'I think you are an enigma, a man with a past, a man with secrets, perhaps a man dangerous to know, but in spite of that, I think you are a good man. It is not me you have to convince of that, but my family and the rest of the world.'

He turned and took her chin in his hand so that he could tilt her face up to his. 'Thank you for that, my darling.'

'But you are in trouble.'

'It will be resolved and when it is, I shall ask my question again.'

'Oh, what question is that?' she asked lightly

'Ah, you cannot resist teasing, I see. You want me to repeat my proposal. You want me to tell you how much I love you, that I cannot contemplate life without you; that with you, life will be a never-ending dream come true, without you a barren wilderness of long days. You want me to say I will never stop loving you, though the sea dry up and the sky fall in…'

'Now who is teasing?'

'I am not teasing. I mean every word.' He cupped her face in his hands and gently lowered his lips to hers. Her arms went up and round his neck and she clung to him, revelling in the familiar sensations of being part of him, fused so closely they became one, two hearts beating as one, one body, one mind, one everything, to have and to hold. It was the need to breathe that drove them apart.

'When you do that to me, how can I doubt you?' she whispered.

'Ah, I did say actions speak louder than words.'

With his arm about her shoulders, they sat quietly for a moment, unwilling to break the spell, but it was Esme that broke it. 'Felix, what are we going to do?'

'Do, my dear?'

'About Ma'amselle Lefavre and Lord Gorridge and the trouble you are in.'

'Don't worry your pretty little head about it. It won't touch you.'

'But it already has. Whatever you do touches me, surely you know that? And the worst of it is I cannot defend you because I don't know what is at the back of it.'

'I cannot tell you. And I would rather you did not attempt to defend me.'

'Why not?'

'It will not help, it might even make matters worse. But thank you for the sweet thought, my darling.'

'It is something to do with the arrest of that man, isn't it? What was his name? It was an Irish name, as I recall. They are saying you gave him money to fund insurrection.'

'Not true. I paid a debt for someone else.'

'Won't that someone else vouch for that?'

'They do not choose to.'

'I seems to me that Juliette Lefavre is not your only enemy.'

'No.'

'I believe it might be Viscount Gorridge.'

'True, he is not overfond of me,' he said laconically. 'But that is because he believes I stand between him and the object of his desire.'

'Which is?'

'You, my dearest one. He has his heart set on marrying you.'

'Then he is bound for disappointment. After what he did to Lucy, I would not even consider him, even if I had not fallen in love with you.'

He grinned. 'You never said that before.'

'I could not, could I? According to Rosemary and the books on etiquette she instructed me to read, it is not a lady's place to declare her feelings.'

'But you have said it now.'

'It just slipped out.'

He laughed and hugged her. 'So what is your solution to our problems?'

'You must put an end to the speculation about your patriotism and I must hold off Lord Gorridge.'

'Yes, do that, my dearest, but do not let him know we have talked, not until I am freed of my obligations and the slur on my character.'

'Will it be before my ball? It is less than a week away.'

'I sincerely hope so. Then perhaps I might be welcome at Trent House.' He paused. 'You will not let Lady Trent change your mind, will you?'

'No, of course not. I would not, anyway, but now Lucy is staying with us, it will be easier.'

He kissed her again. 'If you hear anything else about me or anything that might help, try to find a way of letting me know. Mr Moorcroft can be trusted, I think.'

'Of course he can. One thing I did hear. When I was leaving Viscount Gorridge just now, I heard the Frenchman tell him that Connelly was going to spill the beans if they did not do something to prevent it.'

'Interesting,' he said, standing up and drawing her to her feet. 'I think perhaps it is time you returned to the house before you are missed. I won't come back inside. There is a gate over there that leads to the mews—I'll use that.'

'How shall I know that all is well?'

'You will know.' He kissed her lightly and gave her a little push. 'Now, off you go. My love goes with you always, wherever you are and wherever I am. Always remember that.'

She started back up the path. At the corner just before the end of the shrubbery which would bring her into view from the house, she turned and looked at him. He was standing just as she had left him. She smiled and waved and walked on, but there was a spring in her step that had not been there before and a slight smile played about her lips.

'Esme, where have you been?' Lucy demanded on seeing her. 'I have looked everywhere for you. Everyone has gone home.'

'I was in the garden.' It was said dreamily. 'It was so lovely out there.'

Lucy looked at her closely. 'Oh, I see. Better not let Rosie see that look, or she will begin to suspect.'

'What look?'

'The look of a woman who has been soundly kissed.'

'Oh. I did not know it showed.'

Lucy smiled. 'Only because I know you and understand.'

'You are not to say anything to anyone. Felix—I mean Lord Pendlebury—says we must go on as before until he has resolved his difficulties. Besides, Rosie would throw a fit.'

'I am inclined to agree with him. Now, come along, Myles sent me to look for you. He is becoming impatient.'

They joined Myles who was at the front door, bidding their hostess goodbye. After adding their own adieus, they climbed into a hired carriage. Myles and Lucy chatted all the way home, but Esme did not hear them. She was reliving her precious moments with Felix, feeling his hands about her face, his lips on hers, hearing his low voice telling her what she most wanted to hear. She trusted him, she loved him and now he knew it. There was still much to be resolved, mysteries to be unravelled, conflicts and enemies to be overcome, but that did not matter. She had found a man to desire.

Felix was on a train taking him to Luffenham when the news broke that someone had murdered Patrick Connelly in Newgate prison. According to Rowan, who brought the news to Trent House, an inquiry was to be held to discover if someone had come in from outside or whether it was one of the other prisoners, and though no one said he had actually done the deed himself, it was being suggested that a certain Lord Pendlebury was behind it on account of wanting to prevent the prisoner giving evidence against him.

'He is being sought for questioning,' Rowan told everyone when he came home to dinner that evening. 'But he has disappeared. He was not at home when the police went there and his servants either would not or could not say where he had gone. Nor was he at any of the clubs. Telegraph messages have been sent to the police in Birmingham to apprehend him if he goes to Larkhills or his manufactory.'

'But why suspect Lord Pendlebury?' Lucy asked, looking sideways at Esme who had let out a cry of distress and dropped her knife and fork with a clatter. 'I am sure he can have had nothing to do with it.'

'The evidence is damning,' Rowan went on. 'First there is the fact that he has been seen on more than one occasion in the company of Patrick Connelly, an Irishman known to be a troublemaker who has connections with the revolutionaries in France. They mean to disrupt the peace of this country and what better way to do it than during the Exhibition or even before, when people are coming into London bringing exhibits. Bombs could easily be hidden among them.'

'That is verging on hysteria,' Myles said. 'We have an army and a navy and a police force second to none. The Duke of Wellington is confident the peace can be maintained and her Majesty's subjects can go about their business in complete safety. Connelly was a hothead.'

'Then why would someone want to kill him?' Rosemary asked.

Esme had been sitting perfectly silent and perfectly still through this exchange, but inside she was trembling with fear, convinced her beloved Felix was in mortal danger. Whoever had killed Mr Connelly might turn on him next. She was about to venture that perhaps someone should ask Monsieur Maillet, but decided not to speak. It would mean a cross-examination and she did not feel up to explaining what she had overheard the Frenchman say to Lord Gorridge. She had told Felix and he had pretended to be unconcerned, but it was soon after that he sent her back to the house and made his own way out by a back gate. It might, to her biased listeners, point even more strongly to his guilt.

'The inquiry will establish the truth,' Myles said. 'I, for one, am not inclined to think Lord Pendlebury capable of killing anyone, or inciting anyone else to do so.'

'I must confess I find it difficult to comprehend,' Rowan went on. 'But you cannot deny he has some very strange friends. And why would an innocent man disappear?'

'No doubt we shall learn the answer in due course.' Myles was the only one who seemed calm.

'Then I suggest we drop the subject,' Rosemary said. 'It has nothing to do with us and I can think of more pleasant topics for our conversation.'

Her advice was taken and if anyone noticed that Esme was silently immersed in her own thoughts, they did not comment on it. Felix had asked her to let him know if she heard anything else, but if he had left town, how could she do that? If he was a wanted man, however innocent, he would not dare show his face publicly until he could prove it. And when would that be? The man who could vouch for his innocence was dead. There was Lord Gorridge, of course. He must surely know the truth. Why did he not speak up? Felix had told her it was because they both wanted to marry her. There was only one way to find out if that was so and that was to ask and make sure Lord Gorridge knew she never, never would accept him.

'Esme, what are you dreaming about?' Rosemary demanded. 'You haven't heard a word I said.'

'Oh. Sorry. I was miles away. What did you say?'

'We were talking about your ball gown and I asked you if Madame Devereux said you needed another fitting.'

'No, I think it is nearly finished. Madame said there was only the beading to do and she has several of her assistants working on that.'

'Are you pleased with it?' This from Lucy.

'Yes, it's lovely and I have Rowan to thank for it,' she said, trying to sound animated but not quite succeeding. The dress was indeed lovely, in heavy ivory satin trimmed with gold embroidery and seed pearls, but if Felix were not there to see her in it, what did it matter what she wore?

'I can't wait to see it.'

'We are keeping it a secret until the night,' Rosemary said. 'You must wait and see like everyone else.'

That was the end of that for a conversational gambit, so Rosemary tried again. 'What is everyone doing tomorrow?'

Rowan said he was going to a meeting with Lord Brougham and Colonel Sibthorp; Myles said he had business to conduct though he did not specify what it was. Esme supposed they were both intent on lobbying their point of view before the final vote was taken in the Commons on whether to go ahead with the Exhibition. Rosemary said the florists were coming to decide on the decoration for the ballroom and Lucy said Myles had arranged for a hired horse for her and she intended to go for a ride first thing after breakfast.

'May I come?' Esme asked. 'That is, if Rosie doesn't need me.'

'No, I shall not come down for breakfast,' Rosemary said. 'I am not fit to be seen before the middle of the morning.'

And so it was the following morning Esme was once more in the saddle, riding Blaze into Green Park with Lucy beside her.

'Why did you want to come here and not Hyde Park?' Lucy asked her.

'I am looking for someone.'

'Lord Pendlebury? Do you know where he is?'

'No, I have no idea where he is. I meant Viscount Gorridge.'

'Esme! How could you? You know how I feel about that monster.'

'Yes, but it is the only way. It is partly because of Lord Gorridge that Felix is in this mess and he can save him if he chooses to.'

'How have you come to that conclusion?'

'The money found on Mr Connelly was nothing to do with a revolution. It was to pay Lord Gorridge's gambling debts, though why he could not pay them himself, I do not know, nor why Felix should feel the necessity to oblige him, except that he is his cousin.'

'Did Lord Pendlebury tell you this?'

'Yes. No, not exactly, but I know I am right. I mean to appeal to Lord Gorridge to come forward and explain what happened.'

'You don't think he will do it simply because you ask it of him, do you? He won't, you know, not unless you offer something in return.'

'Money?' Esme turned in her saddle to face her sister. 'Oh, dear, I don't have any. There is my marriage portion, but from what Papa has told me, that doesn't amount to much.'

'And what there is, is intended for your husband. You will have no control over it yourself.'

'Husband? Oh, Lucy, do you mean the only way I can save Felix is by marrying Lord Gorridge?'

'He might suggest it.' She paused and looked closely at her sister. 'But you would never take him on those terms, would you?' She leaned forward to peer into her sister's face to add emphasis. 'Would you, Esme?'

'What am I to do?'

'Nothing. Leave it to Lord Pendlebury to sort out his own problems. I am sure he would not want you to meddle.' She paused a moment. 'What made you think Lord Gorridge would be here today?'

'He asked me if I would ride with him.'

'An assignation! Oh, Esme!'

'Not at all. I did not answer him, we were interrupted by Monsieur Maillet.'

'Who is he?'

'Another friend of Lord Gorridge. He came upon us talking at Lady Aviemore's. He said something very strange. He said, "Connelly will spill the beans if something is not done to stop him."'

'My God! Esme, we must turn round and go home this instant.' She reined in and started to turn her horse. 'Come on.'

Esme hesitated. 'But I haven't spoken to Viscount Gorridge.'

'No, nor will you, while I have breath in my body. Come at once. I must speak to Myles about this. I cannot understand why you did not tell us about that Frenchman before now.'

Reluctantly, Esme turned about and followed her sister from the park. She did not see Edward watching them from the shelter of a copse of trees, the very same copse where she had met and quarrelled with Felix. He had been looking forward to riding with her, wooing her and perhaps venturing something a little more intimate, but as soon as he saw who her companion was, he realised it would have to be another day. Lady Lucinda Moorcroft was the one person he could not manipulate.

Chapter Ten

'But this is wonderful!' Countess Luffenham exclaimed when Felix had unwrapped his Crystal Girl and stood it on the table in the drawing room at Luffenham Hall. 'Beautiful. And you say you made it yourself?'

'Yes, my lady. I call it the Crystal Girl.'

Felix had decided to approach the Earl and Countess through the little glass figure. Talking about it and asking for their permission to show it might give him a lead to ask them something even closer to his heart. He had sent a message from the *Plough* in Luffenham village, saying he was staying there and would appreciate an interview if his lordship would agree to see him. And so here he was, nervous but determined.

The Countess picked it up and ran a finger down its smooth surface. 'It looks like our daughter, Esme. Is it meant to be Esme?'

'Yes, my lady. It is why I have brought it to show you. I would like to exhibit it at the Great Exhibition with your permission.'

She held it out to her husband, who took it from her and turned it over in his hand. 'A very fine piece of workmanship. How was it done?'

Felix explained about the clay model and the metal mould and how the glass was blown. 'I have a small workshop at my home at Larkhills,' he told them.

'Larkhills,' his lordship queried. 'Birmingham way, isn't it?'

'Yes, just outside the town. My father built it to be near the manufactory.'

'Ah, yes, I recall. A manufacturer.'

Knowing the trouble Myles had had about his involvement with the world of the working man, he spoke with some trepidation, but he was not ashamed of his roots and would not prevaricate. If he was to get his way, he had to be open and honest about everything. 'Yes, my lord. When he returned from India and heard the manufactory was about to be closed and hundreds of men thrown out of work, he bought it and made it profitable again. My interest stems from that and when I inherited the title, I also found myself the owner of the manufactory.'

The Earl carefully replaced the figurine on the table. 'Has my daughter seen this?'

'Lady Esme? Not yet, my lord. I came to you first.'

'But how did you manage to make it so lifelike without asking her to sit for you?' her ladyship asked. 'Unless, of course, she did.'

'No, my lady. It was done from memory.'

'You must have a remarkable memory, Pendlebury,' the Earl said. 'Have you been much in her company while she has been in town?'

This was the entry he wanted and he took a deep breath

before replying. 'Not as much as I would have liked, my lord.'

'Oh. Am I to conclude you have a particular interest in her?'

He smiled. 'Yes, my lord, a very particular interest. And I need your approval to pursue it.'

'I knew it,' her ladyship said, laughing. 'That…' and she pointed to the little glass figure '…was a labour of love.'

'Yes, my lady. I am deeply in love with your daughter. It would make me the happiest man in the world if I could make her my wife.'

'And what does Esme think about it?'

'I hope and believe she will agree.'

'Support her, can you?' the Earl asked bluntly.

'Yes. I am in the way of being a wealthy man. My father left me well-endowed and there is the glass manufactory. Glass is coming into its own since the tax was abolished and new techniques for its manufacture developed. It is one of the reasons I made the Crystal Girl, to show what can be done with it.'

'Like making a giant building with it,' the Earl put in, referring to Paxton's design. 'Do you think it will stay up?'

'I do not doubt it.' They were straying from the point and he endeavoured to bring it back on line. 'I am happy for you to talk to my lawyer and satisfy yourself as to my ability to support Lady Esme in the manner you would wish.'

'I am afraid…' The Earl looked discomforted for a moment. 'Oh, dash it, can't beat about the bush. Things are not what they were, the old ways are declining and with it my ability to stump up a dowry of any consequence. Did you know that?'

'No, I did not,' he said carefully. 'But it doesn't make a jot of difference.'

'Hmph,' his lordship said thoughtfully. 'I suppose we are to have another artisan in the family.'

'Why not?' the Countess demanded. 'Myles is a good man, a rock and Lucy is happy, so why not Esme?'

'Very well, Pendlebury, you have my permission.'

'Thank you, my lord.' He did not attempt to hide his relief. 'But I have to tell you something else before I go and it concerns certain rumours circulating in town, which, though untrue, I have been unable to scotch.'

The Earl looked warily at him. 'If you mean there is a scandal or an impediment, I withdraw that permission.'

Felix was afraid of that. 'Will you hear me out first, my lord? Your daughter, Lady Lucinda, has told me you are a fair man who will allow me a hearing.'

'Go on.' It was said quietly, but Felix was aware that some of the goodwill had gone from the interview.

'It concerns work I have been doing for the Duke of Wellington for the safety of the realm before and during the Exhibition. You have perhaps heard rumblings that revolutionaries might use the Exhibition to spread discontent among British workers.'

'Oh, there are always rumblings. Do not tell me there is any substance in them.'

'There might be. You may also have heard that a certain Patrick Connelly had been arrested and that a money draft in my name was found in his possession.'

'No, I had not. I've been too busy on the estate to read the newspapers as thoroughly as I should and I no longer interest myself in politics.'

'The money was paid on behalf of Viscount Gorridge to settle a gambling debt. He is my cousin, you know, and I promised his mother I would look out for him.'

'That worm!' his lordship exclaimed. 'You had better go on.'

'Why did he want you to pay his gambling debts?' the Countess asked. 'He is a very wealthy man.'

Felix managed a wry smile. 'That is what he would have everyone believe, but it is not true. Not yet. The late Viscount Gorridge left everything in the hands of trustees until Edward reaches the age of thirty-five or until he marries, whichever is the sooner. That is why he is pursuing Lady Esme.'

'Esme!' the Earl exclaimed. 'Over my dead body! Surely he has not been encouraged?'

'Only by Lady Trent.'

'Rosemary?' queried her ladyship. 'Surely she knows better than to suppose—' She broke off, evidently distressed.

'He has convinced her and everyone else that the whole thing was a misunderstanding, that he is very sorry for it and has turned over a new leaf.'

'He tried to tell me the same thing at his father's funeral,' his lordship said. 'In view of the solemnity of the occasion I refrained from telling him exactly what I thought of that.'

'And that is why he is saying you have forgiven him and made up your quarrel.'

'The devil he is!' He thought about this for a minute and then something else struck him. 'What was this whatever-his-name-is arrested for?'

'Patrick Connelly. He is a known troublemaker and was arrested speaking to a meeting in a hostelry in Seven Dials and inciting his listeners to violence.'

'And is Viscount Gorridge implicated?'

'If, as I suspect, the gambling debt was a ruse to discredit me and stop me from doing my duty, then I am almost certain he is. Ruining my reputation would bar me from marrying

Lady Esme. That is why he will not go to the authorities and exonerate me, which he could easily do.'

'I am sorry for that,' his lordship said. 'But, you understand, my permission to approach Lady Esme is conditional on you clearing your name.'

'I would not have it otherwise, my lord.'

'Perhaps you should return to London as speedily as possible,' the Countess said. 'Goodness knows what that man will get up to in your absence.'

'I intend to do that.'

'Stay and have a meal first. The Earl will have the gig got out and one of the men will take you to the station to catch your train.'

'Thank you.'

He ate with them and chatted about his work and his plans for the future and the controversy over the Exhibition until it was time to go. It was only after he had gone that the London newspapers arrived and the Earl, perusing them for news of Connelly's arrest, which he had missed before, found the article about the man's death and the hints that it was a member of the British aristocracy behind it, though it named no names, the short biography they printed left him in no doubt it was Lord Pendlebury.

Sir Robert Peel's death, far from putting an end to the Exhibition, increased the enthusiasm of its supporters, who maintained it should go ahead as a mark of respect, and Colonel Sibthorp's motion was heavily defeated, much to the chagrin of Rowan and Rosemary and their neighbours in Kensington and Knightsbridge who would have to come to terms with it. Colonel Sibthorp was reported to have said he advised anyone residing near the park to keep a sharp lookout for their cutlery and serving maids and Rosemary declared she would not be visiting it, considering the riff-raff who were being encouraged to come. 'We are thinking of taking ourselves off to Luffenham Hall for the duration,' she told her sisters. 'We will have a new baby by then and I really could not put up with all the disruption.'

Lucy and Myles did not agree and it might have caused a strained atmosphere in the Trent household, but fortunately Rowan and Myles were out for most of the time and Rosemary was too taken up with Esme's ball to give vent to her feelings as freely as she might otherwise have done. Lucy, ever the diplomat, held her tongue.

As for Esme, she had only one thing on her mind and that was Felix. She was restless and afraid and quite unable to put her mind to the preparations which were at fever pitch. In spite of Rowan saying it was being hushed up, the news that a peer of the realm had engineered Connelly's death to stop him talking was spread across the front of the newspapers. Lucy had told Myles about Maillet, but what he had done about it, she did not know. And where was Felix? Was he in hiding? And why was everyone so determined to make a villain of him, when anyone with any sense must know he was nothing of the sort? How could she communicate with him and he with her? How could she enjoy her ball, when he might be anywhere, might even have been attacked and killed just as Connelly was killed? The very thought of that made her feel sick and faint. Why had they not arrested Maillet?

'My dearest, how can they?' Lucy said, when she asked her on the morning of the ball. 'There is only your word for what he said to Lord Gorridge and they could easily say you misunderstood. They might also say that your passing on what you thought you heard alerted Lord Pendlebury to his danger and that was why he disappeared. It would strengthen the belief that he was behind it.'

'But we know Felix couldn't do anything so dreadful.' They were sitting side by side on Esme's bed; it was the only place Esme felt safe from interruption by Rosemary and even then they were speaking in low voices.

'Yes, we do, but don't forget he has been out of the country and, in spite of his title and manners, he is not well-known to the *beau monde*. Even those who welcomed him earlier in the season are turning against him. You know how they love to gossip and this is a particularly meaty tidbit.'

'Can't Myles do something?'

'He is doing all he can.'

'I wish I could cancel the ball. I wish I could go home. I wish, oh, how I wish Felix would come…'

'He might be arrested if he did, you must see that, Esme. And Rosemary cannot cancel the ball. Everything is ready, the food, the musicians, the flowers, the extra staff and your gown, not to mention invitations accepted. But it isn't just that, it's a question of pride. No one knows how involved you are with Lord Pendlebury and it must stay that way until he clears his name.'

'But I want to defend him, I want to shout it from the rooftops, not pretend I do not know him.'

'I know, my dear, I know. Be patient.'

'And there is Lord Gorridge.'

'Forget him.'

'How can I? He is for ever sending flowers and little gifts, as if he is confident I will accept him. Only this morning a messenger brought a necklace and ear drops which he wanted me to wear tonight.'

'You won't, will you? It would be as good as accepting him.'

'I sent them back. Then he sent a note saying he will bring them himself when he hopes I will be in a kinder mood. Rosie is furious with me. She says it is all very well to keep a suitor dangling, but a man like Viscount Gorridge will lose patience in the end. I am fast losing patience myself and if she says one more word I shall tell her so.'

Lucy hugged her. 'Everything will turn out for the best, you'll see. Now we had better go downstairs and help with the preparations. Rosemary is working herself up into a panic.'

The servants, both permanent and temporary, were dashing hither and thither at the behest of Rosemary. 'Put those flowers on the table there,' she was telling one maid. 'No, on second thoughts put them nearer the dais in the corner where they won't get knocked over.' She turned to another on hands and knees polishing the ballroom floor with beeswax. 'Put some elbow grease into it, Martha, or you'll have everyone slipping over on the polish. And, Daisy, you haven't dusted this chair.' To a couple of footman struggling into the dining room with extra chairs and tables, she said, 'Make haste, Cook wants to put some of the cold dishes out. She hasn't room to move in the kitchen…' And so it went on.

'Do calm down, Rosie,' Lucy said when they joined her. 'There is plenty of time.'

'No, there isn't, and you might lend a hand instead of hiding away. And, Esme, are your clothes laid out ready? You will have to have your underthings on when the hairdresser arrives this afternoon.'

'I know.'

'Rosie, stop worrying,' Lucy said. 'It is not a matter of life and death.'

'I don't want to be found wanting as a hostess. Everything must run smoothly from beginning to end.'

'I am sure it will,' Esme told her. 'So take a rest or you will be worn out. You know Dr Peters said you should not tire yourself. You don't want anything to happen to the baby, do you? It is much more important than my ball.' She took her sister by the arm and led her into the little back parlour and made her sit down with her feet on a stool. 'Now, since the servants are too busy, Lucy and I will fetch something for us to eat and we will sit and talk of anything but the ball.'

They tried. They talked of Caroline Merton's betrothal to Bertie Wincombe, which had taken everyone by surprise. 'Sly little baggage,' Rosie commented. 'I thought he was dangling after you, Esme, but I suppose he could see which way the wind was blowing.'

'I never considered him and would not,' Esme said.

'I hope Rowan is not late back. It would be dreadful if the guests arrive before he does.'

'He said he would return in good time,' Lucy said.

No one mentioned Lord Gorridge, which would undoubtedly set Rosie off again and then she would quarrel with Lucy, who had already said she said she would lose herself in the crowd to avoid speaking to the man. If Esme had had her way he would not even have been invited. Esme, who loved both her sisters, could not bear to hear them quarrelling. She let them talk and went off in a dream world of her own where Felix arrived for her ball and was received as an honoured guest and they danced every dance together and he whispered sweet words of love in her ear and kissed her. She shut her eyes and allowed her imagination to run riot until Rosemary's voice roused her and told her that her bath water was being taken upstairs and she had better go up or it would grow cold and she would not be ready when the hairdresser came.

The Trents, not to be outdone when it came to luxury, had converted two of their upper rooms into bathrooms and it was to one of these Esme went to begin her preparations. She was still thinking of Felix, still hoping he would somehow come to the ball and so her ablutions and *toilette* were made with him in mind. She lay back and soaked in lavender-scented water and imagined Felix kneeling beside the bath, talking to her. He was admiring her naked body and reaching out to touch face and arms and breasts. She was so lost in the erotic sensation this produced that when one of the maids touched her accidentally, she almost jumped out of her skin and began busily soaping herself.

After her bath, she returned to her room and Miss Bannister helped her into her underclothes, her three petticoats, one of which had a padded hem. 'There now,' Banny said, as she slipped on a blue silk peignoir. 'All we have to do now is put your gown on after the hairdresser has been.'

'I don't know why I need someone from outside to do my hair. You always do it very well.'

'I can't do anything elaborate.'

'I don't want anything elaborate. All I want is—' She stopped, fighting back tears.

Banny rushed to comfort her. 'I know, my cherub, I know, but you must stiffen your back and smile. You are the daughter of an earl and must remember your rank and not let your feelings get the better of you.' She turned to answer a knock on the door. A maid stood outside, accompanied by a gentleman with a beard and flowing locks dressed in a suit of black clothes and a huge floppy red cravat. He carried a bag. 'Ah, the hairdresser.'

'Coiffeur,' he corrected her, and came into the room to stand and stare at Esme, who was sitting at her dressing table with her golden locks falling almost to her waist. 'Ah, my lady,' he said, talking to her reflection. 'I think we shall 'ave to use the scissors.'

'No, you do not.' She rounded on him. 'No cutting. Just put it up and be done with it.'

He sighed melodramatically and set to work, pulling, twisting, looping until he had, with the aid of half a pound of pins and several combs, tamed her hair into an artistic creation, into which he threaded gold ribbon to match the embroidery on her dress. It took nearly two hours, after which he took himself off to Rosemary's boudoir and Esme was left to finish dressing.

In spite of her worry over Felix, she could not help a *frisson* of excitement when she put on the lovely ball gown. Rosemary—or was it Rowan she had to thank?—had been generous to a fault. The bodice of the dress, in heavy brocade, embroidered in gold thread interspersed with little pearls, was close fitting, with a deep boat-shaped neckline and narrow sleeves to the elbow, which ended in a flounce of lace. More lace bordered the three tiers of the heavy silk skirt, which, thanks to the underskirts, stood out from her feet and swayed gently as she moved. Her only jewellery was a single rope of pearls Myles had given her, especially for the occasion.

By the time she was dressed and Banny had done fussing round her, Esme could hear the orchestra tuning their instruments and the front door knocker being repeatedly answered. 'It's surely not the guests,' she murmured. 'It is too soon.'

The old lady left the room to find out, but was soon back, accompanied by two footmen. 'No guests yet,' she said, 'But messengers bringing flowers. Look at them all.' She signalled to the footmen to bring them in and put them round the room. 'You are a very popular young lady, you know.'

Esme had never thought of herself as graceful but, as she moved about the room examining the cards that accompanied the flowers, she felt almost regal. She had been transformed from the wayward and excitable young miss into a gracious lady, a true daughter of her father. Whatever happened tonight, she must maintain that poise and if her heart was heavy with longing, no one would know of it.

There was a huge bouquet of white lilies from Edward Gorridge, whose heavy scent was overpowering. She did not want them in her room and asked Miss Bannister to take them back downstairs. The others were from well-wishers and the corsage from Toby Salford, who still believed he was in with a chance. But the posy attracted her attention because it was so simple, a bunch of yellow rosebuds tied with a gold ribbon. She pulled one of them from the bunch to hold to her nose, which dislodged a card nestling in its centre. She saw at once it was no printed card, but a little drawing. Snatching it eagerly from the flowers, she sat on her bed, holding it in her hands, while her heart rejoiced that he had not forgotten her. Savouring the moment, she held it unopened in her hands. The picture was of her, standing alone, dressed in a softly flowing Grecian gown, which clung to her figure and swirled at her feet. One hand was at the back of her neck underneath her hair, which was lying loosely on her shoulders and topped with a circlet of wild flowers. The other hand was hanging by her side, holding a posy with the flower heads facing downwards. It made her look fragile and beautiful. No one could have sent her a better present, however much it cost.

Slowly she opened the card and read the message. 'My beloved Crystal Girl.' Why Crystal Girl? she asked herself. He had never called her that before 'All is well, but I must speak to you before the ball begins. I have something to show you and something to ask you. I shall be at the back gate of Trent House at half past seven. If you love me, be there.' She glanced at the clock. It was twenty-five minutes past. Before Banny could return and stop her, she was flying along the corridor to the back stairs, skittering down them in her haste, the gracious lady completely forgotten. Through the conservatory she went, hardly noticing the banks of flowers or the dank smell of warm wet earth, and out of the door into the garden. Lifting her heavy skirts in both hands, she ran down the garden and wrenched open the gate that led onto the mews. The lane was empty; he had not yet arrived.

Felix had had an exhausting day, beginning with the journey from Luffenham, which was tedious in the extreme because he could not wait to get back to Esme. He had taken a cab from Maiden Lane station to Bruton Street, changed his clothes and set off for Trent House, only to be refused admission because the lady of the house was not receiving on account of preparing for the ball. When he said he would return later, he was told in no uncertain terms by the footman on duty he would only be admitted if he had an invitation.

He had gone back to his house for the little drawing of Esme, written his message and then bought the posy from a flower girl standing on the corner of Piccadilly. Dressing himself in his servant's clothes, he had returned to Trent House and acted the part of a messenger, hoping he might be allowed to take the flowers in and catch a glimpse of Esme, might even, with a little cunning, have a word or two with her. But it was not to be. The posy had been taken from his hands by the same footman and the door shut in his face.

Frustrated, he had gone to Apsley House, where he had found the Duke of Wellington preparing to go out but, on learning who his visitor was, ordered him to be brought to his dressing room. Here, Felix found the great man in breeches and shirt, without shoes or cravat, still tall and upright in spite of his advancing years. He listened attentively while Felix reported all he had been able to discover about the Revolutionaries and in conclusion humbly begged to be relieved of his duty. 'Connelly has been taken, your Grace, and no doubt he will squeak loud enough if he thinks it will get him off.'

'On the contrary, he will not utter a single squeak, my friend. He is dead. Murdered in his cell.'

'Good God! Do we know who did it?'

'According to reports, you did, or commissioned it to be done.'

'Me? You cannot possibly believe that.'

'Of course I don't.'

'Then I beg you to exonerate me publicly. I believe it might be the work of Maillet or those in his pay.'

'Ah.'

He explained the snatch of conversation Esme had overheard. 'I reported it to the Commissioner of Police and he said he would look into it.'

'Why did you not tell me directly?'

'You were not at home and could not be reached. I understood you were at the Palace. I had business outside London and I thought while the man was safely in prison he would come to no harm. Evidently I was wrong.'

'Yes, it is a pity; he will tell us nothing now, but if we can find Maillet, we might yet learn what is afoot.' He rang a bell to summon a servant.

'He might be in disguise. I have been told he had an English mother; he certainly speaks perfect English. He could easily pass himself off as an Englishman.'

The Duke sat at a desk, drew a sheet of paper towards him and began to write rapidly. 'Describe him, if you please.'

'Of medium height, well dressed. I should think his tailor's bill is prodigious. Black hair, probably dyed, black side whiskers and a slight limp. I would put his age at about fifty.'

'Thank you.' The Duke wrote on. A manservant arrived as he finished and was given the note to take to the Commissioner of Police with his Grace's compliments.

'Now, Pendlebury,' he said, after the man had gone. 'You may go about your business. Shall I see you at the Trent ball? I intend to put in an appearance for the young lady's sake. Lovely girl. Have an interest in her, do you?'

'Yes, your Grace. But as for the ball, I do not have an invitation.'

'No invitation! Why ever not?'

'On account of my involvement with the aforementioned shady characters and others of like ilk. That is why I need your public support.'

'You shall have it, young man, but after we have Maillet safely in custody.'

The proviso annoyed him, but he knew it would do no good to argue. He wondered if he had better go and look for Maillet himself, but decided he must see Esme first. If she had heard the rumours surrounding Connelly's death and his supposed involvement—and he did not doubt she had—he must put her mind at rest. He hoped fervently she had read his note and that no one else had seen it and stopped her coming to meet him. And because he also hoped the Duke might persuade her guardians to let him into the ball, he intended to be suitably dressed. He returned home to change yet again. To find Juliette reclining on his sofa as if she belonged there was the last straw.

'I 'ave been waiting for you, Felix, *chéri,*' she said.

'How did you get in?'

'Your man let me in.'

'I'll have his hide.' He came and stood over her, wanting very much to pull her to her feet and bundle her out of the door.

'Oh, do not blame 'im. I told 'im you 'ad asked me to come and wait 'ere for you.'

'Why would I do that? After our last encounter I would have thought even you would understand I did not wish to see you again.'

'Ah, but I know you did not mean it, you were—'ow do you put it?—peeved with me and now you are no more peeved, we can 'ave the civilised conversation. I 'ave finished with those people—'

'Which people?'

'The ones you warned me about.'

'Among them Connelly and Maillet, I suppose?'

'Who are they?'

'You know very well who they are. You introduced Edward to them.'

She shrugged. 'Can I 'elp it if 'e is a poor player? 'e is short of the money and 'e thought 'e could beat them.'

He sighed. 'What do you want, Juliette? I have already made it plain to you, I want nothing more to do with you. Now, will you please leave? I have to change to go out.'

'To the Trent ball.' She laughed up at him. 'You will never get in. I think perhaps you will be arrested as soon as you show your face.'

'Nonsense! I have done no wrong, broken no law, which is more than I can say for you, entering a man's home without a by-your-leave.'

'I 'ad to see you.' She stood up then and tried to wrap her arms about his neck. 'Let us forget them, *mon cher,* they are not important. I 'ave repented of my folly and we can go on as we did in the beginning in France, when life was good.'

He took her hands away from his neck and pushed her away. 'No, Juliette. I advise you to return to France before you are arrested along with your friends. Connelly is dead, probably killed by his own people and you, too, could be in danger.'

'But you could save me, Felix. You 'ave only to—'

'No!'

Furious, she ripped at the bodice of her dress. He grabbed her hands and tried to stop her. 'If you think that will work, madam, you are mistaken.'

They wrestled together for several seconds, while he tried to restrain her without hurting her, but when she became hysterical, he felt obliged to deliver a smart slap. She stared at him in astonishment. Her face was bright pink, his white with anger. He took her by the upper arms and sat her in a chair. 'Now sit there and do not move.' She sat sullenly silent as he rang the bell for a servant and when the man arrived, ordered him to find a cloak to cover her torn garments and hire a cab to take her home.

It was several minutes before that was accomplished and by that time he was very late indeed. He gave up the idea of changing his clothes or even putting on a hat and dashed from the house.

* * *

Esme had been pacing up and down for over a half hour, becoming more and more concerned. Something must have happened to him, something dreadful to keep him from her. She was about to give up in despair, when she saw a figure hurrying towards her wrapped in a cloak. She ran forward, but stopped when she realised it was not Felix, but Victor Ashbury.

'Lady Esme,' he said, stopping to bow. 'Are you perhaps waiting for my cousin?'

She was unsure what to answer, but he had approached her openly, as if he had expected to find her there and only Felix could have told him that. 'Yes,' she said. 'Where is he?'

'Still at home, I am afraid. He has been away and has only just been advised that he is wanted by the police in connection with the death of Mr Connelly. It would be unwise of him to walk the streets and so he sent me to fetch you. Will you go to him? I have a cab waiting at the end of the street.'

She hesitated only as long as it took her to realise if she did not see and speak to Felix before the ball, she would go quite mad with anxiety. And she wanted to find out if there was anything she could do to help him clear his name. 'Yes, I'll come.'

She hardly had the words out of her mouth before he strode off up the mews, trusting that she would follow him. 'Wait,' she called after him. 'I must write a note, or at least leave a message for my sister.'

'No time.' He turned and took her arm. 'Hurry up. He could be arrested, even as we speak.'

She pulled herself away. 'There is no need to manhandle me, Mr Ashbury. I have said I will come.'

She climbed into the cab and he followed. They were instantly borne away. Only then did she begin to doubt the wisdom of going with him, asking herself if Felix would have trusted his cousin, whom he did not hold in any great regard, with such an errand. Her fears were confirmed when, instead of continuing along Piccadilly, the cab turned into Park Lane and then into Upper Brook Street. 'Where are we going?' she demanded.

'To meet your lover. That is what you want, isn't it?'

'But he lives in Bruton Street.'

'He would be a fool to go there, don't you think? It is the first place the Peelers would look for him.'

The cab drew to a halt and he helped her down. She looked up at the house and realised suddenly she had been here before. It was Gorridge House. She looked back in desperation; the cab was pulling away. Victor took her arm. 'Come on, he is waiting.'

'Just who is waiting?'

'My cousin, I told you.'

It was then she realised how she had been duped. Before she could do anything but struggle ineffectually, the door was opened and Edward stood waiting to welcome her, a sickening smile on his face. 'My dear Esme, welcome once again to my humble abode.'

She stopped struggling suddenly, realising it would be better to be compliant and then she might be able to persuade him to go to the authorities and explain that money draft. She stepped into the hall. He stood back to admire her gown. 'Beautiful, beautiful,' he said. 'And all for my benefit.'

'It is for my ball. Everyone will be wondering where I am and when I cannot be found, a search will be made for me.'

'Undoubtedly.' He motioned Victor away and took her hand to lead her into the drawing room where a table had been laid for supper and a bottle of wine decanted. 'But they will discover that note and conclude you have met my not-so-esteemed cousin and he has abducted you. One more nail in his coffin.'

'How do you know about that note?' She realised suddenly that she had taken the card with her into the lane and had dropped it somewhere. Its loss was a blow, but Lord Gorridge must have known about it before that.

He smiled, baring his teeth. 'A certain footman with a grudge. You would be surprised how many discontented servants there are about town. A little flash of coin, especially gold coin, and they fall over themselves to oblige. He has been keeping me well informed.'

'Why?'

'To keep ahead of the game, of course. Now, sit down, my dear, supper will be served shortly and in the meantime we will enjoy an aperitif.' He poured two glasses of wine.

'What game?' she demanded.

'Why, the game of cat and mouse, my dear. It added greatly to my enjoyment to know that Viscount Trent and my cousin Pendlebury are at daggers drawn over the Exhibition. I did not know that before I came to town, of course, and when I did find out, I made full use of it.'

'To discredit Lord Pendlebury.'

'Naturally.'

'Why do you dislike him so?'

'I do not dislike him particularly, but he stood in my way and that I could not abide. When I want something I have to have it—it is my way, you see. And I wanted you.' He raised his glass to her and took a mouthful. 'To my beautiful bride.'

'Whoever she might be,' she said tartly, refusing to pick up the other glass. 'It certainly won't be me.'

'Oh, I think it will. I have the whole evening and the night as well to convince you.'

'Why me?'

'I need to marry and you are by far the most suitable of this year's crop of débutantes: daughter of my father's old friend, the Earl of Luffenham, comely and young enough to mould to my ways. And it gives me a certain satisfaction to have revenge for my exile. I think we shall deal very well together.'

'You know I do not love you.'

'Love! What is love? Nothing but lust in disguise. I will show you before the night is out.'

'If you attempt anything of the sort, I shall fight tooth and nail.'

'I shall enjoy that. I do like spirit in a wench. Your sister fought like a wild cat.'

'She escaped, as I shall.'

'Only because Moorcroft heard her cries. There is no one to hear your cries and no knight in shining armour to come to your rescue.'

'Felix—'

'Felix, my dear Esme, is tucked up in bed with a certain French lady of our acquaintance.'

'That's a lie!'

'Dear, dear, doubting my veracity, are we? I assure you it is true. She, like everyone else, wants her own way and she will do anything to have it. He is only a man, lustful as the rest of us.'

Before she could answer, there was a knock at the door and in answer to his 'Come', a manservant entered with a tray containing some covered dishes. 'Ah, here is our repast. Do sit down, my dear, you cannot eat standing up.'

She sat, but she did not eat, nor did she drink, as sure as she could be that either the food or the wine was drugged. Her whole being was concentrated on escape: how to lull him into dropping his guard, how to get out of the house without being stopped, what to do if she did find herself in the street. Where was Victor Ashbury? Was he standing guard?

'Yes,' he said, as if reading her thoughts. 'Victor is standing outside the front door and there is another man at the back. And I am not nearly as relaxed as you would like.' He laughed and that laughter seemed to ring a death knell in her heart.

Chapter Eleven

He was too late; she was not in the lane, not in the garden, either. Furious with Juliette, he paced up and down, cursing her, cursing all dissidents, cursing Edward Gorridge, Victor Ashbury and Rowan Trent, everyone who conspired to keep him from her. Had she come out at all? He kicked furiously at a stone and then he spied the card he had made from his original drawing of the Crystal Girl, lying in the gutter. She had come and probably tired of waiting and gone back into the house. Was she so annoyed with him she had thrown down that little card? He had to know. The guests would be arriving in their droves; could he slip in with them?

He straightened his clothes, which were certainly not suitable for going to a ball. He would never get past the front door, especially if that eagle-eyed footman recognised him. Opening the little gate, he peered into the garden. That end of the garden was shadowy, but nearer the house it was lit with lanterns strung in the trees and along the path. He heard music and laughter. No doubt Edward was there, fawning all over her and assuming she was going to accept his proposal.

She would not be so foolish, would she? She had promised she would not. If only he could see inside.

He walked quietly up to the house and stood on the paved terrace, trying to see into the ballroom. It was not yet completely dark, but the curtains were already drawn and he could see nothing. He crept round the building until he found a door. Slipping inside, he waited to listen and get his bearings. He was in a narrow passage. There was a door at the end and he made his way towards it. The second he opened it he knew he had made a mistake.

He was in a busy kitchen. A cook and several kitchen maids were working at a table, while menservants came and picked up dishes of prepared food, which they took through another door on the other side of the room. They were making such a clatter and all talking at once that they did not hear him. To get into the main part of the house he had to cross that room in full view and pass through the far door. He calculated it was all of forty feet. He made a purposeful start, intending to pretend to be one of the extra staff that had undoubtedly been taken on for the occasion, but the men were all in livery and he was wearing a plain black suit. Even so, he might have succeeded if the footman he had encountered earlier had not come into the kitchen and seen him.

'Just what do you think you're at, matey?' he demanded.

'Looking for…' Who could he possibly be looking for? 'Mr Moorcroft,' he added in a moment of inspiration.

'In the kitchen!' exclaimed the cook. 'What would he be doing down here?'

'I didn't know it was the kitchen.'

'Evidently not,' the footman said. 'But you did know it wasn't the front door, nor yet the back door. I reckon you were bent on robbing the family and their guests while they were otherwise engaged. A good lay, but not good enough.'

'I am not a thief. Ask Mr Moorcroft to come and speak to me. He will vouch for me.'

'That I won't.'

'Then I shall have to go and look for him, myself.' He dodged past the man and made for the door. It led to a passage with doors on either side, but the one he wanted was the one at the far end that led, he guessed, to the front hall. With the footman and another male servant hot on his heels, he pulled it open and stood blinking as he went from the dim passage to a hall brightly lit with two huge chandeliers. There were guests milling about, some who had just arrived and others being relieved of their cloaks, capes and hats by more liveried footmen. They turned to stare at him.

'Stop him!' his pursuer shouted. 'Stop that thief!'

One or two of the ladies screamed and the gentlemen stood aghast as Felix made for the ballroom. He was on the threshold when he was brought down with a crash by one of the male guests who had stuck out his foot. Before he could rise, the footmen were on to him, one sitting astride his body, pulling his arms up behind him, the other pinning down his feet.

The music continued without interruption, though the dancing stopped as everyone crowded out to see what was causing the rumpus in the hall. 'Pendlebury!' The voice was Rowan's. 'Hold on to him. There's good, fellows. We'll send for a constable.'

'What's happening?' This was Rosemary. 'Good heavens, it's Lord Pendlebury. What on earth are you doing down there?'

'I have little choice, my lady,' he grunted. 'Since two of your men are sitting on my back.'

'I am surprised you had the effrontery to appear here tonight.'

'I want to speak to Lady Esme.'

'Certainly not.'

'She is here, isn't she?'

'Of course. Where else would she be?'

'I don't know, but I need to know she is safe.'

'Safe? Have you taken leave of your senses? Of course she is safe.'

'Then where is she? Esme!' he shouted. 'Esme!' There was no reply, though even more guests crowded out into the hall and the orchestra came to a hesitant stop.

'Please, my lord, do not shout so.' This was Lucy. 'Esme has not yet come down.'

'If she heard my voice, she would be down here like a shot. Lady Trent, I beg you, please go and see.'

'I'll go,' Lucy said quietly, and left to go upstairs. She was back in the time it took for the footmen to be told to get off him and let him stand. 'She isn't there. Her room is empty. Miss Bannister has not seen her since she dressed for the ball over an hour ago. She thought she had come down.'

'Search the house,' Rosemary said, trying to stay calm. 'She can't have gone out.'

'On the contrary, my lady,' Felix said. 'She did go out. I found this in the lane.' He produced the little card. 'I sent this to her earlier this evening. If she did not come back indoors, she is still out there somewhere.'

'Wait there, I'll deal with you in a minute,' Rowan said before herding everyone except Rosemary, Lucy and Myles back into the ballroom and instructing the orchestra to play and keep on playing.

'I have no intention of going anywhere,' Felix said, glowering at the two dishevelled footmen who looked as if they would love to have another go at him.

Rowan returned. 'Now, we will have the whole story before I send for a couple of constables.'

'I haven't time for the whole story. Esme has been abducted, whisked away and we have to find her.'

'Rubbish!'

'Then where is she?'

'Oh, she must be somewhere about,' Rosemary said. 'A fit of nerves, I expect, and she's hiding.'

'She is not a silly schoolgirl, my lady. She does not strike me as a nervous person, at all. On the contrary, she is brave and resourceful, as you very well know, but against some villains she would not stand a chance.'

'What villains? My God, surely you have not involved her in your nefarious activities? Who else is there besides that Irishman? Dead in his cell.' She put her hand to her mouth to stop herself wailing. 'Oh, my poor sister. What have you done to her?'

'I? Nothing. I would never harm a hair on her head.'

'Monsieur Maillet,' Lucy said suddenly.

'Yes, my lady,' he said. 'Or…'

'Gorridge!'

'Oh, Lucy you are becoming fanatical about the man,' Rosemary said. 'He is here.'

'Is he?' Myles asked. 'I have not seen him.'

It took a minute or two for everyone to realise the Viscount had not yet arrived. 'It is early yet,' Rosemary said, unwilling to admit she might have been wrong about him, but there was doubt in her voice. She was even more doubtful when the butler came to tell them the whole house and gardens had been searched and Lady Esme was not to be found.

'I'm going round to Gorridge House,' Felix said.

'You are going nowhere,' Rowan put in, 'except to a cell in Bow Street.'

'My lord, I think you do not care a fig for your sister-in-law, if all you can think of is apprehending me. I give you my word, I will give myself up as soon as Esme is found safe and well.'

'Let him go, Rowan,' Myles said. 'We need all the help we can get to find Esme. She would not go off on her own, knowing how it would upset her sisters. I'll undertake to go with Pendlebury.'

Felix laughed, though it was a hollow sound without humour. 'To make sure I do not escape.'

'If you like. Wait, while I fetch my hat.'

'Has the Duke of Wellington arrived, my lord?' Felix asked Rowan while they waited.

'Not yet, perhaps he will not come.'

'I spoke to him earlier this evening and he was preparing to come, said he was looking forward to it. When he arrives, ask him about me, will you? You might be pleasantly surprised by his answer.' He did not wait for a reply but turned to Myles. 'Ah, here is Mr Moorcroft. Let's be going.'

Esme had watched Edward polishing off a plate of chicken, boiled ham and potatoes with evident relish, though she refused to touch a morsel. Remembering she was her father's daughter, her outward demeanour was haughty, but inside she was quaking. As soon as he had eaten his fill and drunk the rest of the wine, he would start tormenting her again. As long as it was verbal, she could cope, but if he laid hands on her, what could she do to resist him? She needed a weapon. Her eyes strayed to the poker lying in the hearth. It would do, but how to reach it? She began inching herself from her chair.

He looked up. 'Impatient to taste the delights of woman-hood, Esme?' he asked.

She froze. 'Certainly not. You disgust me.'

'Now, that is a pity. You will have to adjust that opinion or your life as Viscountess Gorridge will be far from con-genial. Better to bend a little with the wind, don't you think?'

She was about to tell him that nothing on earth would persuade her to marry him when the door opened and Juliette came into the room. She was wearing a large black cloak, which covered her from head to toe. 'He's gone. I couldn't keep him.' She flung off the cloak to reveal a thin silk dress whose bodice was ripped to the waist.

'Where's he gone?'

'To look for her.' She pointed at Esme, who was simply staring at the state of the woman's dress.

'Damn.' Then he shouted, 'Victor!' His cousin appeared in the doorway. 'Make sure the police know he's on the loose. Tell them to go to Trent House and make haste to arrest him. Tell them Viscount Trent and his lady are in danger.'

Victor left and Juliette sat down at the table and drank Esme's untouched wine in one gulp. Esme, realising that with Victor out of the way and Edward facing Juliette, she had been given an opportunity to make her escape, slipped from her seat and made for the door. She did not reach it before he grabbed her, proving he had not relaxed his vigilance one iota. She struggled to free herself, calling him all the names she could think of, while Juliette laughed and refilled her glass. 'You should have locked her up,' she crowed. 'Or fed her to the fishes in the Thames. Why don't you do it now? It would be one more murder Felix Pendlebury has to answer for.'

'You are mad, woman. You don't think I took all this trouble to have her only to throw her away, do you?' He sat Esme roughly back in her chair and pulled off his cravat to tie her to it with her hands pulled painfully behind its back. Once that was done, he went to a bureau and took a small bag from a drawer and thrust it down the front of Juliette's torn dress. 'Here, take this for your trouble and leave.'

'Leave?'

'Yes, go where you like.'

'What are you going to do?'

'Make sure this little lady becomes my wife. Tonight, in fact if not in name.'

'But you said you would marry me. You said I would be Viscountess Gorridge and mistress of Linwood Park. All I had to do, you said, was help.'

'I lied.'

Esme began to laugh. She was in the most perilous situation of her life and the laugh was more of hysteria than amusement. 'He lied. He lied to you, he lied to me, he lied to Felix and my sisters. The man is a born liar. Surely you did not believe him?'

'Shut up, both of you!' Edward shouted. 'I want to think.'

'It is a pity you did not do more of that before you started this business,' Esme said. Her arms were hurting her and she could hardly feel her hands and the more she pulled at her bonds the tighter they became, but she was defiant. 'You must know you cannot get away with abducting me, let alone murdering Mr Connelly.'

'I murdered no one and I did not abduct you. You came of your own free will.' He turned to Juliette. 'You still here? Make yourself useful. Go and fetch a cab, one of those large closed carriages. We can't stay here. I cannot rely on the police arresting Felix; he might talk them out of it and when he discovers his lady love is not at her ball, he will come looking for her.'

Juliette left them and Edward began pacing the room, glass in hand. Every now and again he stopped in front of Esme and regarded her with his head on one side. She returned his gaze with eyes full of hate, but neither said a word. She could not leave her chair or pick up the poker and wondered where he meant to take her and how she could leave a message for Felix. Would he believe she had come here willingly? But her biggest worry was how to preserve her virtue.

A knock at the door made him look up. 'The cab,' he said, untying her from the chair, though he retied one of her hands to one of his own.

'Where are you taking me?'

'You'll see.'

If he expected her to go simply because she was bound to him, he was mistaken; she hit him with her free hand, kicked at his shins, pulled his hair, scattering her hair pins and the pearls embroidered on her gown across the floor. His answer was to untie the cravat that bound their hands so that he could pick her up bodily and carry her out to the cab where he dumped her on the seat, gave the driver an order and climbed in beside her. Neither gave a thought to Juliette Lefavre, nor did they take any notice of another cab turning into the street as they turned out of it.

Felix, who had brought Myles up to date about his visit to Luffenham and his interview with Wellington while they travelled, jumped down before the vehicle had come to a stop and ran to the door, intending to demand admittance and brook no refusal. But it was wide-open. He stepped into the hall and listened, but there was no sound. There was a light in the drawing room and he strode into it, but there was no one there. There was the remains of a meal and two empty wine glasses and, flung on to a chair, the cloak he had wrapped round Juliette. She had come here when she left him, undoubtedly to report what had happened. He supposed she was meant to keep him busy all night. But had Esme been here?

He stepped forward to retrieve the cloak and felt something crunch beneath his feet. He bent and picked up a small pearl. There were others scattered about and hair pins, too. He gathered them up, certain they belonged to Esme and that she had put up a struggle. Where, oh, where had that monster taken her? He turned to Myles who had followed him in and showed him the pearls. 'These are Esme's, I'm sure.'

'You are probably right; Lucy said she had pearls embroidered on her gown. Where do you think he's taken her?'

'I have no idea.' He looked round wildly, but there was nothing to suggest a destination. There was no one in the servants' quarters; they must have been given the night off. A trip to the nearest mews revealed the empty Gorridge carriage and the horses Edward had hired contentedly munching hay in their stalls, so they had not taken that. Some stage coaches still left London at night and there were a bewildering number of trains, going all over the country. 'We need help,' he said, running his hand through his hair. 'More men to spread out and search the coaching inns and railway stations.'

He realised, even as he spoke, that if Edward had taken Esme out of London, he would be too late to stop him. He had learned in a hard school to control his feelings and not panic when in a tight spot, but this situation was testing him to the limits. He wanted to rush about, scream to the heavens, thump someone, especially his cousin. He took several deep breaths, telling himself Esme would not meekly give in, that she would fight, might even find a way of tricking Edward into letting her go. She might even lure him into dropping his guard by promising to marry him. Would such a promise be enforceable? Would he take her to Linwood? Would his mother condone what he had done? It was she who had suggested he should marry Esme.

'If she is proving difficult to handle, would he risk taking her so far?' Myles queried, when he put it to him on the way back to the cab. 'He would want to take her somewhere close at hand but secure while he negotiates terms.'

'You have a point.'

'What about Victor? Do you think he knows anything?'

'Victor! Of course!' He ordered the driver to take them to Clarges Street, but neither Mrs Ashbury nor Victor were at home. They had, so they were informed, gone to the Trent ball. It was very late by the time they arrived back at Trent House where Felix elected to wait outside while Myles went in.

It was hot and stuffy in the cab and he got out and began pacing up and down the street. The second time he returned to the cab, he found his way blocked by Juliette. She had changed her dress and was wearing a short cape and a feathered hat. 'Not you again. Why can't you leave me in peace?'

'You won't find her, you know. Not without some help from those who know.' She tapped the side of her nose with her forefinger.

He seized her upper arms and shook her. 'If you know anything…'

'I won't tell you anything while you treat me like a serving wench. You are as bad as that lying cousin of yours.'

He dropped his hands. 'Very well, let's sit in the cab.' He helped her in and got in beside her. 'Now, tell me, where is she? What has he done with her?'

Esme could not see where she was being taken; Edward had drawn the blinds. She wondered if he had a plan or whether he was simply riding round, not knowing which way to turn. Perhaps he was taking her home, after all. What would everyone say? They would know she had left the house willingly. Would her reputation be ruined forever? Even if it was, she would not consent to marry him. Never. Never. Never.

Suddenly he rapped on the roof and they came to a halt. He got down, paid the cabman and held the door for Esme to alight. She paused on the step, looking about her, wondering where she was and which way to run. It was very dark, but she realised they were no longer in among buildings, but in a park. The moon and stars were obscured by clouds, trees threw out strange shadows as the wind made the branches sway and ruffled the leaves. Not far away, she saw the glint of water. They had not be travelling more than a few minutes, so it must be Hyde Park. He grabbed her arm and pulled her down to stand beside him and shut the door. The cab rolled away.

Had he decided to take the Frenchwoman's advice and throw her in the lake? Well, let him! She could swim, though with all the clothes she was wearing it was going to be difficult. And he would not stand by and allow her to climb out, would he? She was proved wrong about his intentions when he put his shoulder to a dilapidated building and burst the door open.

'In you go.' He pushed her in the back and she stumbled

over the step. It was pitch dark and she could see nothing, but he seemed to know where he was going. 'This will do for the moment.' Keeping her in front of him, he fumbled for a moment with a match. It flared up and revealed they were in a tumble-down shack containing nothing but a table and a couple of rotting chairs. The place smelled stale and musty. He found a candle on the shelf above the fireplace and lit it. 'Sit down.'

'I will not.'

'Stand then.' He went to the door and secured it shut.

'Now what?' she demanded, going towards the window, but that was shuttered and she could see nothing. She was very frightened, but determined not to show it; he was behaving like a cornered man and such men were dangerous. 'You are in a fix, aren't you?' she went on in a pleasant tone. 'Nothing has gone to plan. Wouldn't it be better to let me go?'

'No, it would not.'

'Do what you will, I will never consent to marry you. I loathe you.'

'Pity,' he said. 'It was my mother's dearest wish.'

'Not yours?'

He shrugged. 'It was all one to me. I needed a wife and the daughter of the Earl of Luffenham would have silenced those who perpetuated the rumours about me and your sister.'

'Is that all?'

'It was enough, but I am beginning to revise my opinion. I do not think I want a harpy for a wife.'

She was foolish enough to let her relief show. 'So you will take me home.'

'No. I want something out of this little adventure. It has cost me a pretty penny and my bills must be paid.'

'I have no money. Neither has my father.'

'He has Luffenham Hall. I've always fancied adding that to my estate.'

'He would never part with Johnny's inheritance, you must know that.'

'There is such a thing as a mortgage, but to tell the truth I think that has already been done. No, I think my best course is to apply to Lord Pendlebury.' He looked mockingly at her. 'He might pay well to have you released, but would he want to marry you? After all, we have been alone together for some hours and if you were to look outside, you might see dawn is breaking.'

The door burst inwards with a suddenness that shook them both. The candle guttered and went out, but not before Esme had recognised Felix. He was dressed in a rough suit of clothes, wore no hat and his hair was wild, but that did not matter. She threw herself into his arms.

'Are you all right?' he asked, as Edward slipped past him and out of the door. 'Has he hurt you?'

'No. Oh, how glad I am to see you.' She could just see him in the light from the open door, because Edward had been right about the dawn.

'And I you, my love.'

They stood holding each other, oblivious to the sounds of a struggle coming from outside. He kissed her forehead, her eyelids, her cheeks. He rained kisses on her hair, now tumbling about her shoulders. He took her hands one by one and put them to his lips. 'Thank God, thank God,' he murmured.

'How did you find me?'

'Juliette told me where you were.'

'Ma'amselle Lefavre? I saw her earlier.'

'I know. Edward had promised to marry her if she would help him to ruin me, but when she realised he had lied, she was furious. She stayed around long enough to see him take you out to a cab and hear him tell the driver where to go. Then she came to Trent House and spilled the beans. I left her talking her head off to the Duke of Wellington.'

'Hold me tight. Don't let me go. I need to know you are real.'

'I'm real.' He laughed and kissed her again and the glorious shudders that ran up and down her body testified to how real he was. He stood back from her at last, though he still held her hands. Her hair was down, her dress torn, but nothing could take away her loveliness in his eyes. 'You look beautiful, sweetheart. The belle of the ball.'

'My ball. Oh, my ball. What happened? Is Rosemary very angry?'

'I believe a grand time was had by all. The entertainment was especially appreciated.'

'What do you mean?'

'He means he caused a hullabaloo trying to get in to see you.' This was Myles. 'Being chased and sat on by footmen. When you could not be found, everyone at last agreed that something must have happened to you and we set out to find you.'

'And you did. How clever you are and how grateful I am.' He still had hold of one of her hands. It felt warm and strong and she felt safe at last. The nightmare was over.

'Did you get him?' Felix asked Myles.

'Yes. He's been taken away by the bobbies. There will be no third chance for him.'

'Let's get out of here,' Felix said. 'It stinks.'

He led the way outside and it was then, as she was taking great gulps of fresh air, that she realised they had been in Annie Hicks's abandoned shack. 'Why did he bring me here?'

'He didn't have time to take you any farther afield and I suppose he remembered this place was empty.' He handed her into the cab and climbed in beside her.

'I think I'll walk back,' Myles said, grinning at them. 'I could do with the exercise.'

Felix kissed her again as they moved off. 'I thought I'd lost you.'

'He said no one would have me after we had been together all night and then I would have to consent to marry him. I never would have, never. Never. She gave a little laugh, which showed how frightened she had been and how relieved she was. 'He did not touch me except to grab my arms and tie me up. That made me angry. He didn't like that.'

'No, I don't suppose he did, my fearless one. And as for not wanting you, I want you and need you more than ever. Do you remember I said when my difficulties were resolved, I would ask my question again?'

'Yes, are they resolved?'

'Yes. Now I am free to explain everything and to ask you once again to make me the happiest man in the world and consent to marry me.'

'You know I will. It is what I want most in the world, too.'

He laughed delightedly and kissed her again. And again. And again, until she was tingling all over and thought she would burst. 'You do not need to explain anything to me,' she said. 'But perhaps my sister…'

'Lady Trent knows it all. We are reconciled.' He smiled wryly. 'Though she is a little put out that the ball did not go according to plan.'

'What a pity. She did so want to make it memorable.'

'Oh, it was that, never fear. I doubt anyone who was present will ever forget it. There was me fighting with a footman…'

'The one who was in Gorridge's pay? He said there was one.'

'Probably. Only he could have known about my note and given Edward the idea of kidnapping you. I took the flowers to the house about four o'clock this afternoon, but I discovered from Miss Bannister you did not receive them until seven, ample time for the footman who took them from me to take the card to Edward, who evidently told him to take it back and sent Victor to meet you.'

'How did you know that?'

'I didn't at the time, but I knew something had happened when I found my card in the lane. I flattered myself you would not willingly have thrown it away.'

'No, I dropped it.'

'It was a good thing you did, or I might not have gone up to the house and convinced them to make a search for you.'

She snuggled down into his arms. 'What else happened?'

'The Duke of Wellington arrived and told them how I had been employed to spot malcontents out to cause trouble for the Exhibition. When the troublemakers realised that, they tried to implicate me with rumour and when that did not altogether work, to have me wanted for murder.'

'I knew you could not do anything so dreadful.'

'I thank you for your faith in me.'

'Was Viscount Gorridge a part of the plot?'

'Only in so far as Juliette used him to help her come to England. She introduced him to Connelly and Maillet, who really did mean trouble. I don't think he set out to become part of it, but decided to go along with them to discredit me.'

'What for?'

'He knew I loved you. He was afraid you loved me. It would have put an end to his hopes.'

'He was right to be afraid.'

He hugged her again as the cab drew up outside Trent House. He helped her down and escorted her to the door. Before they reached it, it was flung wide and Rosemary ran out to meet her, still wearing a rose-coloured heavy silk ball gown. 'Oh, Esme, you are safe. Thank God! Thank God.' She took her arm. 'Come inside and let us look at you. Are you hurt? Did he…'

Esme smiled and repeated the assurance she had given Felix that Lord Gorridge had not harmed her. She was guided into the house where Lucy, Miss Bannister and Rowan were all gathered. She was hugged by each in turn, even Rowan, and then Lucy took charge. 'Come on, let's get you out of the gown and into a bath. And then bed. You need to sleep before answering any more questions.'

She looked back at Felix, who had followed her indoors. He was smiling. 'Go on, my love,' he said, taking her hand and kissing the back of it. 'You need to rest. I will come back later.'

With Lucy, Rosemary and Miss Bannister fussing about her, she was soon tucked into bed. So much had happened to her in the last twenty-four hours she did not think she would sleep. She lay for a few minutes, looking at the card Felix had sent in his posy, admiring the picture and reliving the precious moments coming home in the cab with his arm about her, his breath warm on her cheek, his soft voice telling her he loved her and asking her again to marry him.

The next thing she knew was Banny drawing her curtains.

'Wake up, sleepy head. It's the middle of the afternoon and everyone is waiting downstairs to hear your story.'

'Everyone?' She sat up, blinking in the sunlight filling the room. 'Felix?'

The old lady laughed. 'Yes. His lordship could not have had more than a couple of hours' sleep for he was back here before noon.'

She sprang from her bed. 'Quickly, help me dress, Banny. I must go to him.'

Miss Bannister seemed to take ages to fetch out a dress for her to wear, debating which would be the most suitable, when she did not care tuppence what she wore, and then she insisted on arranging her hair in coils and ringlets and threading it with ribbon. It was another hour before she appeared in the drawing room.

They were all there, waiting for her. She hesitated in the doorway, searching out Felix, who came forward and took her hand, bowing over it in a formal manner that made her laugh.

'I believe Lord Pendlebury has something to ask you,' Rowan said. 'You have your sisters' permission to receive him privately in the library.'

She led the way, but as soon as he had entered the library behind her, she turned and flung herself into his arms. He hugged her, then put him from her. 'Now, we have to do this properly, Lady Esme.' He was doing his best to keep a straight face and not quite succeeding. His delight was evident as he led her to a chair and then knelt before her. 'Lady Esme Vernley, will you do me the inestimable honour of consenting to be my wife?'

'Yes, oh, yes, please.'

'Do you not need to think about it? I believe that is the usual reply.' He was delighted by her quick response but could not resist teasing.

'I have thought about it. I have thought about nothing else for weeks, ever since I decided you would make a most desirable husband.'

'Desirable?' he queried, one eyebrow cocked.

She laughed. 'Desirable is much better than suitable, don't you think? Suitable is too stuffy. And if you do not get up from the floor, you foolish man, I shall join you on the carpet.' And suiting action to words, she dropped down beside him.

He pulled her into his arms and smothered her face with kisses. Her response was all he could hope for, and it was only when he ran out of breath that she sat back on her heels and regarded him seriously, though her eyes twinkled mischievously. 'Is this what you call doing it properly?'

'It was your fault. You should have maintained a cool hauteur.'

'Oh, you know I could not do that. Not when we have already been through so much.' She paused, becoming more serious. 'Are your difficulties all resolved?'

'Yes, every one, except—' He stopped.

'Except what? Tell me at once.'

'I'll show you.' He got up and left the room, leaving her feeling puzzled and not a little alarmed. Surely there was nothing standing in their way now? He returned in less than a minute, holding something behind his back. She scrambled to her feet and faced him. 'What have you got there?'

'My exhibit. I said I would show it to you.' He brought the figurine out and stood it on Rowan's desk. 'There she is. There's my Crystal Girl.'

'Oh… Oh.' It was a long drawn-out sigh. 'Oh, Felix, it's the same as the drawing on the card. It's me, isn't it?'

'Yes. Do you like it?'

'It is wonderful. Beautiful. But I am nothing like as graceful as that.'

'Oh, yes, you are. In fact, I do not think I have done you justice.'

'Oh, Felix, you make me want to cry.'

'Oh, please do not do that. I can't bear you to be sad.'

'I am not sad, I am happy.'

'Crying with happiness, that's a strange thing to do. Do you laugh when you are sad?'

'Sometimes, because it makes it more bearable.'

'From now on, I hope you will only laugh with happiness, my darling, but the question is, will you allow me to put it into the Great Exhibition?'

'I would be honoured and delighted.' She paused and stood on tip-toe to kiss his cheek. 'Do you not have another question?'

'Another?'

'To name the date?'

He laughed. 'Oh, that. I hope fervently it will be very soon.'

'As soon as the arrangements can be made, so shall we go and tell everyone the good news?'

She grabbed his hand and led him back to the drawing room. While they had been gone, Rowan had ordered champagne and glasses to be brought and, amid congratulations, hugs and kisses, they drank a toast to Felix and Esme, soon to become Lady Pendlebury.

They were married in Luffenham church in November, the earliest her mama and sisters said they could be ready. She wore her lovely ivory ball gown, refurbished with new pearls and an added train. A circlet of pink rosebuds topped the coils and ringlets of her hair. Watched by a large congregation of family, friends and villagers and attended by her sisters in apple green and Master Harry Moorcroft proud in his sailor suit, she walked up the aisle to join Felix, waiting nervously

with Myles, his groomsman. Her smile was a little tremu-
lous as he came to stand beside her and took her hand, but
its warm pressure reassured her. The rector came forward and
the service began.

It passed in a whirl for Esme, who could not quite believe
that her dreams had come true and she had the love and
devotion of the man she adored and most desired. Afterwards, eyes shining with happiness, she left the church on
his arm, the new Lady Pendlebury, and returned in an open
carriage decked with flowers to Luffenham Hall for the
wedding breakfast. As they circulated among their guests,
she kept looking up at Felix and found him regarding her in
the same quizzical way he had studied her when they first
met. To him, she would always be his beloved Crystal Girl,
fragile yet tough, transparent yet mysterious, for ever young.

Epilogue

Thursday 1 May 1851

London, indeed the whole country, was in a fever of excitement. After all the months of wrangling, the arguments about unrest, about the site and the elms, about the price of tickets, about travel and accommodation and public conveniences, about the thousands of exhibits and where they should be housed, about who should and should not be admitted on the first day, the Crystal Palace was ready and waiting for the opening ceremony.

The day dawned bright but blustery and by the time it was fully light, the streets along the royal route were crammed with spectators waiting to see the Queen and her consort travel in state to open the Great Exhibition of the Industry of All Nations. The people had been arriving from all over the country and their numbers were swelled by thousands of foreigners. Extra trains had been put on, hotels and guest houses were full to overflowing. Some had hired cabs the better to see over the milling crowds, some had taken over omnibuses and sat on the top decks and even delivery vans had been put to use as platforms. Those whose homes and offices overlooked the route had invited friends and relatives to see it from their windows. Six thousand extra police had been drafted in and five cavalry regiments were on standby in case of trouble, but they were not needed.

Felix and Esme were among the privileged who were to be allowed inside for the opening ceremony and they left their London home in Bruton Street at nine-thirty in order to be in their places well before the Royal party arrived. It was a slow progress; the crowds seemed determined to cheer every carriage that rolled by them whether they recognised the occupants or not. Delightedly, she laughed and waved back at them.

'To think the Queen has this reception very time she ventures out,' she said, reaching for Felix's hand. 'It makes me feel quite regal.'

'And you look regal, my darling,' he said, turning to survey the wide-skirted green silk gown she wore and the dainty diamond tiara that sat on her golden curls.

'Oh, look, Felix,' she exclaimed as the carriage pulled up at the entrance gates to Hyde Park directly in front of the Crystal Palace, from where they would make their way on foot. The park was a milling mass of humanity, but over their heads she spied something huge and colourful. 'There's a balloon being inflated. Do you think it's our balloonist?'

'I don't know, but we cannot stand here, we are blocking the way.'

She took his arm to enter the great glass building. The sun had gone in and a light rain was falling, but even so the light playing on such a huge expanse of glass made it sparkle and shimmer, now bright, now shadowy as a cloud moved across, a truly magical sight. 'Such a lot has happened since we went up in a balloon, hasn't it?' She said. 'What with my come-out and all that trouble over revolutionaries and you-know-who.' She still could not say Edward's name without a shudder. He could have been charged with abduction and attempted rape and probably treason, for which he could have been deprived of his title and his lands. But she could not bear the prospect of giving evidence in court, nor did she want Lady Gorridge to suffer and so the trustees of the estate decided to send him off to Australia for life which would probably have been his punishment had be been formally tried and found guilty. The estate would remain in their hands until, in the fullness of time, the next in line, a grandson of the late Viscount's younger brother, could inherit. 'But it turned out all right in the end, didn't it?'

He squeezed her arm into his side. 'More than all right, my darling. Perfection.'

All their difficulties had been overcome, the objectors silenced just as the difficulties and objectors over the Crystal Palace had been overcome and silenced. The first iron columns had arrived in September and the great glass building had begun to rise on its appointed spot. Only one small dispute had marred its construction, when at the end of November, one of the glaziers fitting the huge sheets of glass called a meeting to incite his fellow workers to strike for more pay. Felix and Esme were on their wedding trip to Venice at the time and did not learn of it until they returned, but he could not have done anything about it; the man was not one of his employees, but someone who had obtained employment with the builders, specifically to cause trouble. Fortunately, the police had been on hand to prevent trouble between the handful of strikers and the main body of men who wanted to work as usual and St Clair was arrested. The work went on and the completed building had been handed over to the Commission in February.

Exhibits had begun arriving long before it was finished, but warehouses and storerooms had been found for them and now they were all in the appointed places in the building waiting for the Queen to declare the Exhibition open.

Once inside, Felix and Esme found Myles and Lucy talking to Rowan and Rosemary, whose fears over insurrection had not come to pass and who had finally been won over by the magnificent building. Together they found seats where they could see the ceremony to advantage. Only then did they look about them. Felix and Myles had been many times during its construction and it was not such a wonder to them, but it was the first time the ladies had been inside and they marvelled at it.

It was almost like a great cathedral with a wide nave and a transept one hundred and eight feet high that enclosed the three majestic elms, which had been the subject of so much debate. The ironwork was painted in pale blue and yellow. In the centre of the building where the aisles crossed was a twenty-seven-foot pink-glass fountain. The displays were on two levels, the ground floor and a gallery that ran all round it. There were statues everywhere and potted palms and myriads of flowers. Soon after they had taken their seats the Duke of Wellington, whose eighty-second birthday it was, arrived in full military regalia, and was cheered to the echo.

By noon the rain had stopped and those inside heard the sound of guns which told them the Royal party had arrived. An organ played the National Anthem, as they made their way to the centre of the building. Prayers were said and a choir sang the 'Hallelujah Chorus'. After speeches, which only those close enough could hear, the Great Exhibition was declared open and at that exact moment, a balloon rose high in the sky above it.

Everyone inside set about viewing as many of the one hundred thousand exhibits as they could. Esme insisted on going straight to the Larkhills Glassworks stand to look at the Crystal Girl, taking pride of place among exquisite examples of the glassmaker's art. She stood hugging Felix's arm and gazed at it in wonder that he had loved her so much, even when they were quarrelling, to produce something so beautiful. Only three copies had been produced: one stood in the centre of a special glass shelf in the dining room at Larkhills, where it was always noted and commented upon by their dinner guests; one had pride of place in the drawing room at Luffenham Park; and the third had been placed in the foyer of the Larkhills Glassworks in Birmingham.

'Come on, sweetheart, there is lots more to see,' Felix said. 'And you must know every line of that by now.'

'It still makes me want to cry.'

'With happiness, I hope.'

'Of course.' She allowed him to draw her away. 'Do you think you could do one of our son when he comes?'

'I intend to try, but we might have a daughter.'

'Will you mind? A daughter, I mean.'

'Lord, no! She might grow up to be as lovely, as good and as brave as her intrepid mother.'

'Oh, let us go and see as much as we can before you have me in floods of tears.'

It was impossible to see more than a fraction of the exhibits in one day. There were printing machines, textile machines, machines for spinning cotton, machines for making envelopes, pumps, turbines, microscopes, cameras,

telegraph machines, locomotives, including the one from the
Moorcroft engineering works in Peterborough. There was a
Medieval Court, an eastern section where the Koh-I-Noor
diamond was displayed; ornate eastern furniture, beautiful
silks. There was a model of Liverpool docks, and ordinary
household products, agricultural machinery, threshers and
reapers and steam engines. There were strange curiosities
like furniture made from coal, false teeth hinged to make it
possible to yawn without dislodging them, stuffed animals,
a semi-circular clock and strange musical instruments. All
five continents were represented.

It was tiredness, not boredom, that sent them home, but
in the weeks to come, using their season tickets, they came
back again and again. In July the price of tickets, which had
in the beginning been a pound and then reduced to five shillings, was down to a shilling and it was then the workers, who
had been saving up for over a year, came in their droves.
Esme derived as much pleasure from watching their wonder-
ment as she did from the exhibits. By the time the Exhibition closed in October, over six million visits had been made
and it was universally acclaimed a huge success.

Charles Robert Pendlebury was born at Larkhills in the
first week of December and the whole family, Rowan and
Rosemary with John and little Rowena now a year old, Myles
and Lucy with Henry and Victoria, the Earl and Countess of
Luffenham with thirteen-year-old Lord John Vernley, and the
dowager Lady Pendlebury, who was thrilled with her
grandson, all gathered at Larkhills for the christening and
stayed for Christmas.

They ate and drank and played games and drank toasts to
each other, but the one that gave Esme the most satisfaction
was the one Felix proposed to the family and its future, a

future in the hands of the younger generation who would grow up to see many more inventions and discoveries. 'But may they never lose sight of their humanity,' he said, raising his glass. 'To us.' They drank, echoing his words. He turned to Esme, who was standing beside him, and murmured, 'And to my Crystal Girl, who has brought me all the happiness a man could wish for.' He smiled and, noticing the tears sitting on her lashes, added. 'And don't you dare cry.' It made her laugh and then everyone was laughing.

On sale 5th October 2007

TO THE CASTLE
by *Joan Wolf*

A powerful knight and his innocent bride...

Just weeks from taking her holy vows, Nell de Bonvile
is swept from the convent, and ordered to marry
Roger de Roche, heir to Britain's most powerful earldom.
Lovely and naive, Nell bravely faces her uncertain future.

Roger is prepared to wait for his innocent bride, yet as
he watches Nell blossom from timid girl to courageous
mistress of his keep, his desire grows. But war gives
no quarter to newfound passion, testing every
whispered word and each unspoken promise...

Medieval

LORDS & LADIES

COLLECTION

VOLUME FOUR

CHRISTMAS KNIGHTS

Share the magic of a Medieval Christmas!

King's Pawn by **Joanna Makepeace**

The handsome Earl of Wroxeter, powerful and commanding, had no intention of marriage. But when the king ordered him to take a bride, he had no choice but to obey. Cressida, a beautiful innocent, caused fireworks at court. It was the Earl's task to rescue her…and make her every Christmas wish come true!

The Alchemist's Daughter by **Elaine Knighton**

A chance meeting in the Holy Land gave Isidora a means of escape. But she would have to watch her beloved Lucien continue the experiments that claimed her father's life. And how would such an exotic flower fare in the cold depths of an English winter?

Available 5th October 2007

www.millsandboon.co.uk

M&B

Victorian London is brought to life in
the stunning sequel to Mesmerised

London, 1876

Though Kyria Moreland is beautiful and rich enough to attract London's most sought-after gentlemen, she has yet to find love and refuses to marry without it. When she receives a mysterious package, she is confronted with danger, murder and a handsome American whose destiny is entwined with hers...

Rafe McIntyre has enough charm to seduce any woman, but his smooth façade hides a bitter past. Still, he realises Kyria is in danger, and he refuses to let her solve the riddle of this package alone. Who sent her this treasure steeped in legend? And who is willing to murder to claim its secrets for themselves?

Available 17th August 2007

FREE!

2 Books
and a surprise gift!

We would like to take this opportunity to thank you for reading this Mills & Boon® book by offering you the chance to take TWO more specially selected titles from the Historical series absolutely FREE! We're also making this offer to introduce you to the benefits of the Mills & Boon® Reader Service™—

- ★ **FREE home delivery**
- ★ **FREE gifts and competitions**
- ★ **FREE monthly Newsletter**
- ★ **Exclusive Reader Service offers**
- ★ **Books available before they're in the shops**

Accepting these FREE books and gift places you under no obligation to buy, you may cancel at any time, even after receiving your free shipment. Simply complete your details below and return the entire page to the address below. You don't even need a stamp!

YES! Please send me 2 free Historical books and a surprise gift. I understand that unless you hear from me, I will receive 4 superb new titles every month for just £3.69 each, postage and packing free. I am under no obligation to purchase any books and may cancel my subscription at any time. The free books and gift will be mine to keep in any case.

H7ZEF

Ms/Mrs/Miss/Mr ....Initials ....

Surname ....

Address .... **BLOCK CAPITALS PLEASE**

....

....Postcode ....

Send this whole page to:
UK: FREEPOST CN81, Croydon, CR9 3WZ